THE ALCHEMY
OF BLOOD

THE ALCHEMY
OF BLOOD

A Scientific Romance

BRIAN STABLEFORD

WILDSIDE PRESS

I

The upper floors of the town house overlooking Holland Park were almost completely dark, because the windows were shuttered in the continental style and all the shutters had been closed. Chinks of white gaslight showed through the wooden slats in one of the ground-floor rooms—Sir Julian Templeforth's study—and it was just possible to glimpse the ruddy glow of firelight in the master bedroom, which was doubtless being made comfortable in advance of the baronet's retirement. The unshuttered windows of the servants' quarters in the basement were, by contrast, all aglow with yellow candlelight; the staff still had two hours of the working day ahead of them.

Mathieu Galmier paused outside the railings of the house, no longer certain of what it was he wanted to say to the baronet. He had made his resolution before setting forth, complete with supportive arguments: he had to continue, come what may; he had to see it through; he was so close; he could not possibly stop. But now he remembered thinking exactly the same thing last time he had come to beg for money, and since then, the costs of his failure had multiplied, spiraling out of control. It was not so much the material repercussions that he feared, although those might be bad enough, but the costs to his soul, into which remorse and shame had already penetrated deeply.

His hiding place was no longer secure; although the letter that had reached him, asking for a meeting, had promised complete confidentiality, it had been a bombshell. If its writer had been able to locate him, then others could, and surely would, if they had a mind to do so. Unidentifiable threats were lurking in the darkness, perhaps closing in.

And yet, he really did feel that he was *so close*.

Dare he trust that feeling, which had proved so treacherous before, or should he be finally be prepared to admit that it was reckless egotism, verging on madness, and already over the line of criminality?

He actually turned around, but stopped dead. That would be to accept defeat. If he had been going to accept defeat, he should never have sent the note to Sir Julian asking to see him before tomorrow's treatment. The one thing he must not do, whatever the final outcome might be, was show weakness to the baronet, whose wrath was only barely contained as things were. If it were to burst forth…the man was capable of anything.

He took off his hat before he rang the bell at the gate, acutely conscious of the fact that a Frenchman—even a physician once attached to the famous Pasteur Institut—was expected to be humble in this part of London, even before lackeys. It was a long time since Britain and France had last been formally at war, but no one in the British Isles had forgotten the name of Waterloo, and those who read the newspapers knew that any vestiges of French dignity that had survived Bonaparte's fall had been shattered and ground into the dust at Sedan, less than twenty years ago.

The porter, Reilly, scowled at Mathieu as he opened the gate for him, and did not trouble to accompany him to the perron, to which Sir Julian always referred as "the front steps". Cormack, the butler who answered the door in response to the second bell, was too haughty to scowl, but that did not mean that he looked upon his master's guest with any conspicuous approval. Cormack was duty-bound to accompany Mathieu to the study door and introduce him, once he had collected the visitor's rain-soaked coat and hat, but he was not required to purge his conscientiously-schooled voice of all disdain, and he took full advantage of that license.

Sir Julian was endeavoring to relax in a leather-upholstered armchair with a glass of hard liquor and a volume from Mudie's library, but he gave the impression of having a great deal on his mind. He made no show of being glad to see his visitor, but he did not allow any anxiety to become manifest either. He simply got to his feet, smoothed the creases in his blood-red waistcoat and adjusted the ruffed sleeves of his old-fashioned shirt.

"Come in, Doctor," the baronet said, suppressing a sigh and inviting Mathieu with a casual gesture to take his armchair's twin, positioned on the other side of the fireplace. "Is there a problem with regard to tomorrow's appointment?"

Mathieu sat down. His heart was beating rapidly, although he tried with all his might to match Sir Julian's discipline and conceal his anxiety. That was by no means easy, although he had surely had practice enough concealing it from himself before his conscience had begun to break through the carefully-constructed wall of his scientific objectivity and cultivated inhumanity.

The baronet went to the sideboard, where there was a crystal decanter of whatever he was drinking—probably Irish whiskey—and refilled his glass. Sir Julian invited Mathieu to take a glass by means of a quasi-theatrical gesture, to which Mathieu endeavored to reply in the negative, albeit a trifle tiredly, in kind.

The baronet held up his glass so that the crystal caught the light, in a hand that did not tremble at all; the slight overabundance of its contents might have betrayed something of his concealed alarm Mathieu thought, or might simply be evidence of a habitual overindulgence.

Cormack was waiting by the door for further orders. The baronet waved him away; the butler closed the study door behind him, ostentatiously clicking the catch to emphasize that his master's privacy was guaranteed.

"Well, spit it out," Sir Julian said, sitting down again. "What's wrong now?"

"If fear that there *is* a problem, Sir Julian," Mathieu said, hesitantly. "As I warned you at the time, I was unable to retain enough of the agent following the last administration to continue the principal course of the experimental scheme for longer than a few days. Given the desperate need to find a means of reproducing the agent, if the project is not to reach an impasse...."

"What you mean," Sir Julian said, cutting him off rudely, "is that you want me to bring you more money tomorrow."

"I do need more money, Sir Julian," Mathieu said, still trying not to let his anxiety show, "but..."

"But that's not all," the baronet finished for him. "You also need an extra...volunteer. In one sense, that's less problematic than the money, at present, but in another...well, you know as well as I do that if those purchases go on, people will talk, add things up, and word will get around. The law can't touch me, or Cormack, but if there's a scandal...well, this isn't the way it was supposed to be when we made our deal. This isn't what you promised."

Mathieu was very well aware of that, and it frightened him in more ways than one. If the experiment had only gone to plan...but it hadn't, and now he was counting the cost in more ways than one. If he had been able to back out of his arrangement with Templeforth, he would do have done so before now, but they had both come too far. Sir Julian knew that there was no way for him to go now but forward, and hope that his hireling achieved a complete success, at least with regard to his own treatment, before the situation became critical. And while Sir Julian saw things in that light, he would not tolerate Mathieu seeing them any differently, no matter how great the corollary human costs became. For the baronet, even deaths were simply a cost to be borne, not to be regretted in the slightest, provided that they could be concealed. The minor losses, in his eyes, were trivial...as long as they were not his.

"My promises were reckless, it seems," Mathieu murmured. "I..."

Templeforth cut him off. "Promises have to be kept," he said, sternly. "You've had considerable success, or else I'd never have brought you out of France and funded your laboratory. I'm the living proof of the accuracy of your theory. The snag is most unfortunate, but as you've said yourself, all along, the solution is merely a matter of time and effort. That's up to you—but you know that tomorrow's treatment absolutely has to go ahead as planned. There can't be any delay."

"I'm not asking for a delay," Mathieu was quick to put in. "As for time and effort. I'm working as hard as I can, believe me. But we're both prisoners of the logic of the situation in which we find ourselves. If your need for the agent continues to increase—and I'm fearful that you'll need increasingly frequent doses to maintain your condition...."

"Then the supply has to be increased commensurately," Sir Julian finished for him. "But when will it end?"

"I told you when we began this project that I couldn't put a firm price on the achievement, nor specify a time-limit," Mathieu protested, weakly. "Organic chemistry is in its infancy, as is microbiology. Believe me, I'm doing my best—but I'm not a magician. Science can't be done with a magic wand, even when its effects duplicate those of ancient legend."

Templeforth scowled. The expression emphasized his nascent wrinkles, but in essence, it simply made him look ugly—the worst imaginable effect, in the circumstances. There were certain effects of circumstances and temperament that the agent could not counter. The baronet was familiar with the effect, and he always tried suppress his surges of ill humor, in order to remain serene and handsome—but his powers of self-control were limited.

"I don't understand your obsession with inducing the so-called agent to reproduce," Sir Julian said, when he had regained his impassivity. "The point is to make the effect last, to make it permanent. You should be searching for a medicine that will prevent it from decaying in my body. That's the key to the problem."

From your viewpoint, yes, Mathieu thought. *But from mine, you're not the only one who matters. You're just as much a trial subject as the poor donors....*

"Originally," he said, babbling slightly. "I thought the extract might function like Jenner's vaccine, that one dose might confer lasting immunity...and even when the effect proved temporary, I hoped to find a means of stabilizing *in vitro*, but it seems to me now that the agent is definitely alive, and mortal—in which case, finding a means of reproduction becomes vital to its preservation as well as its multiplication."

Templeforth waved his hand, airily. "If you say so—but you'd better be right, and you had better deliver the answer soon. If not..." He let the sentence die there, not so much because he wanted it to sound like a threat, although he did, but because he did not want to contemplate the consequences of Mathieu's ultimate failure. He had too much at stake.

After a brief pause, he went on. "I understand that explorers don't always find what they're hoping to find right away, Dr. Galmier, but when they don't, they have to adapt their plans, or perish. Cormack can get you more raw material easily enough, and I have no alternative but to keep funding the operation, but don't expect my patience to last forever. East End sluts are cheap enough, and there's no shortage of supply, but you're costing me dear in rent, laboratory supplies and living expenses. There's a limit to the indulgence you can expect in terms of messing about with your damned serums and substrates."

Sir Julian was now staring at Mathieu in a markedly insistent fashion, as if he were attempting to mesmerize his visitor, or at least to dominate him by the power of his will. The stare was difficult to resist, even though it had no occult force. Mathieu had to admit that the baronet presently had the appearance of an idealized natural aristocrat, possessed of an innate right to rule. Sir Julian's title was meager, but his bearing was not; he gave the impression, for the moment, of being a seventeenth-century Cavalier displaced into the nineteenth century by some freak of time, reminiscent of a lush Dutch portrait of Prince Rupert of the Rhine, and he seemed genuinely to believe that if he only handed out his orders firmly enough, they would simply be obeyed, without regard to the limits of possibility.

Sir Julian Templeforth was a handsome man nowadays, Mathieu thought, proudly. There was nothing in the least unmasculine about him—indeed, he had an exceptionally robust and virile frame—but only a few days ago his face had had a particular perfection of form and complexion that was rarely seen in a male of the species. His black hair had been sleek and glossy, with a hint of a natural curl, and his sky-blue eyes had a clarity that was quite marvelous, even in the Celtic type that routinely combined dark hair with blue or green eyes. The tarnish that was now beginning to set in was slight, as yet, but no one looked in a mirror quite as sensitively and scrupulously as Sir Julian, and the baronet was well aware by now how rapidly his trivial symptoms deteriorated. By the end of the week, if the treatment were not renewed, he would be manifestly unhandsome even to the most casual glance.

If ever there was such a thing as an irresistible stare, Mathieu thought, the one presently aimed at him surely qualified; but he knew that he had to resist it, if he could. Given that it was, in a sense, his invention, or at least his production, he felt that he ought to be able to do it.

"I *am* making progress, Sir Julian," he hastened to add, as much to convince himself as his client. "The extraction process runs much more smoothly now that I've mastered it. I've also improved the filtration gel considerably, and if the color is a reliable guide, the purity of the agent is much greater now—which might help to stabilize it, with luck. The purification is vital, because some of the girls that Cormack has brought were carrying multiple infections, none of which we understand fully as yet."

Sir Julian's eyes narrowed again. "Are you saying that, in spite of all your precautions, I might *catch something* from one of your injections?"

Mathieu cursed himself for leaving an opening for Templeforth to take that inference. "That's highly unlikely, Sir Julian. The filtration is highly effective, with regard to bacteria."

"But not for your damned agent, which you now claim to be alive. If that can get through...."

Templeforth was not a stupid man, and his argument was by no means unsound. Mathieu fell back on the standard tactic of the scientific smokescreen. "It's true that the range of microbial agents now seems to be wider and more varied that was first believed," he said, judiciously. "I've been keeping close track of the Institut's publications, especially Elie Metchnikoff's immunological work, Monsieur Pasteur's quest for new vaccines and the latest advances in apochromatic microscopy. The new findings, however, seem to support my theory that the great majority of entities in the blood that can be considered independently alive are inoffensive or benign. Pathogens are the exception, not the rule. Thus far, you haven't shown any symptoms of accidental infection."

Sir Julian got to his feet, perhaps hoping to increase the dominating effect of his stare, but after looking down at his visitor for a few seconds he turned away. His eyes went to the portrait hanging over the fireplace: the portrait of his father, who had fought at Waterloo as a mere subaltern and had subsequently commanded a brigade in the Crimea, where he had somehow avoided being singled out by *The Times* as yet another glaring exemplar of British military incompetence. Sir Malcolm Templeforth had not been a handsome man, and his son did not resemble him at all. His own army career had taken him to India, but had surely involved far more strutting and socializing than fighting. It was there that he had become a dandy, as well as bringing his monumental arrogance to a curious perfection.

"Things are bad in Ireland and getting worse," Sir Julian said, suppressing another sigh and allowing his train of thought to deviate. "Ever since Gladstone gave the rebels that first inch they've been determined to take far more than a mile. Even with an honest steward in place, the estate's revenues are sinking like a stone. The poor fellow's under siege. Even bog-Irish peasants are taught to read nowadays, it seems, and are encouraged to delude themselves that they're capable of philosophical thought. What they read, alas, is the radical press, and the form their philosophy takes is an obsession with the so-called rights of man, trades unions and all that nonsense. My tenants have formed some sort of association, it seems, and they're badgering my steward daily with lists of grievances. He's demanding, on their behalf, that I go over there—not requesting, you understand, but *demanding*. He won't believe me when I say that I can't, although we both know full well that I can't leave London for any length of time now. It wouldn't do any good, of course, if I did go over—the wretches complain bitterly about what they call absentee landlords, but they make it impossible for anyone to operate comfortably in residence."

Mathieu did not know how to respond to that tirade, and began to wish that he had accepted the offer of a glass of whiskey, if only to have something to do with his hands.

"Anyway," Sir Julian went on, "my purse isn't bottomless, and I'm feeling the pinch at present. There's no way I can increase my funds, except perhaps by marrying again, but the marriage market isn't what it was twenty years ago. I could probably snag some American bitch in heat whose father's in steel or oil, although they all seem to want an earldom, at least, but that would take time." He paused before adding: "You're not thinking about looking for another backer, are you? You do realize how unwise that would be?"

The way the two questions were phrased made them appear to be defensive moves in the face of a hypothetical threat, but Mathieu knew that they constituted a serious threat in themselves, and perhaps a deadly one. He had always known that Templeforth was a dangerous man with whom to deal, untrustworthy as well as violent, but he had not been in a position to argue when the Englishman had offered him a refuge outside France. The Sûreté had been on his heels, and Paris had become unsafe.

Unfortunately, it seemed that London might become even less safe, even though no one here had been able to track his early experiments with the same facility as certain interested parties in France. Here, he was a foreigner, and automatically under suspicion, just as poor Metchnikoff was in Paris, in spite of his well-deserved reputation for benignity.

When he had first arrived in the English capital, Mathieu had been utterly convinced that he was on the very brink of the crucial breakthrough, that the victory was only months away—a year, at the most—and that Sir Julian Templeforth would be the perfect advertisement for his capacity to improve the human condition. Now he was nearly three years older, and the ultimate objective of his research seemed to be as far away as ever, in spite of all his efforts. He was no longer able to set a hypothetical time-limit on his project, and was uncomfortably aware that it might, in fact, take forever. Except, of course, that it couldn't, because the corollary damage was too great, and every casualty of his endeavor added to the heavy burden on his conscience.

No, he thought, he could not go on forever, or very much longer. It was a truism of his profession that doctors could bury their mistakes, that their diplomas were, in effect, licenses to commit murder—but that was on condition that they committed their murders by the book, and not by effecting novel treatments that awoke an instinctive revulsion. It also required the cultivation of a particular kind of arrogance and an anesthetization of the conscience that Mathieu had never fully acquired.

After a long pause for thought, Mathieu said, softly: "There's no need to threaten me, Sir Julian. You might think of yourself as my backer, as me as a pawn in a risky speculation, but so far as I'm concerned, you're my patient, and it's my duty to do everything possible to maintain your health for as long as humanly possible."

"It certainly is," the baronet retorted, "given that my present...troubles are partly of your making. It's the faults in your own treatment that you're trying to repair."

That was not strictly true, Mathieu knew. On the other hand, he was even more fully aware than Sir Julian of the risk of iatrogenic aftereffects. If the treatment were to stop now, for whatever reason...

The baronet sat down again. "I sometimes wonder whether you might be playing me like a fish," he said, "keeping me hooked by deliberately doling out your drug in doses that become less effective by degrees, simply in order to keep extracting money for me to fund your greater ambitions. Your obsession with so-called progress and the greater good of humankind is unhealthy as well as absurd. The only kind of progress either of us should be interested in is personal progress: our own goals. If that's egotistical so be it...but you need to look out for your own interests if you're going to see this through"

"I'm trying," Mathieu assured him. "And I'm certainly not deceiving you, in any way. You know full well that I'm no charlatan, that the treatment does work, within its limitations. It's just a matter of overcoming those limitations. We need to trust one another."

That was true, but it was an unrealistic hope. Neither of them had ever trusted the other, and the awkward progress of the experiment had not contributed to the burgeoning of any trust within their wary relationship.

Templeforth did not have time to comment on that fact, if he had any intention on doing so, because there was a discreet knock on the door, which Mathieu was now capable of recognizing instantly as the product of Cormack's knuckles.

The butler waited for his master to call out a summons before he opened the door, and came in, hesitantly. "I'm very sorry to disturb you sir," he said, "but I thought you ought to know that there is someone watching the house from the bushes in Holland Park. According to Reilly, he took up his post immediately after Mr. Galmier's arrival, and might perhaps have been following him."

Sir Julian fixed Mathieu with a different kind of stare, which testified eloquently to the extent of the lack of trust between them.

"I had no idea!" Mathieu protested. "I wouldn't have been able to get a hansom, even if I'd tried, because of the rain...."

"That wouldn't have made a damn bit of difference, you fool," Sir Julian said, hotly. "The point is, who is he? And how did you attract his attention in the first place?"

Mathieu shook his head, helplessly.

Sir Julian was a man of action, and not one to waste time in procrastination. He went to the cabinet beside the door and took out his father's old saber, with a promptitude that implied very strongly that he always relished an opportunity to do so. Mathieu knew that rumor suggested that the baronet had killed at least three men in duels—though none, as yet, on English soil—and he was prepared to believe that, for once, the rumor was not exaggerated.

"Tell Reilly to work his way around behind the fellow if he can," Templeforth instructed Cormack. "He'll need a stout cudgel, but tell him not to wield it too brutally. We want to question the man, not split his skull. We'll leave five minutes, and then we'll come out of the front door and make directly for the spy."

Cormack nodded, and hurried away to relay the order. Sir Julian raised the saber and weighed it in his hand, in eager anticipation.

"The fellow can't see anything, with all the shutters closed," Mathieu pointed out. "His vigil will be wasted."

"Even if he didn't follow you here," Sir Julian said, "he'll probably follow you home, given the chance. If appearances are correct in suggesting that he's aware of our association, and interested in it, it means that he probably knows too much—enough, at any rate, for us to need to know exactly how much he does know, and what his interest is."

The baronet put on his black coat, handed to him by Cormack. His bearing assumed a kind of emphatic swagger that he probably thought of as "Wellingtonian". The butler had brought Mathieu's coat too, which was shabbier by far, along with his hat and his cane.

When the five minutes had elapsed, Sir Julian made for the main door of the house, beckoning to Mathieu as if he were commanding a footman. Mathieu followed him, quite content to remain three paces in rear.

Sir Julian bounded down the steps and raced through the open gate, crossing the deserted street in three strides—but there were iron railings around the park, and the nearest gate was ten yards to one side, requiring an awkward detour. As Sir Julian headed for the gate there was a flurry of movement in the bushes beyond the railings, and the quarry set off like a startled hare.

Reilly, alas, was no greyhound. By the time Sir Julian had reached the place where the watcher had been stationed, the porter had already engaged the spy in a brief scuffle, but had been knocked down without being able to bring his cudgel into play.

When Mathieu finally caught up with his patron, the baronet was fulminating at his aged retainer. Reilly complained in vain that the unknown man had been considerably taller, younger and stronger than he was, and that the grass had been exceedingly slippery after the rain.

Sir Julian rounded on Mathieu then. "This is your fault," he declared, although he had no real reason to suppose that to be true. "Make sure that no one follows you home, if you can. I'll come tomorrow, at seven, as arranged. You'll have the usual delivery before noon, and I'll make provision for another before the end of the week. I'll bring some extra money for you—but I warn you that I expect results. You'd better find a means to grow your vaccine in a flask pretty damned quick, else you and I will need a further reckoning."

"This kind of adventurous research can't be done to order," Mathieu said, tiredly, feeling obliged to mount some kind of formal protest. "There's no precedent to guide us."

"Necessity," Sir Julian stated, with not a hint of irony, "is the mother of improvisation. It was you who put yourself under its spur—where I've long grown used to living. There's no use complaining that you need more time when the sand has all but run through the hour-glass. If that was a policeman, he's far more likely to be after you than me—which means that you need me even more than I need you, and not just for money. Whether you walk back to your lodgings or take a cab, *keep looking behind you*."

II

In fact, Mathieu did not return to his lodgings at all, although he told himself as he walked that that was probably the wiser thing to do. But fear and curiosity were stronger than sagacity. He needed to know who had sent him the letter, and why. He needed to know exactly how many kinds of trouble he was in, and how imminent the threat was.

It was late now, but the letter had assured him that the writer would be glad to receive his visit at any time. That detail suggested a certain urgency on the part of the other, which was probably not a good sign, even though the tone of the letter had been courteous and imploring, with not the slightest hint of a threat.

Whether or not the letter had anything to do with the fact that someone had been watching Sir Julian Templeforth's house, Mathieu had no idea, but that possibility added to the alarming quality of what had just happened. He could not believe that the lurker in the bushes had been a policeman, although he assumed that Scotland Yard had a hired rabble of petty criminals to do its dirty work just as the Parisian Sûreté had, but if he really was being followed, then he had to assume that he was in real danger.

As he walked along Holland Park Avenue in the direction of Shepherd's Bush he followed Templeforth's advice and kept looking behind him at intervals, but he could see no evidence of anyone dogging his footsteps. On the other hand, the rain had stopped and the street was far from deserted; there was enough of a crowd for any determined observer to remain unobtrusive. He turned off Shepherd's Bush Green on to Rockley Road, where the Brook Green Hotel was located, approximately equidistant between Sir Julian's house and the unassuming terraced house in a side-street off Hammersmith Grove in which his laboratory had been installed. That intermediate location now seemed ominously suggestive.

Mathieu gave his name to the clerk at the registration desk, who sent a bell-boy to announce the presence of a visitor to the mysterious individual who had sent the request for him to call.

Perhaps it's just a patient in need of medical attention, he told himself, not for the first time—but it was a forlorn hope. He was not in practice in London, and had not advertised his medical qualifications to his neighbors.

The bell-boy returned and then escorted him up two flights of stairs and along a corridor illuminated by a single oil-lamp. The employee knocked on the door, and then abandoned Mathieu on the threshold. The door was opened by a tall young man with an athletic build. He seemed to be in his mid-twenties, about five years younger than Mathieu; his hair was black and his complexion bronzed: a southerner, Mathieu guessed.

"Do come in, Dr. Galmier," said the hotel guest, in French, ushering Mathieu into a reception room that was more brightly illuminated than the corridor, and which seemed relatively plush by comparison with the hotel's modest exterior.

Mathieu tried to formulate an apology for calling so late, but stumbled over the phrasing. "Not at all," said the other, making every attempt to seem welcoming. "It's very good of you to come. I'm Philippe de Valcoeur."

The letter inviting Mathieu to call at the hotel had borne that unfamiliar signature, so Mathieu was not surprised to find the writer speaking French, and the distinct accent, which had a hint of Basque about it, seemed to fit his appearance perfectly.

Philippe de Valcoeur took Mathieu's coat, hat and cane, and invited him to sit down on a sofa. As he did do so, the physician darted a rapid glance around the room. Almost everything was as he would have expected it to be in a respectable hotel but there were two small paintings on the mantelpiece that surely must have been placed there temporarily by the guests. One was a portrait, a miniature of a woman whose features could not be distinguished at the distance from which Mathieu was viewing it, but the other was like an illuminated illustration of a cross, whose intersection was covered by a red rose.

Before Mathieu could formulate a mental response to that symbol, one of the reception room's two internal doors opened, and a young woman appeared on the threshold. She was tall and slender, with the same dark hair and amber complexion as Philippe de Valcoeur: an evident family resemblance. She was not unusually beautiful, but she certainly did not resemble a potential client for Mathieu's as-yet-dubious wares. Her serene expression suggested contentment with herself, and with the world; she seemed to be one of those fortunate people, surprisingly rare in Mathieu's experience, who seemed at ease in a life of relative ease.

"My sister Myrtille," said Valcoeur, as Mathieu stood up again. "Myrtille, this is Dr. Mathieu Galmier."

"At last," said the young woman, coming forward and extending her hand to be shaken in the English manner. "You're a hard man to find, Dr.

Galmier."

"I'm sorry," Mathieu replied, although the apology seemed rather ridiculous, and the lie with which he followed it even more ridiculous. "I wasn't aware that anyone was searching for me."

With scrupulous politeness, however, no mention was made by the Valcoeurs of any of the people who might be looking for him, in a desultory fashion, in Paris. Gestures of invitation were made, and he resumed the seat that had already been offered to him.

"Will you take a small glass of Bordeaux?" Philippe de Valcoeur asked.

This time, Mathieu accepted the offer, less fearful of wine than he had been of the whiskey, and suspecting that he might have more need than before of something to occupy his hands.

Philippe sat down in an armchair, and his sister—who seemed to be the older of the two siblings by two or three years—took its twin.

"We would have written long ago," Philippe said, "had we known your address, but you do not seem to have given it to any of your former friends at the Institut, including Dr. Metchnikoff."

"You know Metchnikoff?" Mathieu parried.

"We've met. I'm a physician, like yourself, and I've visited the Institut. He's not the one, however, who gave us details of your research. Let's not bother with incidental details, though—it's late and you'd doubtless like me to get to the point as quickly as possible. In sum, we know of your work, in which we have a strong interest, and we sympathize with your present situation. France, alas, has always been ingrate to its pioneers of science. If Louis XIV had not revoked the Edict of Nantes and sent all the Protestants packing, France, not England, would have led the Industrial Revolution. More recently, Napoléon III exiled Republican intellectuals, including Raspail, and nowadays the fashionable panic concerns Anarchism, again sending several of our great minds into exile."

"I'm not an Anarchist," Mathieu observed, warily.

"I intended no accusation," Valcoeur said. "I was merely illustrating an unfortunate pattern. Your experiments in blood transfusion, like my own, only became possible because a ridiculous ban was recently lifted, and the lifting of the ban has not prevented the attempts at suppression from which you suffered, and which I might well suffer too were I not working a long way from Paris, in relative isolation. But France must not be allowed to cut her own throat in that fashion. A man like you, Dr. Galmier, should not be working as a fugitive in London. He ought, ideally, to be funded by the State, working in the best laboratories in Paris, but since that has become difficult, I'd like you to consider the possibility of working in the Midi, in collaboration with me. I think such a collaboration might prove very fruitful, and the location ideal. Paris has become the center of global civilization, the *avant garde* of progress, but Aquitaine once held a similar position, and its oldest families can trace their ancestry back to that time. There are regions that have been relatively untouched by the centuries of strife that have destroyed so much of the cultural heritage of ancient Aquitaine…including its alchemical traditions."

"I'm no more an alchemist than an Anarchist," Mathieu remarked, a trifle sharply. He could not help glancing at the picture on the mantelpiece, and he noticed that Myrtille de Valcoeur had observed his attention.

Philippe de Valcoeur was about to issue another reassuring assent, but his sister interrupted him, leaning forward. "But you *are* a modern alchemist, are you not, Dr. Galmier," she said. "And circumstances have obliged you to conduct yourselves as the ancient alchemists were often forced to do, working covertly and furtively. Sometimes, however, those alchemists of old found powerful patrons, who supported them in their quests—for the secrets of transmutation, for spiritual enlightenment, and…"

She deliberately left the sentence dangling, perhaps in the hope that Mathieu would complete it.

He did not. He steeled himself, as he had at Templeforth's house earlier. "I fear," he said, "that it's quite impossible for me to leave London at present. I have a patient…"

"Sir Julian Templeforth," said Philippe. "We're aware of that. We're also aware that your treatment has been successful in his case.

Not successful enough, Mathieu thought. *Appearances can be deceptive.* He was beginning to suspect that the Valcoeurs not only thought that he was in search of the legendary elixir of life, but that he had found it. Did they also know, he wondered—or at least suspect—what kind of costs the production of his own less ambitious elixir required?

"The treatment isn't concluded," he said, aloud. "I can't leave London at present, or in the foreseeable future, and even if I could…"

He left the sentence unfinished, feeling that they had set the rules of the game, and that he might as well use the same strategy of vague implication.

Once again, it was Philippe de Valcoeur who assumed the responsibility of picking up the thread of the conversation and directing it.

"You do not know us," he concluded. "Well, you can research our ancestry, if you wish, in the British Museum Reading Room, if that is what concerns you, but I believe you to be a practical man who puts little store in status and reputations. More importantly, I am a graduate of the University of Toulouse, and a qualified physician, involved in research on the analysis of human blood and the possibilities of its transfusion. My sister is a scholar in her own right, albeit in more esoteric fields. My mother is a great reader, and since suffering an accident some twenty years ago that left her paralyzed from the waist down, she too has become a very assiduous scholar. My late father was a graduate of the École Normale, an engineer who played a considerable role in the south-western extension of the railway system.

"All of that is incidental, however. The point is, Dr. Galmier, that we are in a position to offer you a place in which to work infinitely more comfortable than your present lodgings, and funding for your research more generous than Sir Julian Templeforth. Our estate, including our château, is situated in a truly beautiful landscape, and although it is certainly isolated, it is not deprived of good intellectual company. I think you would find it preferable in every possible way to foggy London."

Mathieu suspected that he might—but Philippe de Valcoeur was presumably unaware of the precise nature of the dependency that Templeforth had on his physician at present, and was probably also unaware of the exact nature of Mathieu's dependency on his client.

"I really am sorry," he said, "but I'm simply not free to consider other offers of support for the moment. I have a duty to my patient, and until his treatment has reached a satisfactory conclusion, I cannot leave London, fog or no fog." His tension increased as he wondered whether his refusal might lead to a change of tone and tactics on the part of his mysterious interlocutors.

It was Myrtille who took up the thread, leaning forward and staring at him intently.

"Are you really content, Dr. Galmier," she said, softly, "to serve the cause of Sir Julian Templeforth's personal vanity and lust, when there are higher causes that your work might and ought to be serving?"

That was not a direction from which he had expected the attack to come. Nonplussed, he could not meet the young woman's stare, and his gaze flickered to the mantelpiece.

"Do you know what that symbol is, Dr. Galmier?" she asked, softly.

That question, he could answer. "A Rose Cross," he said. "There was a fictitious seventeenth-century fraternity of scholars, supposed custodians of occult wisdom, who adopted that name, but I believe that their rose was white, not red. The symbol has recently been taken over by several masonic sects in Paris, and at least one in London."

"Indeed," she said. "But the symbol is much older than the seventeenth century. The specific Fraternity identified by the *Fama fraternitatis* was, as you say, largely fictitious…but the choice of its symbolism was significant, and not inapt. It's late, Dr. Galmier, and I fear that it would take far too long to explain now exactly what it means to us—but I am very anxious to do so. Could you come back tomorrow, perhaps, during the day or earlier in the evening, so that I can offer you that explanation, and Philippe can tell you more about his research?"

Mathieu suddenly felt a trap yawning beneath his feet. He wanted to know who had found him, and why, but he also wanted to get rid of them, if possible, as quickly and cleanly as possible. He did not want to become bogged down in an argument about "the cause of Sir Julian Templeforth's vanity and lust," which he surely could not win, and he certainly did not want to be ensnared by some kind of modern mystical cult.

"I'm sorry," he said again, "but I have a very full day tomorrow...."

"The day after, then?" Myrtille de Valcoeur's mesmeric determination was a quieter and more effective variety than Sir Julian's, but it was evidently just as powerful.

"There are complications...," he began weakly.

"All the more reason, Dr. Galmier, why you might need our help and support. Whatever complications there are, I'm sure that we can help you to solve them. You're not alone, Dr. Galmier—not any more. If you cannot leave London for the moment, then please accept our help here; but above all, please listen to what we have to say. I can assure you that it really is in your best interests."

Mathieu could not shake off the feeling that a trap was being extended for him—but nor could he escape the feeling that it was unavoidable. And the assurance that he was not alone, that help might be available to him when he needed it most, promised soothing balm to a stinging wound...if only he could trust it.

As he hesitated, Philippe de Valcoeur stepped into the breach again. "We sympathize fully with your sense of duty to your patient, Dr. Galmier. We understand that you want to complete his course of treatment. But when that treatment is finished, we are prepared to do everything necessary to facilitate your return to France, and to smooth over any subsequent difficulties that might arise with the French authorities. When the time comes, we can arrange the transfer of any equipment and personnel that you need or want to take with you. We can board a ship in the port of London, bound for Bordeaux, as soon as you feel free to do so, but by all means take all the time you need to make a decision—and please, as my sister says, come back to see us again, so that we can explain more fully the nature of our interest in your work. We are content to remain at your disposal in the meantime."

Mathieu continued to hesitate, uncomfortably aware of the Valcoeurs' seeming blissful ignorance of the real difficulty—the horror, even—of his present situation. What would their reaction be, he wondered, if or when he explained the costs his work involved, and the manner in which he had accepted them?

His gaze flicked back and forth between the bother and the sister, anxiously.

"The girls in our homeland are exceedingly pretty," Myrtille observed, almost as if it were a matter of complete indifference, a mere detail of the décor.

Mathieu felt a sudden frisson, The possibility that the Valcoeurs knew about the casualties of his endeavor, and might be horrified by them, suddenly seemed less ominous that the possibility that they did know, but did not care—and might, indeed, be just as willing as Sir Julian to supply his experiments with "raw material."

Mathieu could not help flinching, and blushing. He knew that Myrtille had seen his reaction, but she seemed surprised, as if she had not expected to touch such sensitive nerve. Perhaps, he thought, she only knew abut the girls in Paris, and not the ones in London. But if Philippe de Valcoeur was involved in research parallel to his own, with some result, he might have encountered the same snag, and if that were the case…

"Further explanations are clearly necessary," said Myrtille de Valcoeur, virtually echoing his own thought. "We need to understand one another fully. There will be time for explanations, while Sir Julian Templeforth's treatment continues…but may I ask you when that treatment is likely to conclude?" She was still leaning forward, and her stare was intense, as if she were trying to read in his mind an answer that she did not expect him to spell out orally.

"I really can't tell," he admitted. "The treatment is experimental, and there's no basis as yet for me to calculate a timetable. It's possible, in fact, that it might not be concluded at all…that further treatment might be required indefinitely."

The explicit statement seemed like a confession…a confession of a mortal sin, for which there might be no possible absolution. He thought he could read disappointment in Philippe de Valcoeur's eyes, and decided that the brother, at least, had hoped to discover that he had made more progress than he had. Myrtille's reaction was more difficult to evaluate, but she did not seem surprised by the possibility that Sir Julian might require continued testament permanently.

"We understand the difficulties of such projects only too well," Philippe said, "but I repeat that if we can help in any way to bring matters to a conclusion, or at least to a point where a pause might be appropriate, we will be only too glad to help. Mother has urged us to do everything possible to bring you to Valcoeur, at least for a short visit, but if that is not practical at the moment, we shall adapt our plans accordingly. In the meantime, we can be patient."

Mathieu was about to stand up and take his leave, but hesitated. There was too much he did not know, too much that might be cause for alarm. He glanced again at the image of the red Rose Cross on the mantelpiece. "Forgive me if I'm being presumptuous," he said, "but I can't help suspecting that you might be laboring under a misapprehension as to the exact nature of my discovery and my research. I fear that you might have been misled by rumor, or even by appearances, to think that I can work wonders beyond my actual compass. What I have discovered is not an elixir of longevity, or even a fountain of youth."

"We are not under that illusion," Myrtille assured him, flatly. "I think, when I have explained our own objectives, you will understand that we have far more in common than you imagine."

"But on the other hand," Philippe interjected, "how can either of us tell how far our work might eventually progress, now that we have modern equipment and modern experimental methods. Our present limitations might be temporary, and the breakthrough might come at any moment. Once the crucial obstacle is overcome, perhaps a true fount of youth or elixir of longevity will not be beyond our reach. Mother is trapped by the ideas of long tradition, but we might well be able to break free from those shackles. If we can combine our efforts, Dr. Galmier, who can tell what we might achieve?"

Mathieu had the impression that that speech had been aimed as much at Myrtille de Valcoeur as at him. He inferred that whatever traditional thought had "trapped" Madame de Valcoeur's ideas also had a grip on her daughter's, and that there was a degree of disharmony within the family. On the other hand, it appeared to have been the mother who had sent the children to find him, and to bring him to Valcoeur.

"My brother is an optimist," Myrtille de Valcoeur put in, "and I admire him for it—but please don't be intimidated. Dr. Galmier. We do not expect miracles from you. We know that yours is an honest endeavor, which showed genuine promise before you felt obliged to quit Paris, but we also know that promise of that kind sometimes flatters only to deceive, and can be frustratingly slow. The path of progress is steep and winding, and hedged with thorns, but it does lead upwards, toward the light. We would like to enable you, if possible, to walk that path in tranquility, and to favor your march as best we can. All that we ask of you—all that anyone can reasonably ask of you—is that you make what progress can presently be made, by means of your intellect and labor. We believe that it would be greatly to your advantage to work with us…

with all of us."

"That's very generous," Mathieu murmured, still uneasy. He groped for rational arguments to shore up his unease, but none came readily to mind.

"You need time to complete your current operations," Philippe supplied. "We understand that, and we will gladly grant you all the time you need. But please think about what we have said, and please come back to see us as soon as possible, so that I can explain my present research, and the historical background to it, more fully, and answer the questions that you will undoubtedly have to ask. As I said, we shall remain at your disposal in London for as long as necessary."

After that careful repetition, Philippe de Valcoeur stood up, although his sister waited until Mathieu had done likewise before standing up herself. The three of them parted in the most cordial fashion imaginable, on Mathieu's promise that he would come to see them again when he had the chance, in order that they could discuss their mutual interests further.

As he went down the hotel stairs, Mathieu honestly could not tell whether he had just been thrown a lifeline that might save him from drowning, or whether he was being invited to jump from a sizzling frying-pan into a blazing fire—and he criticized himself bitterly for a fear that seemed entirely unworthy of him or the situation.

I've lost my self-confidence, he thought, *and my courage has fled with it. I have to pull myself together. I'm going to need my wits about me tomorrow.*

As he walked home, Mathieu lost himself in urgent thought. He dismissed as too absurd the hypothesis that the Valcoeurs might be working for the police, endeavoring to lure him back to France in order that he might be arrested. And having rejected that, why should he not take everything that they said at face value? How, in fact, could he avoid doing so, given that he could not imagine any other motive for them to lie?

One way or another, obviously, rumor of the work he had begun at the Institut, and had made no attempt to hide in its early stages, had spread far and wide. Sir Julian Templeforth was far from being the only man in the world liable to be attracted by the promise it had apparently held, and there was a certain category of women who would undoubtedly find that lure even more powerful than Templeforth. Might that include Madame de Valcoeur? But the hopes he had awakened had so far had proved more than a little treacherous, and the cost, in human terms, far higher than he had initially anticipated. Could he continue to allow potential patients to entertain those mercurial hopes? If he could solve the present problems with the maintenance of Templeforth's condition, then yes, undoubtedly—but if he could not, and the worst came to the worst, that would be another matter entirely.

The fact that one of the London prostitutes had died was only part of the problem, although it *was* a part, even though he had not actually killed her or even contributed directly to the cause of her death. It was the ones who were still very much alive who were the real problem, the very image of his ironic failure. And if he continued his present program he would have to bleed at least two more…no, *only* two more; he had to fix his determination in that regard. If the breakthrough did not come, this time, he surely had to change direction…if he could. If he had been able to multiply the number of donors, and reduce the donation made by each individual, the side-effects could undoubtedly be reduced, but how could he possibly cast his net wider, without attracting attention?

And even if Sir Julian could be persuaded by buy prostitutes by the dozen rather than one at a time, simply reducing the side-effects on each individual would not make any contribution to solving the fundamental problem, and if the problem persisted, the dozens might become hundreds. It was all very well to think, glibly about "changing direction," but he could not do that without first defining another direction to take. He could not simply stop Sir Julian's treatment while he went back to basics and tried to plot another course toward the objective. Quite apart from the form that Sir Julian's wrath might take, if his worst fears regarding the consequences of a cessation of treatment proved justified, a physician really did have a sacred duty to his patient, a duty not to abandon him, even if that meant…

But he did not want to think about that. He had turned off the Gold-hawk Road some time ago, and had now reached his front door, in a street of terraced houses. Belatedly, he remembered Sir Julian's recommendation that he keep looking behind in order to ascertain whether he was being followed. The street was deserted at this late hour, but it was also very dark. As he scanned the two rows of houses, the quantity of dark doorways and coverts where a watcher might be hiding seemed ominously numerous—but there was no sign of movement.

Again, he cursed himself for his fears. *Pull yourself together*, he commanded himself, sternly. *This is no time for weakness.*

He turned the key in the lock and went into the gloomy, lonely house, where he dared not employ a servant—especially a maidservant, no matter how ugly—and dared not even hire a laboratory assistant by the day.

He lit a small lantern, which provided an illumination more lugubrious than the one in the corridor of the Brook Green Hotel, until he had turned into the ground floor laboratory, where he lit both the readily-available lamps. He checked the blinds before turning them up, however; he did not anyone peering in, or even being surprised by a brightness in his window that seemed excessive to eyes accustomed to the vulgar nocturnal illumination of tallow candles. Even in the supposed Age of Enlightenment, in the heart of a great metropolis like London, rumors of necromancy and diabolism were far too easy to generate and spread.

After disposing of his coat, hat and cane, however, Mathieu did not go to work immediately. His ideas were too confused, still confronted by alternatives that would have to be weighed and evaluated. He knew that he ought not to allow that confusion to undermine his concentration and inhibit his work, but knowing it and achieving it were two different things.

He sat down in an armchair, and put his head in his hands—but he could not afford dejection, let alone despair. Only a few minutes later, he got up again, picked up his large magnifying-glass, and began inspecting his precious cultures, hoping, as he had hoped so many times before, that this time, the alchemical gold would not have faded away, and might instead have intensified its gleam....

III

Cormack brought the girl early the following morning, as had been promised the previous evening.

"She's bought and paid for, all day," the butler said. "She's all yours."

Mathieu gritted his teeth. Cormack knew perfectly well what the girl would be required to do, and had had been instructed to explain it to her in sufficient detail to obtain her consent, but the butler was privately convinced that Mathieu used the prostitutes in more orthodox ways as well. Mathieu wished that the fat man was entirely wrong about that, but his own flesh was, alas, as weak as the next man's, and scientific rectitude had not always counterbalanced temptation. He had only succumbed once in the three years since he had arrived in London, but once was surely too many, especially as he had been fully aware by then of the consequences of the extraction and his inability to ameliorate those consequences. When he had nightmares, the lost face that haunted him was the face of the girl he had used, and defiled, in more ways than one.

On this occasion, however, he was determined to be rigorous, all the more so as the girl was little more than a child. She might only have been thirteen, in Mathieu's judgment, although she claimed, when asked, to be sixteen. Either way, she seemed unlikely to reach twenty, whatever was done or not done to her in the meantime.

She told Mathieu that her name was Judy Lee, which he had no reason to doubt. Prostitutes who used invented names, as many did, tended to use more fanciful ones, and usually did not bother with surnames at all.

"Do you know why you're here, Judy?" Mathieu asked, when Cormack had gone, leaving him alone with the girl in the laboratory, which she was inspecting with more wonderment than anxiety.

"Going to bleed me," the girl said. Her accent was barbaric. "Been cupped afore—didn't do me no good, though they said it would."

Her gaze was flitting hither and yon, surprised but not unduly intimidated by the profusion of glassware and apparatus. She had surely never been to a public lecture at the Royal Institution, so the only place she might have seen such an assembly of equipment before was on the stage of some cheap theatre. Quasi-alchemical laboratory equipment had been a clichéd décor of exaggerated melodrama ever since Mary Shelley's *Frankenstein* has been adapted for the Porte-Saint-Martin in Paris more than sixty years before and had quickly migrated back to England in imitative pieces. If she had seen such apparatus on the stage, however, it had not given her cause to be frightened. Cormack had evidently impressed upon her that Mathieu was a doctor, a healer, a man who could be trusted.

"I'm not going to cup you, Judy," Mathieu said, as soothingly as he could. "I'm going to insert two hollow needles into veins in your forearms. They've been sterilized in an autoclave—that's a high-temperature boiler—and I'll swab the flesh with alcohol first to sterilize that too. The cooling effect of the alcohol's evaporation will help numb the pain. I'm going to leave the needles in place for some time, so that I can put the blood I draw from one vein through a special filter, and then return it to the other. It might seem rather horrid, but it's quite safe. You can watch if you like, or look away, if you'd rather. One day, in the not-too-distant future, such procedures will be standard practice in hospitals all over the world, and everyone will be familiar with them."

"I had worse done to me," Judy Lee reported, making an effort to remain laconic. Mathieu had no reason to doubt that, either. He thought it best to keep talking, not so much by way of paying lip-service to the principle of informed consent as to reassure her that this was something that he had done before, many times, and that it really would become a normal aspect of medical practice one day—*scientific* medical practice, not quackery or the obsolete traditions that the majority of practicing physicians still insisted on following.

"You're contributing to an important study, Judy," he assured her. "You and I are adventurers on the path of progress."

The girl attempted to smile, but she had not been a whore long enough to have mastered that kind of insincerity. She was still beautiful, as much because of the pallor of the consumption that had already begun to eat her away as in spite of it. The disease gave a certain semi-transparent gloss to the skin and sculpted her lean features, exaggerating the eyes in a strangely soulful fashion.

Mathieu told himself that she would not have been beautiful for much longer, whether he intervened in the process of her deterioration or not, but he was not sufficiently hypocritical to wonder where it might be good for her to become less attractive, perhaps even to be saved from a successful career in prostitution. He knew that the only thing worse than being a whore who had an overabundance of clients was being a whore who could not find enough.

Soon, he thought instead, he would be able to pay back what he took from his "volunteers," with abundant interest. If he were only given time and adequate financial support, he would surely find a way to isolate the agent and feed it *in vitro*, so that it would be able reproduce itself independently of its host. Then the transactions in which he dealt would no longer be a matter of robbing Petronella to pay Paul, but a matter of assisting in the evolution of humankind, of building a hitherto-unimaginable Utopia on the rickety foundations of London's slums.

"French, ain't yer?" the girl said, as the second needle went in, causing her to grimace with pain. The original syringe, having injected the anti-clotting serum, had been hooked up to the pump and the filtration apparatus. Mathieu hooked up the second modified syringe, completing the circuit, with the utmost care.

He had good grounds, nowadays, to be sure that he could feed at least six liters of the girl's blood through the machine without undue risk, and return it to her body, although he would have to give her instructions to limit subsequent blood-loss, given that the anti-clotting agent would remain in her bloodstream for anything up to three days. It had been an induced hemophilia that had caused the two fatal casualties in Paris, not the extraction process itself, but a Parisian tribunal would have been unlikely to appreciate the nice distinction, and an English court would doubtless take an equally harsh view. There had only been the one fatality since he had decamped to London—but that might well prove to be one too many, if the spy who had been watching Sir Julian's house the night before really had been a policeman investigating his activities.

"Yes, I'm French," Mathieu admitted, without looking up from his work. "I worked with Louis Pasteur in Paris before I came to London."

"Heard o'him," Judy Lee boasted. "Germs'n'that."

"That's right," Mathieu said, approvingly. "He's developed a method of sterilizing milk, and a treatment for rabies. A great man—a very great man, although François Raspail actually deserves the credit, not merely for developing the germ theory of disease, but also for pioneering the hygienic precautions that have done so much to prevent infection."

"Don't know him," the girl observed, without any undue shame or disappointment. She was watching her blood flow along the tubes without any evident horror or faintness, and a certain avid fascination.

"Pasteur's greatest gift has been the founding of the Institute that is continuing and extrapolating his work and Raspail's. That's where experiments in blood transfusion are being carried out, now that the legal prohibition has been lifted. We lost two hundred years of potential progress in that regard, because the scientific method came into conflict with the law. The first human blood transfusions are said to have carried out within walking distance of this very spot, by Sir Christopher Wren—the man who designed Saint Paul's Cathedral—in 1657."

The date seemed meaningless to Judy Lee, who provably did not have an adequate knowledge of arithmetic to carry out a subtraction of that magnitude.

Mathieu plugged on, thinking that if he talked with blithe confidence, the incomprehensibility of much of what he said would only add to his apparent authority, and help to maintain his patient's confidence. "Wren was hoping to find a method of rejuvenation, but it soon turned out that one man's blood is sometimes another man's poison. My countryman, Jean-Baptiste Denis, was sued by the widow of a man who died in the course of one of his transfusion experiments, and the practice was outlawed. The prohibition was relaxed temporarily early in the present century, when a surgeon named Jamee Blundell used a syringe to carry out infusions in order to counter heavy blood loss after women gave birth. Many of his attempts were successful, but some ran into catastrophic problems because of unexpected incompatibilities between the transfused blood and the recipient's. My former colleagues at the Institut have been working hard to understand those incompatibilities and to draw up classification of blood types that will enable transfusions to be made safely.

"That could have been done long ago—even the primitive microscopes of the eighteenth century would have been adequate to the necessary investigations—but the work wasn't done because no one dared take the risk of prosecution. If the early experiments had persisted, all kinds of surgery would have become safer and more effective more than a hundred years ago—the metalworkers and glassworkers of the day would have been easily able to produce hollow needles and Pravaz syringes, if only there had been a manifest need for them. As things turned out, though, it has taken a long time to put together the kind of apparatus that can replace blood lost in surgery, just as I'm now replacing yours, and its use in hospitals is still rare.

"The removal of blood from the body, the prevention of its clotting and its reintroduction may seem bizarre to you, but they'll very soon be routine procedures in medical practice. In the twentieth century, there will probably be nothing in the least unusual in people selling their blood for the use of others, probably for less than the guinea you were paid.

"Scientific medicine might have made vast strides in the eighteenth century, if only medical scientists had been permitted to experiment rationally. Instead, there was a Golden Age of quackery, when all kinds of bizarre patent medicines flourished, while orthodox physicians fought tooth and nail to defend their own superstitions. The possible deaths of a few dozen or a few hundred volunteers in controlled experiments were prevented by the ban, while hundreds of thousands of people who had no choice at all died by virtue of licensed but misguided treatments, and millions more by virtue of ignorant inaction. Things are different now—very different—but the necessary research requires time, and money, which is direly hard to come by. If the governments of Europe would only take their responsibilities seriously, instead of spending all their time and revenues plotting and preparing for war, there'd be no need for self-serving buccaneers like Sir Julian Temp...."

He stopped abruptly, realizing that his tongue had run away with him, and that it was perhaps as well that the girl could not be expected to understand what he was saying. "I'm sorry," he said. "What I mean is that you're helping in a great cause, and have every reason to be proud of yourself."

"Just doin' it for the money," she observed, dully. "You can buy a girl in Bethnal Green for a shilling—a guinea's good scratch. Done worse for far less."

Mathieu gritted his teeth again. "One day," he said, in a low voice, "my work will do wonders for girls like you. You'll be its true beneficiaries, at the end of the day. The twentieth century will be a new Age of Miracles, not just for the rich but for everyone."

She was hardly listening. Her eyes were glued to the apparatus—not to the flowing red blood now, but to the extract oozing from the gel compartment into the collection tube, which was beginning to form golden droplets.

"What's that yellow stuff?" she asked.

"The red color of blood is due to a pigment carried in corpuscles," he told her. "It's only red when it's oxygenated—if you look at the veins on the back of your hand you'll see that they're blue, because that's the color the corpuscles have when they're not oxygenated. You never see blue blood outside the veins, though, because the moment the corpuscles are exposed to the atmosphere by a cut, they turn red. If you take the corpuscles out of the blood, the fluid in which they float, the plasma, is the color of straw. But plasma is still a complex mixture of dissolved substances and living cells. The particular substance that my special filter is removing and diverting is golden yellow."

"Not real gold, then?" said Judy Lee, in jest.

"More precious than that," he murmured. "Alchemical gold."

"Really?"

Mathieu collected himself, not wanting to mislead the girl by the use of metaphors that she might take too literally. "No, not really," he said, apologetically—that's just a manner of speaking. Our techniques of chemical analysis aren't yet capable of determining a precise formula for the golden fluid, but it's not simply an inert solution. It doesn't consist of corpuscles visible through a microscope, but I suspect that there are many kinds of living cells, and perhaps living entities that don't consist of cells, that are too small for microscopes to distinguish.

"The filter is the key to the whole process. That was the one stroke of luck I had that no other researcher has found, and it might have remained undiscovered for decades if I hadn't stumbled upon it. It doesn't work like a sieve—in fact, as you can see, it lets the red corpuscles and other cellular components through—but it soaks up the vital ingredient in which I'm interested. At first, I had hoped to make use of the orthodox filters used in chemical analysis, but I soon realized that not only do they trap far too many components, but that the particular biological agents I was trying to isolate are extraordinarily delicate, and very easily destroyed. Some of them, it seems, can only survive in contact with living tissue. I began experimenting with filters comprised of networks of fungal hyphae, and then with gels made from fungal protoplasm. I was fortunate enough to find a gel that not only absorbed but preserved the golden fluid that became the focal point of my future research, at least temporarily. And there it is."

"But not real gold?" she said "I don't have real gold in my blood—just fool's gold."

That was not an analogy with which Mathieu was comfortable.

"It's not metallic gold," he said, "but it really is exceedingly precious."

"Worth more than a guinea, then?" Without waiting for a reply, though, the girl added: "Obviously, or you wouldn't bother. Not worth anything to me, though, without a buyer. Like other things I could name, if I weren't in decent company."

Mathieu did not want to discuss the other objects of her traffic, even though he was far from sure that he qualified any longer as "decent company." He continued talking about remoter matters.

"The whole *raison d'être* of the Institut Pasteur is to substitute a new scientific medicine for the alchemical medicine of old, and to replace the occult version of the human microcosm with an image based on the findings of microscopy and organic chemistry. We knew at the outset, of course, that the microcosm in question would not be simple, but we had no conception of the awesome extent of the complexity that we would discover—although *discover* may be too strong a word, given that we have barely begun the process of exploration.

"John Donne once proclaimed that no man is an island, and he was right—every man is, in fact, not merely an island but a universe, entire and unique, which plays host to all manner of microbiological life-forms, and other agents whose nature seems to be ambiguously suspended between life and inertia. You might have heard talk of bacilli and protozoans, but we'll require a terminology far more elaborate than that to get to grips with the complexity of the multitudinous entities that dwell within a human body, the vast majority of which remain invisible to the most powerful microscopes."

Judy Lee was looking at him carefully, with a certain wonderment. He knew that she could only understand a tiny fraction of what he was saying, but would be all the more impressed by it in consequence, all the more inclined to believe that he knew what he was doing, that he could be trusted. In any case, he needed to keep talking, for his own benefit rather than hers. He felt a need to summarize, to clarify, to remind himself what not only of he was doing, but why—to remind himself that the poor child wasn't simply "raw material" to be used, discarded and forgotten but a collaborator in a great and magnificent enterprise, of which she should and ought to be proud.

She was prepared to listen to him meekly and patiently, not merely because she was a captive of the apparatus, for the time being, but because she doubtless had to be prepared to listen meekly and patiently to other clients who liked to talk while they used her flesh for their own purpose, putting on a show of understanding, of being interested, of giving value for the money they were paying her. For a guinea, she was prepared to manifest a lot of docility.

"Thanks to François Raspail and Louis Pasteur," Mathieu continued, "we now have good grounds for believing that many, if not all, infectious diseases are caused by micro-organisms of one sort or another. Thanks to Edward Jenner, we've begun to find ways of countering the pathological activity of those invaders, sometimes by means of other micro-organisms. The vast majority of the entities that live within us are, however, benign. It is quite possible that we couldn't exist without them—that the life we think of as our own is actually a collaborative enterprise, and that the processes of progressive evolution that the Chevalier de Lamarck and Charles Darwin have identified and explained are collaborative too. At any rate, our internal populations are as subject to the principle of natural selection as we are, and far more intensely, by virtue of the brief life-spans of the individuals comprising them.

"When I was at the Institut I agreed with my colleagues in thinking of aging and death in terms of disease. Like them, I entertained the hope that we might one day find ways to combat the disease of aging, perhaps to find a medical elixir of life. That was why I went to the Institut in the first place. Once there, though, I began to think in somewhat different terms, wondering whether it was really accurate to imagine youth and health in terms of the mere absence of, or resistance to, agents of decay.

I began to wonder whether good health and the common attributes of youthfulness might more accurately be considered as positive results of the tireless endeavor of active agents, while old age and death are merely the consequences of the eventual fatigue and failure of those collaborative commensals.

"There was nothing unreasonable about that kind of eventual failure, I realized, in terms of the logic of Darwin's theory. Like all living organisms, the primary imperative of our indwelling multitudes is to reproduce themselves, not merely within the context of a particular human microcosm but in terms of the further reproduction of the microcosm entire. Natural selection exerts strong pressure on our indwelling micro-organisms—especially those which, unlike disease-causing bacilli, can't easily transmit themselves from one microcosm to another by infection or contagion—to do whatever they can to further the cause of human reproduction. Once the reproductive phase of human life is over, however, such micro-organisms would no longer be subject to pressure maintaining that aspect of their activity, and their own mortality would tend, in consequence, to be fragile and limited...."

He broke off, not because the argument was complete, but because the extraction process had nearly run its course. The collection tube was almost full of golden liquid. He inspected it closely, trying to measure the exact color, the presumed purity. He was convinced that the fragility and mortality of the substance was at least partly due to impurities that earlier versions of his filter had retained. The sample extracted from Judy Lee, however, seemed perfectly clear to the naked eye, and the color was beautiful.

"You don't get much for your guinea," Judy Lee observed, measuring the size of the collection tube with her bleak blue eyes.

Not nearly enough, he could not help thinking. *But for you, unless you're very lucky, far too much.*

The effects on the donors of the removal of the golden fluid had been very variable, apparently in accordance with some mysterious law or pattern that he could not yet predict. Some girls were less disfigured by the diminution of their beauty than others. Younger ones tended to fare better, and also to have more capacity to regenerate fluid to compensate for the removal; it was the riper, more mature forms of beauty whose loss was more striking, more despairing. He hoped, with all sincerity, that Judy Lee would not come out of the process too badly.

Initially, he had assumed that the golden fluid would be regenerated fully, in exactly the same that blood removed from patients by means of leeches, lancets or syringes was renewed by the body's own mechanisms. Even when he had realized that the recovery was always partial, he had hoped that the deficit might be reparable by means of conventional tonics and cordials, that if the general health of the patient could be improved, the golden fluid might recover the level and effect that it had had prior to the extraction.

He had clung to that hope for a long time but it was gone now. He knew, now, that the extraction process inflicted permanent damage—damage that he had not yet found a means of repairing The beauty he stole from the donors in order to improve Sir Julian Templeforth's good looks—in the service, as Myrtille de Valcoeur had reminded him, of the aristocrat's vanity and lust—was for them a permanent diminution.

Some of the earlier patients who had come back to see him—not to accuse him of anything, at least directly, but simply because he was the only doctor they knew, and someone to whom they could turn for help—had gained some benefit from the tonics he had devised, but none had recovered her former attractions in full. Meanwhile, the benefit transferred to Sir Julian was always temporary, and the duration of the effect declined with each new treatment. The arithmetic of the exchange never added up; there was always a deficit in the total.

He did not know how long he could keep telling himself that he was on the very brink of the breakthrough that would enable him to maintain Sir Julian's condition without increasingly frequent transfusions, and begin to repair some of the damage that he had inflicted upon the victims of his vampirism. He did not know how long he could ward off the confrontation with the possibility that the breakthrough in question might never some, that the moment might arrive when he might have to tell Sir Julian that he was not prepared to continue his treatment, and that he too would have to suffer the fate of his victims, perhaps in an exaggerated fashion.

"Do you mind if I leave you alone for a few minutes, Judy?" he said. "The process is almost finished; I'll come back to unhook you very soon. I'll be within earshot, so if you need anything, just shout."

Judy Lee nodded. Mathieu knew that he really ought to stay, but her taciturnity was putting undue stress on his lecturing skills, and the atmosphere in the subterranean laboratory was becoming foul with the reek of blood. He needed a few breaths of fresh air—and today, fortunately, was one of the rare days on which London's air really was fresh. Yesterday's rain had washed the lingering smog-particles out of the atmosphere, and a brisk south-westerly breeze was preventing its reformation. Although the new network of sewers had not yet taken up the entirety of the river's burden, the days of the Great Stink were long gone.

Mathieu went up the steps to the pavement of the street and leaned against the railings protecting the hollow in which his front door was set. There was a faint unsteady vibration beneath his feet, which was primarily a side-effect of the construction-work on the underground railway, although the excavation of the sewers still had a minor contribution to make. London's Underworld was a complex hive of activity nowadays, with countless workers toiling round the clock in shifts, largely unnoticed by the denizens of the surface.

Men of science, Mathieu thought, were not unlike those subterranean laborers, their patiently heroic endeavors being largely unheeded by journalists and historians alike. The chroniclers of the modern world, like those of the Middle Ages, paid close attention to the actions of kings, statesmen and generals, but rarely noticed the subtle revolutions in technology that were the true motor of history.

Mathieu realized, however, that he was not unobserved at present. There was a tall, thin man bundled up in a dark blue overcoat leaning casually on the railings of the house opposite, who never looked at him directly but never excluded him from his field of vision either. Mathieu had no idea whether it was the same man who had been watching Sir Julian's house the previous evening, and he had no way of determining whether or not the watcher might be a police detective, but he was suddenly in no doubt that he and his lodgings were under surveillance.

The laboratory was only visible from the street when the blinds were raised, as they hardly ever were, and only partially then. It was completely invisible from the back yard too—the only other ground floor window was that of the kitchen—but that did not make him feel any more comfortable.

He went back inside immediately, and hurried back to the girl, who was drowsy but seemed as well as could possibly be expected. He fed her a small measure of port wine, holding the glass to her lips so that she did not have to move her arms.

"Nearly over now, Judy," he said, mustering his best bedside manner. "I just have to take the needles out and tidy everything up."

"Don't mind," she replied, valiantly. "It don't hurt." She did not bother to add, once again, that she had done worse for less. For the moment, at least, she thought it was less. Perhaps she still would when the full cost became evident, even if it was worse than he hoped. The likelihood was, in any case, that she would not connect the delayed effect with this particular cause, and would not bear any grudge against him at all. But he felt sure—and his meeting with the Valcoeurs the previous evening had only confirmed his conviction, in spite of their careful circumlocutions—that other people would soon been able to put two and two together and arrive at the correct total. His carefully sterilized hands were far from clean, even if the young women he injured—the children he injured, in some cases—did not realize it.

When he had detached the needles and bandaged the residual wounds, he gave Judy Lee a generous cup of hot sweet tea and a slice of toast with marmalade before allowing her to go on her way. He advised her to go home and rest, but he did not suppose that she would take the advice. She was a little unsteady on her feet but she could walk perfectly well. She looked around as he ushered her through the hallway, taking what note she could of the circumstances of his life.

"I can come back later, if you like" she said, as he opened the door. "For company, not blood." She sounded genuinely hopeful, perhaps because he seemed a substantial cut above her usual clients, one she would be glad to see regularly, or perhaps because she was optimistic enough to think that he might pay her as generously for the use of her meager flesh as for her rich blood.

"No," he said, brusquely. "That's not necessary." He suspected that she would be back eventually, for one reason or another, but he had learned to steel himself against such occasions, and to send the visitors away with whatever meager prescriptions he could provide. He was always discomfited, nevertheless, by the sight of the consequences of his work.

The watcher on the other side of the street did not budge from his station when Mathieu escorted the girl back up to the pavement, and did not follow her when she made her way back toward Goldhawk Road. The tall man watched the girl attentively as she walked away, though, before returning his eyes to Mathieu's lodgings, abruptly enough to catch Mathieu's gaze for a moment.

Mathieu judged, as the two of them locked stares, that the other man knew perfectly well that he had been spotted, but did not care. The watcher's eyes were dark and keen. The uneven coloring of his face suggested that he had recently shaved off a well-grown beard and moustache, in the habitual fashion of a seaman recently returned from a long voyage. He was lean but seemed muscular, and if he really was a mariner, he was probably strong and physically capable.

Mathieu hurried back to his laboratory, to begin work on the filtrate; it was a few minutes after three o'clock, and he was anxious to get the preparatory work done before Sir Julian arrived. He wanted the laboratory to be spick and span, to present an image of efficient, dedicated and productive labor. He wanted Sir Julian to feel confident that his money was being well spent, and would eventually prove, in spite of temporary snags, to be an excellent investment, on his own behalf and the world's.

Mathieu split the filtrate into two unequal parts: one for Sir Julian and one for the continuation of his *in vitro* experiments. He would dearly have loved to retain the larger fraction for the latter purpose, but he did not dare. Sir Julian's need—if *need* was the right word—was increasing too rapidly. Had the baronet been given the choice, Mathieu would probably have been instructed to reserve all the filtrate for his use, but Mathieu still had power enough within their relationship to insist that the broader purpose be maintained. Sir Julian had had plenty of opportunity to see what happened to the "volunteers" who provided him with the means to maintain his condition, and he knew exactly how valuable Mathieu's expertise was.

As a last resort, Mathieu knew, the baronet might take the chance of replacing him with some ambitious graduate of Guy's or St. Thomas's—but only as a last resort. Parties to the kind of Faustian bargain that Sir Julian Templeforth and Dr. Mathieu Galmier had made could not easily be substituted, on either side. On the other hand, he thought, the Valcoeurs of ancient Aquitaine might well be correct in suggesting that they could play Mephistopheles more convincingly than a minor Anglo-Irish landlord whose fortunes were apparently in decline.

He held the collection tube up to the lamplight, to try once again to assess the quality of the alchemical gold. The sample seemed pure, and beautiful, but he knew that it was not only Judy Lee's beauty that had been compromised by the extraction; the golden color would begin to tarnish too, in a matter of hours. Once in Sir Julian's veins, his fraction ought to be stabilized to some degree, but invisibly, it would gradually begin to lose its force, its alchemical power. The fraction that remained in the tube would follow a more visible deterioration, gradual but inexorable—unless he could find a way to nourish it, to maintain its mercurial vitality, and perhaps to multiply it.

He began, patiently and meticulously, to distribute droplets of the golden fluid in Petri dishes, whose lids were carefully marked to indicate the make-up of their substrates. The substrates were mostly transparent, but even in those, the yellow color was hardly visible once the droplet had spread out.

When all the dishes had been prepared he placed them carefully in the incubator, in order to maintain them at body temperature. There were only a dozen. Tomorrow or the next day, when Cormack brought him another patient ready and willing to be bled, he might be able to prepare as many as thirty, or even three dozen....but with the necessary replications, and the potential number of substrates whose effects had to be explored, that was still a very small number. He was in desperate need of a stroke of luck, a single crucial success on which to build. If he could only obtain that...

In the meantime, there was nothing he could do but keep trying, to keep working as hard as he could.

IV

While Mathieu was working on the filtrate, the lamps illuminating the laboratory began to run out of oil. One of them went out, but it was the more distant of the two and he did not immediately get up from his work-bench to refill it. His reserve supplies of fuel were at a low ebb; it would be better to make do with one lamp, if he could, at least until Sir Julian had handed over the promised cash.

His work would have been more brightly served by gaslight, of course, but the laboratory was only fitted with a single gas tap, which he reserved for his Bunsen burner.

Had Mathieu's rooms been located under the eaves of the house, instead of a ground floor so far between the level of the road outside that it almost qualified as a basement, he would have been able to work by daylight, but when he and Sir Julian had selected his place of work they had both thought a room whose blinds need never be raised best suited to their purpose.

At that time, they really had imagined that a single dose of the "vaccine" might suffice to work a miracle that could be repeated a hundred times over, but the combination of Jenner's practice and Pasteur's theory had not been as simple as Mathieu had hoped. The fundamental thesis had been sound enough—it really did seem to be the case that Jenner's vaccine worked because it transmitted a biological agent of some kind, rather than by observance of some strange homeopathic principle—but it had proved impossible to construct a strictly analogical procedure with respect to the agent that Mathieu's fungal gel filters had trapped and diverted.

The human microcosm was, it seemed, far more complicated than the macrocosm that scientific astronomy had recently begun to reveal, with the aid of photography, spectroscopes and increasingly powerful lenses. If the alchemical principle of *as above so below* specified a strict equivalence, it now seemed that every aspect of the universe contained infinitely more than was manifest to the naked eye, and that the scientific quest to elucidate its mysteries might be far more challenging than primitive occultists such as the imaginary fraternity of the Rose Cross had ever dared to believe. The spiritual ideal that such scholars had allegedly sought might be exceedingly difficult of attainment by merely human intelligence.

When Mathieu heard the click of a catch in the corridor outside the laboratory he immediately looked up at the clock, which indicated half past six. Sir Julian had a key to the front door, of course, and was not given to ringing doorbells, but he was a punctual man and it was unlike him to be early, even when he was anxious.

Mathieu looked around for something that might serve as a weapon, and picked up a scalpel from the bench. He moved to the door, but did not reach for the knob; instead, he positioned himself so that he would be concealed behind it if it were opened.

It did open, very quietly, and swung inwards slowly. That, too, was not Sir Julian's way—he was a man more inclined to throw doors open and march in boldly, no matter what the circumstances of his arrival might be. Whoever was opening the door now was peering in gingerly, attempting to look around before setting foot across the threshold. Had the intruder been anyone with a legitimate reason for being there, he would surely have called out, but he seemed intent on maintaining the strictest silence.

Mathieu did not wait for the invader to step inside, but put his shoulder to the door while the other was still within the compass of its swing, and shoved it with all his might. The other, quite unprepared for such an abrupt assault, cursed loudly and yielded ground—but he did not fall over and immediately began to shove back.

It was obvious to Mathieu that his adversary was the stronger man, for he felt himself gradually pressed back toward the wall, threatened with being trapped there by the pressure of the solid wooden door. He reached round the batten and slashed downwards with the scalpel. The thrust brought forth another curse, but the blade had caught the sleeve of a thick overcoat, and it was not a wounding blow. The other leaned on the door even harder, forcing him back against the wall and trying to crush the breath from Mathieu's body.

Mathieu cried out for help, although he had no reason at all to think that any assistance might be close at hand. The crushing pressure continued, and he shouted again, knowing that he might not have enough breath left for a third appeal. He lashed out with the scalpel twice more, but now that his assailant knew that the instrument was in his hand, the thrusts cleaved empty air.

Mathieu knew that he was beaten, and had just decided to issue his surrender and beg for mercy when the weight pressing on the door was suddenly relieved. There was the noise of a sudden furious tussle on the other side of it, and then the sound of running feet as one of the two combatants—presumably the one who had been using the door to crush him—scrambled for the front door.

Mathieu moved around the door, ready to greet his rescuer, assuming that he would see Sir Julian—but the man standing in the corridor, wearing a puzzled expression as he watched his erstwhile opponent beat an ungainly retreat, was the man who had been leaning on the railings opposite a few hours before, watching the house.

For a moment, Mathieu wondered whether the wrong combatant might have been bested, and raised the hand clutching the scalpel as if to stab his enemy—but then he realized that the watcher really had run to rescue him, and that the man who was now running up the steps beyond the front door was completely unknown to him.

It seemed to Mathieu, on due reflection that he really had had a narrow escape, because the man who was running away was every bit as tall, and considerably more heavily-built, than the man who had come to his aid.

Mathieu hesitated over what to do next—and while he hesitated, the watcher from the far side of the street grabbed his wrist and disarmed him, saying: "No need for that, Frenchy." His accent had a distinct cockney twang, but that was no guarantee that he was not a policeman.

At close range, Mathieu was able to estimate that the darker parts of the man's complexion were the consequence of exposure to tropical sunlight. The dark blue overcoat was, in fact, the sort worn by merchant seamen, and his heavily-callused hands provided further evidence that he was a sailor recently returned from a long voyage.

"Who are you?" Mathieu finally found the courage to demand.

"A friend, it seems—at least for the moment."

"Why were you watching my house? Have you been following me?"

"As a matter of fact," the tall man said, "I started off following the fellow who brought the little girl this morning. I had just about made up my mind to knock on your door, after a long hesitation, when I saw that fellow open it surreptitiously. When you called for help, I answered the call."

While this terse conversation was taking place, the newcomer's gaze had made a careful tour of the gloomy laboratory. His dark eyes did not give much away, but Mathieu judged that he had not had the slightest expectation of seeing this kind of apparatus, and was now wondering what kind of wizard's den it was that he had stumbled upon.

"Why were you following…the man who brought the girl?" Mathieu asked, bluntly.

"Because I was told in Stepney that he had once collected another girl in exactly the same fashion, for a similar fee—a girl who hasn't been seen since, at least by her mother, sister or aunt."

Mathieu's heart sank. *Not the police, then*, he thought. *At least not yet—but trouble all the same. On the other hand, he can't be certain that the other girl was also brought here, and in any case, he saw Judy Lee leave, apparently safe and sound, and has no reason to suspect that she was brought her to do anything other than offer her usual services.*

"What do you want with me?" he asked, aloud.

"That, I don't quite know, as yet," the stranger replied. "What did *he* want with you, do you think?" He nodded towards the door through which the other invader had made his escape, which still stood open.

"A common sneak-thief, I suppose," Mathieu said, wishing that he sounded more convincing.

"This place reeks of blood," the tall man observed. "What in God's name are you doing here?"

"Medical research," Mathieu retorted, taking slight offense at the other's tone. "Work for the benefit and progress of humankind."

Perhaps remarkably, given that he seemed no better educated than the young whore, the stranger did not seem disinclined to take that statement at face value. "What kind of...?" he began, albeit not disrespectfully.

The seaman did not have time to complete the sentence before a new voice cut in, saying: "I do not think, sir, that the doctor's work is any concern of yours."

Mathieu and the stranger both turned to the open doorway, where Sir Julian Templeforth was now standing. The briefest sideways glance at the clock told Mathieu that the baronet was as punctual as ever.

The stranger looked the baronet up and down, and lowered his eyes reflexively in the face of that blue-eyed stare, seemingly brilliant even in the poor light.

"Who is this, Mathieu?" Sir Julian demanded, with a note of accusation in his voice.

"I don't know his name, sir," Mathieu was quick to say, "but he came to my aid when I called for help just now, and frightened off a man who was attacking me—a burglar, I suppose, who must have thought the dwelling empty, having seen no light from the front."

"I'm Thomas Deangate, merchant seaman," the tall man supplied, promptly, "lately second mate on the SS *Hallowmas*."

Thomas Deangate waited politely, but Sir Julian did not introduce himself. Instead, he reached toward his inside jacket pocket, groping for his wallet, saying: "We're grateful for your help. Perhaps..."

"I don't want your money," the seaman interrupted, his voice turning harsh. "I want to know what's going on here. I want to know what that girl was doing here this afternoon, and whether the same thing that happened to her, whatever it might be, also happened to my sister Caroline."

Sir Julian's eyes narrowed, and his hand fell away from his jacket pocket towards his britches, where there was a very conspicuous bulge. If Sir Julian wanted to carry a revolver, Mathieu thought, he might do better to wear looser-fitting trousers with more capacious pockets—like the ones the sailor had on.

He found, somewhat to his alarm, that he could remember a Caroline quite clearly, although she had never told him her surname. His heart began to beat even faster as his alarm increased. At least, he thought, desperately, she had not been the girl who had died. He had no reason to think that the sailor's sister was not alive and well, albeit perhaps difficult to recognize at first glance.

"Mr. Deangate followed a man who brought a young girl here this afternoon," Mathieu said, trying to let his patron know, without giving the game away, that the seaman did not appear to be aware of the connection between Cormack and Sir Julian. He made a private observation that the lack of any such awareness made it unlikely that Thomas Deangate had been the man who was watching the house in Holland Park on the previous night, before adding: "He thinks the same man might have taken his sister away. If so, Mr. Deangate, he certainly did not bring her here. He probably supplies girls to more than one client." He hoped that the lie was plausible, but was fearful that it might have seemed far too blatant.

Deangate's gaze went from Mathieu to Sir Julian and back again, and then made another thoughtful tour of the laboratory through the open door. He made no attempt to hide his suspicions, and he suddenly seemed far more villainous that when he had obligingly come to Mathieu's aid. "In that case," he said, "I'd best take what I know to Scotland Yard, and let the police…"

It was probably an empty threat, but it was a very unwise move. Thomas Deangate had no idea of the kind of man that he was trying to intimidate.

Mathieu prayed silently that the baronet would simple laugh off the threat and keep calm, but Templeforth was not in a calm mood, and was the kind of man who was always likely to overbid any attempt at intimidation with unnecessary excess.

The seaman did not attempt to pick up the sentence where he had deliberately left it dangling when Sir Julian produced the revolver from his pocket, but a slight smile flashed across his lips. Mathieu inferred that Deangate's vague suspicions had just been turned into an impression of certainty. He was now convinced that the aristocrat and the scientist had some guilty secret to hide, and equally convinced that his unlucky sister had, indeed been brought to the laboratory, perhaps for something other than to provide sexual services. But he had seen Judy Lee walk away, Mathieu reminded himself. He had no reasons yet to think that his sister had come to any harm here.

As an officer on an ocean-going vessel, Thomas Deangate was presumably required to carry a gun himself on occasion, and he did not seem to be in the least intimidated by the weapon that the aristocrat was holding. Mathieu, on the other hand, knew that Sir Julian was as expert with a pistol as he was with a blade, and was certainly reckless enough to make use of his expertise if the impulse came upon him. He guessed that the baronet had leapt to the mistaken conclusion that Caroline Deangate *had* been the girl who had died. He never asked the names of the girls that Cormack procured.

Sir Julian closed the door of the house behind him and turned the key in the lock. "You should have taken the money, lad," he said, softly. "By the look of you, I doubt that your blood has anything to contribute to the professor's research, but a man of science can always find a use for such stuff, if it comes to that. If you behave yourself, though, we'll settle for tying you up and putting you to bed in the professor's cupboard for a little while."

Mathieu groaned audibly, knowing that the situation was now beyond all possibility of control. "What about the other one?" he murmured. "What if *he* turns out to be the one who was watching us in Holland Park?"

Sir Julian evidently had not considered that possibility. After a moment's pause, though, he shrugged his shoulders. He waved his gun to indicate that Mathieu and Deangate should move into the laboratory, which they did. He followed them, but did not close the door behind him. He was obviously thinking hard, but Mathieu had no confidence in any conclusion that his limited intelligence might reach.

"We can't stay here now, in any case," the baronet said, finally. "Your hideout has been found, and not just by this fellow. It looks as if we'd best be Ireland-bound as soon as possible, no matter how much trouble the goddam rebels are causing over there. We'll have to go ahead with tonight's treatment, as planned, but as soon as Cormack comes back. I'll mobilize my entire staff in packing up here and at the house. Do you have some rope with which to tie this fellow up?"

"Only twine," Mathieu said, looking towards the shelf that accommodated a stout ball of sturdy string.

"Best do a good job, then," Sir Julian said. "He's a sailor, after all, well used to dealing with knots. If he gets loose, I'll have to shoot him—

and that's not what any of us wants." That statement was, of course, intended to impress the logic of the situation upon Deangate rather than Mathieu, but Mathieu could see, as he reached for the ball of string, that the seaman had made his own estimate of that logic.

Mathieu had quite forgotten the scalpel, and Sir Julian evidently had not noticed that Thomas Deangate was carrying anything. The instrument was, after all, quite small and the seaman's hand was larger than average. Mathieu's blood ran suddenly cold as the sailor suddenly flipped his wrist and sent the scalpel hurtling towards Sir Julian's face. The baronet saw it coming too late, and probably had no idea what it was until the object struck him full in the face. The sharp blade sliced into the cheek, about an inch below his right eye, and cut through the flesh until its progress was arrested by the cheekbone.

Sir Julian howled, more in wrath than in pain, and jerked his head to one side.

The wound bled copiously, but Mathieu could not imagine that it was serious. The blade fell to the floor, but Sir Julian had closed his eyes reflexively even as he raised the pistol in order to take aim.

Before the baronet could open his eyes again, in order to complete the threatening gesture, Deangate had grabbed Mathieu and pulled him into position as a human shield. Deangate's left arm was now around Mathieu's neck, while the right held a much larger knife, with a curved blade and a serrated edge, which he must have had concealed about his person.

As Mathieu felt the point of Deangate's knife digging suggestively into his neck, not far from the carotid artery, Sir Julian tried to stem the blood coursing from his cheek with his left hand, while holding the revolver as steadily as he could in his right.

Eventually, the baronet fished a handkerchief from his pocket and pressed it to the wound. The white cotton turned red, but the further flow of blood was inhibited. The baronet's eyes were livid with anger, but he was in control of himself again and his right hand was not trembling.

"Now," said Deangate, a trifle hoarsely, "let's take stock. It seems that the man I put to flight might not have been a common-or-garden burglar after all—in which case, he might come back. In all likelihood, though, we won't be disturbed for a little while: time to complete the introductions, at least. Who are you?"

"Go to hell," Sir Julian said.

If Mathieu could read the sky-blue eyes correctly, Sir Julian was weighing up the possibility of taking a shot anyway, carefully weighing up his chances of hitting the seaman in the head without Mathieu ending up with a cut throat. He felt that he ought at least to calm things down.

"I'm Mathieu Galmier, a graduate of the Sorbonne and more recently on the staff of the Institut Pasteur," he said. "I'm doing research in immunology, in parallel with Elie Metchnikoff in Paris. I didn't hurt your sister, although I did put some of her blood through a special filter to remove certain infectious agents. If she never went home thereafter, it certainly wasn't because of anything I did." Again, he was by no means convinced that the new lie would sound plausible, but he hoped that his word as a man of science might carry some weight with the seaman.

"And who's he?" Deangate demanded, meaning Sir Julian.

"He's my patron," Mathieu said, carefully refraining from supplying a name. "He's also my patient—which is to say, one of my experimental subjects. As you can see, no harm has come to him by virtue of his involvement in my work."

"I've rarely seen a man in such good trim," the seaman admitted, suspiciously. "What are you treating him for—the pox?"

"That's not your concern," Sir Julian put in. "If I put the gun away, will you put down the knife, so that we can discuss the matter as civilized men?"

"It was you who uncivilized the situation in the first place," Deangate pointed out. "It's not as easy to mend things as it is to break them, alas. If you had nothing to hide, you'd hardly be planning to tie me up and flee to Ireland, would you?"

Silently, Mathieu cursed Julian Templeforth's loose mouth and propensity for hasty action. "You don't understand, Mr. Deangate," he said. "So many people simply *don't understand,* even though the notion of drawing blood is perfectly familiar in medical practice. My syringes are neater and safer by far than leeches or cupping, but hollow needles still seem to intimidate the popular imagination, and the mere concept of experimentation seems to send shivers down the backs of many common folk. Have you any idea of the abuse that Louis Pasteur, the greatest benefactor of humanity this century has seen, has had to endure in the course of his researches, for his temerity in regarding the human body as a legitimate object of experimental study? If you had the least conception of the persecution that Ignatz Semmelweis underwent at the hands of hidebound physicians, for proving the necessity of sterile technique and demonstrating to surgeons that they were infecting their patients with mortal diseases, you wouldn't be in the least surprised that I prefer to work in secret, or that those who depend on my work might be a trifle over-anxious to preserve that secrecy."

Thomas Deangate had probably recognized Pasteur's name, as Judy Lee had, and Mathieu thought that he was probably capable following the argument that he had put forward—but the gun had spoiled everything. There was no longer any chance of persuading the seaman that nothing untoward had happened to his sister.

"I'm working for the betterment of the human condition, Mr. Deangate," Mathieu continued, "and I would far rather do so in the open—but I need blood to feed my investigations, which no one is willing to supply except prostitutes who are willing to sell it. If some misfortune really has befallen your sister, it is most likely the result of some infection that might have been curable a hundred years ago, if only the Age of Reason had been allowed to extend its viewpoint to the human body. If you want to blame someone for that, blame the acolytes of ignorance, superstition and horror who have surrounded medical research with all manner of prohibitions!"

"Caroline isn't a prostitute!" Thomas Deangate growled, although his lie was far more blatant than the ones Mathieu had told.

Mathieu did not attempt to contradict him, even though he knew from personal experience that Caroline Deangate sold sexual favors as well as her blood…or had. She had been an exceptionally pretty girl, he remembered, and she had been considerably older than Judy Lee. Although he had not seen her since the extraction, the calculus of probabilities suggested that the extent of her loss might well have been drastic.

"That isn't the point," he said. "The point is that if something *has* happened to her, I might be able to help her. You'll have to look for her elsewhere, I fear, but if you find her. I'll be glad to do whatever is possible, as a doctor." He honestly wished that he were wholly sincere, rather than merely trying to gain time.

Mathieu felt the pressure of the knife-point relax somewhat, and knew that he had made an impact of sorts. The seaman was no fool; whether or not he had ever heard of Pasteur and Semmelweis, he had definitely followed the gist of the argument, and did not find it implausible or horrific. On the other hand, he had been given evidence enough that the doctor and his patient had something to hide, sufficiently serious to make the patient think seriously about fleeing to Ireland.

Sir Julian, in the meantime, was still pointing the gun as if he were avid to use it. The cut on his cheek was not serious, but he was exceedingly sensitive about his appearance, and he was not a man to take such an insult gracefully.

"Listen!" Mathieu said, speaking to them both. "There is, I think, a way to set Mr. Deangate's mind at rest. Let him witness the treatment for which you came here tonight, my lord. Let him see that there is nothing to fear in the mere process of drawing blood and reinserting it into the body. Let him see, at any rate, that *you* are not afraid, and that you trust me to work in your best interests. Then perhaps, we can all agree that there is nothing truly sinister going on here, let alone anything diabolical, even though we have reason to be fearful of the possible superstitious reactions of our neighbors."

Sir Julian only needed a few seconds to see the wisdom of the move, if only as a temporary delay, and he was presumably already regretting the hastiness of his overreaction. He had already offered, albeit in a somewhat cavalier fashion, to put his gun away in order that he and Deangate might discuss matters like civilized men, and Mathieu's suggestion was only one step further.

"I'm agreeable to that," the baronet said—but he flashed a warning glance at Mathieu, as if he were afraid that the scientist might give away too much. "If the fellow wants to watch, he can—but he can't do that while he's holding a knife to your throat. I'll keep hold of the gun, just in case, but I won't use it unless I have to. It's in everyone's interests that no one gets hurt…any more than they already have been." He dabbed his cheek with his bloody handkerchief, to remind Thomas Deangate that the only person who had suffered any harm thus far was him.

Thomas Deangate was evidently curious. Slowly, he lowered the knife—but he did not put it down. "All right," he said. "I'll settle for that, for now. You can show me what you want to show me. Afterwards… we'll see."

V

Once that relaxation of the situation had been agreed, it proved pos-sible to negotiate further reductions in threat. After a little further discus-sion, Sir Julian agreed to deposit his revolver on the coat-stand in the hallway, while he remained stationed beside the open door for the time being. Thomas Deangate placed his knife on a shelf in the laboratory, and took up a position in front of the shelf unit, distant from the door to the hallway.

That was done, and it seemed that the tension had drained away from the situation. There was a pause while Mathieu checked that his front door was properly locked, and that they were safely isolated. He took time to inspect the cut on Sir Julian's cheek, which he sealed as carefully as he could and dressed with gauze.

"It might open again when I replace your blood, because of the anti-clotting agent," he said, anxiously, "but you should be able to staunch the flow without overmuch difficulty."

"It's only a scratch, damn it!" the baronet growled. "Better a little bleeding than go without the treatment."

The seaman watched, with evident fascination, as Mathieu sat the baronet down in the chair that had recently been occupied by Judy Lee, and carefully inserted the hollow needle into his right forearm. Sir Julian did not flinch, although it was becoming far harder to connect with his vein than it had been to get into the girl's. From the corner of his eye, Mathieu saw the scowling seaman bite his lip in apparent sympathy. He switched on the pump that would assist the extraction.

Mathieu had set aside the apparatus that had circulated Judy Lee's blood through the filtration matrix, having already abstracted the filtrate from the matrix. The filtrate intended for infusion into the baronet's veins was now being held in a rotating flask dipped in lukewarm water-bath. When Mathieu had drawn off half a liter of Sir Julian's blood he put it in a second flask, which had already been warmed to body-temperature in the same water-bath. He detached the first flask, added its contents to second, and then set the second flask to rotate for a moment.

"The agent requires dilution before reinjection, in order that its ef-fects may be properly generalized," Mathieu informed the seaman, although he knew that it was not really an explanation.

"What effects?" Deangate wanted to know, understandably.

"Increased resistance to certain infections," Mathieu said, employing deliberate circumlocution.

"That doesn't make sense," Deangate protested. "How can taking blood from a sick child-whore—and I saw the girl who was brought here this afternoon, Dr. Galmier, so I know that she was already showing signs of consumption—help increase resistance to disease in a healthy man?"

"It might seem strange," Mathieu told him, smoothly, "but one of my former colleagues at the Institut Pasteur, Elie Metchnikoff, has demonstrated that the body has its own innate defenses against infection. The reason that Jenner's vaccine against smallpox works, we now believe, is that exposure to the relatively-harmless cowpox stimulates the production of some kind of reactive agent, which is also effective against the much more dangerous smallpox. Even when the reactive agents within a human body are fighting a losing battle, they can be filtered out and concentrated, and used to arm a healthy body against the same infections that were defeating them in their original host."

Deangate was, indeed, no fool. He was able to take the argument a step further than Mathieu had assumed. "And what effect does the removal of the *reactive agents* have on the *original hosts*?" he demanded, after only a moment's thought. "More exactly, what effect did it have on my sister? Did it weaken her, and make her more vulnerable to disease, hastening her on the road to death?"

"We're not aware of any such effect, Mr. Deangate," Mathieu was quick to say, hoping yet again that the lie was not transparent. "Indeed, I believe that my filtration process removes infective agents as well as reactive ones, preserving exactly the same balance as before in the donor—but the infective agents are held in the gel filter while the reactive agents are leached out, and I'm careful to sterilize the gel before reuse. Your sister left here in no worse condition than she arrived, and perhaps better."

He could see that Deangate did not believe that, but he could also see that the seaman was trying hard to think through the implications of what he had been told.

"If what you say is true," Thomas Deangate said, slowly, "it seems to me that if you were to reinject the separated reactive agents back into the donor…"

"Her condition might well be improved," Mathieu agreed, making haste to get the half-truth out of his mouth, in order to return to safer argumentative ground, "and that is, of course, my long-term goal. The eventual aim of my research is to find a means of multiplying the reactive agents in isolation, so that they can then be redeployed, not merely in their original host or a single new host, but in a hundred or a thousand individuals. Given time, and sufficiently effective filters, we might not only put an end to dozens of infectious diseases, but might be able to slow down the aging process and…" He paused in response to Sir Julian's warning glare, and then finished, a trifle lamely: "…and accelerate the healing process in wounds inflicted by bullets and blades."

"I see," the seaman said, studying Sir Julian's face and figure carefully. "Well, your patient certainly looks well on the treatment—all the more so if he really did have the clap before you started the treatment."

Sir Julian scowled at that, but Mathieu moved to fill yet another Pravaz syringe from the contents of the warm flask, and made ready to reinject the baronet's blood, hoping to distract his attention and soothe his quick temper.

"I can assure you that my patient is not suffering from syphilis or any other life-threatening disease," Mathieu was quick to say, as he connected the syringe to the needle that was still in place and began to depress the plunger.

"That's very good news," said a voice from the doorway, in a pronounced Irish brogue. "Indeed, we could hardly have hoped for better."

Mathieu, Sir Julian and Thomas Deangate turned simultaneously to the man who had just stepped into the room, carrying Sir Julian's revolver carelessly in his right hand. He was as tall as Thomas Deangate, and somewhat broader, but much older—perhaps as old as fifty. Mathieu recognized the man that Deangate had earlier put to flight. He was not alone, this time; he had brought reinforcements with him: two younger men, hardly out of their teens, but seemingly robust and vigorous.

It occurred to Mathieu, somewhat belatedly, that he had locked his front door after bidding farewell to Judy Lee, and that the "sneak-thief" from whom Thomas Deangate had saved him must therefore have had some way of turning the key in the lock from the far side of the door, without making any appreciable noise, other than the click of the latch when he actually opened the door.

He guessed, too, that the man who had been watching the house in Holland Park—the older man or one of his companions—had not followed him *to* the house at all, although he must certainly have followed him to the hotel in Rockley Road and then to his home, in spite of his cursory precautions.

"Never fear," the newcomer said. "I'm no hooligan, and I've not the least intention of using this toy—although I confess that I'd rather have it in my hand just now than see it in someone else's."

"Who the hell are you?" Sir Julian demanded.

"I'm Sean Driscoll, Sir Julian, the president of your tenants' association—of *our* tenants' association, at any rate. My friends here are two of my deputies, Michael MacBride and Padraig Reilly. You've long been acquainted with Mr. Reilly's great-uncle, I believe, although I met him for the first time myself last night, under circumstances that were admittedly awkward. We've been engaged in talks with your steward for some time, and have urged him as powerfully as we could, but in vain, to fetch you back to your estates so that we might include you in the negotiations. Now, we're following the advice of whatever wise fellow it was who said that, if the mountain will not come to Mahomet, then Mahomet must go to the mountain—although I hasten to add that we're all good Catholics."

"Get this thing out of my arm," Sir Julian said to Mathieu, tersely. Then, to Driscoll, he said: "What on Earth do you think you're doing, coming after me here, of all places?"

"Well, sir," the Irishman said, "that's a slightly embarrassing matter—although I have to confess that we weren't sure what sort of a welcome we'd get if we rang the bell at Holland Park, even though young Padraig here is kin to your gatekeeper. The truth is that there are all kinds of rumors running around your estate, sir, about your having made a deal with the Devil, selling your soul in exchange for eternal youth. I never believed them for an instant, of course, being a man who can read and figure as well as most, but I had to admit that I was very surprised when I caught a glimpse of you last night, for the first time in twenty years. I knew your father, you see, and I had abundant opportunities to observe you in the days when you used to favor us with your presence over the water, although I doubt that you ever noticed me. I did not mistake this gentleman for the Devil, of course, even though he's a foreigner, but I *was* curious to discover what dealings you had with him. It's a wise tenant who knows his landlord, sir—especially when he has protests to lodge and polite requests to make. I'd be truly glad to find that your friend is no more than a common-or-garden physician, and that your unnatural good looks are purely attributable to good health…if that really is the case."

"You've got a damned nerve," Sir Julian retorted. "I think you'll find that Irish rebels are by no means welcome on English soil, and that you'll likely end up in jail if I call the police."

"I'm not a rebel, sir," Driscoll replied, equably. "I really don't care one way or the other about Home Rule. What I do care about is justice between landlord and tenant. If I'm fairly treated, it doesn't matter overmuch whether the land I work is owned by an Englishman, an Irishman or a Chinaman—but given that my fellow tenants and I are not being fairly treated, in my opinion, then I feel obliged to make our position clear. You may call the police if you wish, sir—but if my guess is right, that's not something you're overly enthusiastic to do. This other gentleman sent me packing a little while ago, when I thought myself outnumbered again and made another tactical retreat, but if what I've overheard in these last few minutes is anything to go by, he has grievances of his own against you, and against your physician too. I have sisters myself, and daughters too, and I know well enough how a man's ire can be roused when he loses one, or finds one in dire straits through no fault of her own."

The Irishman paused, and then added: "Would it interest you to know, by any chance, Mr. Deangate—I believe I heard you called by that name—that the man sitting in front of you is fifty-nine years old, and that he looked almost as old when he was thirty-and-one as he does now, and was far less good-looking."

Mathieu could tell that Thomas Deangate was, indeed, interested to hear that item of information, even though he did not know quite what to make of it.

While the seaman was still puzzling over the unexpected revelation, Driscoll handed him the revolver. "I think this had best be committed to the care of a neutral party," he said, "while my companions and I explain our grievances to our landlord. With all due respect to the owner of all this fine apparatus, this room seems to me to be a trifle cramped and gloomy for our purposes, so I think it might be best if we and Sir Julian removed ourselves to somewhere more comfortable—perhaps a public house if, as I suspect, he does not care to invite us to his home."

"You can get drunk wherever you please," Sir Julian said, standing up, a little unsteady on his feet but evidently determined to stand as firm as he could. "I have no intention of negotiating with you, on English or Irish soil. Any grievances you might have must be taken up with my steward. If you do not leave this house immediately, I shall certainly summon the police—and I think you'll find them unprepared to take your word for it that you have no rebel sympathies or criminal intentions, given that you're guilty of breaking and entering."

Sean Driscoll's florid face put on a fine show of theatrical insincere distress in response to this declaration, but Mathieu had the impression that the big Irishman had little or no idea what to do next. He was far from home, and must know very well that he would be in a weak position if his contest with an English baronet really did become an issue for English law to settle. Mathieu noticed, too, that there was now only one man standing behind him—although the two of them were just as capable of blocking the door, should they see fit to do so, as three. The young man who had disappeared was the one who had been introduced as Michael MacBride.

"I broke nothing," Driscoll said, mildly. "The key was in the lock, and it has too long a shaft, allowing it to be turned from the wrong side. What you need, my friend, is a strong bolt, or a sturdy bar."

"Just a minute," said Thomas Deangate, finally. "Are you saying that Dr. Galmier really has discovered an elixir of youth? That he's stealing the health from the blood of young girls and injecting it into his paymaster?"

"Well, now," Driscoll said, with a slight spontaneous smile, "Dr. Galmier's certainly not injecting it into himself, is he? Unless, that is, he's a hundred years old instead of thirty-some."

"It's not as simple as that," Mathieu was quick to put in.

"Be quiet!" Sir Julian commanded him, intemperately. "That's our business, and no one else's. All these men are trespassing, Doctor, having invaded your lodgings uninvited, whether they broke your door or not. This one has held a knife to your throat and now has a gun. Will you go to Goldhawk Road, if you please, and find the policeman patrolling that beat. Tell him to summon help, and to come armed, prepared to meet violent resistance."

Mathieu eyed the route to the laboratory door apprehensively, not at all sure that he would be allowed to walk out without meeting violent resistance himself. Nor was he sure that he wanted to leave his apparatus—but he knew that he could hardly round on the baronet and tell him to go in search of a policeman himself if he really wanted one to come.

Instead, he opened his mouth to say that there was no need for any trouble, hopeful that he might be able to find further arguments to support that assertion, but he was interrupted by the noise of movement in the hallway. Padraig Reilly came further into the room as Michael MacBride reappeared in the doorway, in company with another person, who was definitely not a policeman.

It was direly difficult to tell, at first glance, exactly what the other person might be, given that she was clad in a capaciously-hooded cape which, in combination with a thick woolen scarf, hid every feature of the face within, save for the faint gleam of feverish eyes. Mathieu, however, was not in the slightest doubt that the person must be female. The hood testified to that even more clearly than her short stature. Set between the three burly Irishman she looked incredibly frail, even though the bulky cape blurred the sharp lines of her emaciated frame.

Mathieu's heart sank, and he had a vertiginous feeling of being utterly lost. It was by no means the first time that one of his former "volunteers" had returned in search of help, usually for some condition other than the one he had induced, and they almost always returned in this part of the evening, when the cover of darkness was fully secured but before the London streets became truly hazardous for those incapable of self-defense. None had ever come when Sir Julian was undergoing treatment, however.

Instinctively, Mathieu looked at the clock, and pricked up his ears waiting for the carriage that would doubtless come to collect Sir Julian very shortly, although he no longer hoped that the butler's mere arrival might save the situation, which had become far too complicated for any kind of easy disentanglement. Mathieu found that he had his mouth open, in the expectation of having something to say, but that he was quite incapable of speech.

"Girl wants to see the doctor," MacBride reported, laconically. "Hadn't the heart to tell her that he was busy. Best take her to another room, though, sir, if you have one, while we continue our discussion with Sir Julian."

Mathieu felt dizzy, and feared that he was about to faint. He could not help staring at those fugitive eyes hidden in the shadows of the hood, even though he was terrified by the idea of meeting their accusatory stare.

He felt a peculiar surge of relief as he realized that he did not have to do that. The gaze of the terrible eyes was not fixed on him at all but on something else—some*one* else.

Three seconds of awful, pregnant silence went by, while Mathieu observed strangely similar expressions of puzzlement forming on the faces of Sir Julian Templeforth and Sean Driscoll, neither of whom had begun to comprehend what was happening.

Then the girl spoke, and her voice, although it was inexpressibly feeble, struck Mathieu with all the impact of a bomb—because what she said was: "Tom? Is that you?"

Thomas Deangate's Caroline, Mathieu realized, was definitely still alive, if not necessarily well. That fact would confirm part of his story—but not, alas, the most important elements. For all he knew, Caroline Deangate might have vanished from her family's ken simply by virtue of the shame of her prostitution, or for some other reason entirely, and must surely made the decision to stay away before the after-effects of her condition had begun to show. He was sharply aware, however, of the fact that the change in her appearance might have made the prospect of going home even less bearable. In a way, the confirmation that she was alive was certainly good news—but in another way, it might be anything but good. Thomas Deangate was still holding Sir Julian's revolver, and he now knew more than enough about Mathieu's experiments to know, even if she did not, who was responsible for any deterioration in her appearance.

The seaman did not waste time with idle repetition of his sister's querulous question. He had a more direct means of discovering whether the girl in the hood was known to him, and he only had to take one long stride reach out his arm to push back the hood.

She flinched, reflexively. She actually raised her hands in order to try to fight him off when he tried to pull down the scarf, but she could not do it.

Mathieu anticipated the general gasp of astonishment a split second before it actually sounded within the room, and the anticipation made it even worse. He knew that there was really no cause for that astonishment, given that Caroline Deangate did not look nearly as ugly as one or two of his other volunteers, but the situation was conducive to melodramatic clichés—and in all fairness, the poor child did look remarkably plain, and considerably older than he knew her to be. He could remember her face quite clearly now: the face that she had lost forever, that is. It had been beautiful. So beautiful that…

He stepped backwards, pressing his spine against the wall in a narrow gap between two sets of shelves.

Thomas Deangate's automatic response was to exclaim: "You're not Caroline!"

The girl made no attempt to assert her identity, and seemed to be biting her bloodless lips in anguish over the fact that she had given herself away. She tried to turn and run, but MacBride and Reilly were still blocking the door, and were too stunned to remove themselves from her path.

Sean Driscoll swore, softly. Sir Julian's handsome face was uniformly white, save for the red stain on the dressing applied to his cut—which did not make it any less handsome, but somehow contrived to augment the insult.

"Caroline?" said Thomas Deangate, helplessly, admitting the truth at second glance in spite of what must have seemed blatant evidence to the contrary. Then he raised the gun, and pointed it at Mathieu. "You did this," he said, hoarsely. "You really are the Devil."

"You don't understand," Mathieu protested, although it was obvious that everyone in the room understood the fundamental fact perfectly well, however incredible they had found the possibility when voicing it before. They had been no more able to believe in any kind of elixir of youth than they had been able to believe that Sir Julian Templeforth really had made a bargain with the Devil, despite Sean Driscoll's observation regarding the remarkable transformation of the baronet's appearance. In isolation, even given what they now knew about what went on in the laboratory, that appearance had merely seemed an oddity, a strange stroke of luck. Now, juxtaposed with its counterpart, it seemed to be something very different, and literally diabolical.

Except, Mathieu insisted to himself, it was not diabolical at all—not literally, or even metaphorically. It was authentically hopeful: a highly significant step on the path of progress; a staging-post *en route* to the Age of Miracles. *That* was the understanding he had to convey to them—not just to the dangerous man with the revolver, but to all of them—if they would only give him time.

However dangerous he might be, however, Thomas Deangate was not a stupid man. He did not squeeze the revolver's trigger, although his stance and expression suggested that he would be perfectly prepared to do so. Instead, he said: "Reverse it! Right here, right now. Take back what you stole, and return it."

Mathieu knew that he must have gone pale in his turn, but he knew how futile it was to protest when he stammered: "No…you don't understand…it doesn't work like that.…" While he forced the words out, his gaze darted around the company, taking in Sir Julian and all three Irishmen before settling on Sean Driscoll's face.

Even if Thomas Deangate had been alone, Mathieu thought, the gun would have given him the means of backing up his demands, although he would probably have had to put at least one bullet into Sir Julian's body to force his cooperation. The fact that he was not alone, though, increased his advantage vastly, in moral as well as material terms—and he was not alone in any sense of the term. The Irishmen were outraged on his behalf; they shared his distress, and sympathized with his anguish.

The Irishmen had no reason to love Sir Julian, and certainly would not defend him. Indeed, they might even imagine that they might benefit, in the short or long term, were the baronet to be robbed of his unnatural virility. Even if they had had no advantage of their own at stake, though, they would still have sided with Thomas Deangate and backed him up. They had never seen Caroline Deangate before she had accepted Cormack's guinea, but they had imagination enough to assure them that she might—must—have been as pretty as any young girl on the brink of puberty. It required little or no creative effort for them to exchange, in the mind's eye, Sir Julian's preternatural beauty for her dismal plainness, restoring her lost purity at the expense of his.

In a single visionary flash, Mathieu saw that it really was going to happen. His four unwelcome visitors really were going to force Sir Julian back into the chair, tying him down if necessary, in order to demand that Mathieu must draw out his blood, as he had drawn Judy Lee's that afternoon, and Caroline Deangate's some little while ago. Then they were going to force him to inject the filtered produce of Sir Julian's blood into the girl, just as he had injected the filtered produce of Judy Lee's blood into Sir Julian mere minutes before.

And he would have no choice but to do it. They would not give him a choice. If he refused, Thomas Deangate would hurt him, and keep on hurting him until he complied. They had no fear of the police now; they were obedient to what they considered to be a higher law.

But they truly did not understand the finer details of the situation. They were thinking in mystical terms; they did not understand the way that the natural world was made. They did not understand the logic of blood incompatibilities and clotting factors, and a thousand other problems; they did not understand that Mathieu's process was science, not magic, and could not comprehend the harsh implications of that distinction.

"Sir Julian's blood isn't compatible with Caroline's," Mathieu said, hastily. I can't inject it into her without harming her. I'll explain...."

But Thomas Deangate was inspecting the tangle of apparatus and remembering the explanations he had already been given. "But you have blood here," he said, pointing to the residue of Judy Lee's blood. "In any case, you isolate what you call the agent from the blood you leech. You can take a little blood from Caroline, as you did from this fellow, in order to dilute the fluid you extract from Templeforth's blood, before injecting it back into her...."

A ship's mate, Mathieu realized, had to be a quick learner, a quick thinker and a man of action. The Irishmen probably could not have connected up the argument so rapidly, and Caroline was still completely at sea, but the seaman was confident...perhaps unreasonably so. What he was asking Mathieu to do was something he had not tried before, and he was all too well aware of the fact that new ventures did not always turn out as expected, even when the logic supporting them seemed sound.

More seriously, even if the reinjection did compensate, partially or wholly, for Caroline Deangate's loss, there would be side-effects, one of which was all too predictable....

Everything, Mathieu realized, was about to collapse: the entire edifice of his work and his life. Catastrophe was looming, unavoidably.

"You haven't thought this through," he said. "You mustn't do it. Believe me...."

He realized, even as he voiced the final phrase, though, that there was no way that Thomas Deangate, or anyone else, was going to believe him now. He had told too many lies already. He did not deserve to be believed. He had betrayed his own principles, and those of science. The reckoning was nigh, and it would be disastrous. Nothing he could say would be sufficient to persuade the seaman and his new allies that his anxieties were anything more than mere bluster, or that any consequence he identified beyond the one for which they hoped—perhaps in vain— ought to deter them. Their notion of justice outweighed mere practical considerations. Even if he did explain the whole truth, and managed to persuade them of that truth, it would not stop them. It would not stop Sean Driscoll, let alone Thomas Deangate. This was the kind of night- mare from which there was no escape, from which there could be no awakening.

And when it was over, what then? What would become of him—and, more importantly, of progress?

VI

Sir Julian Templeforth was probably not as quick-witted as the seaman, and Mathieu had not been entirely honest with him either, but he had been living with the theory and the experimentation for three years, and he knew, at least to an extent, what was likely to happen to him if Thomas Deangate forced Mathieu to do as he asked. The baronet could, had he been so minded, have added the weight of his voice to Mathieu's, to appeal for calm and reason, to demand that Mathieu set out the scientific arguments clearly, so that the situation could be assessed in full, accurately. But he was not that kind of man. He was an aristocrat, an absentee landlord, and a habitual bully.

Sir Julian turned to the self-proclaimed leader of his tenants' association, and said: "You haven't yet stepped over the line, Mr. Driscoll. All you've done thus far is request a meeting to discuss the situation of my tenants. That's fair and just. But if you help this madman to force my doctor to assault and injure me, you'll be accessories to a hanging matter. Your two friends might be too young to have families, but I do remember the Driscolls, no matter what you might think, and I know that you have a great deal at stake in this matter. If you help me, you'll earn my gratitude; if you don't…I'll send you all to hell, along with your parents, wives and children. That's the choice you have to make."

He stared Sean Driscoll in the face, doubtless expecting to instill terror in him—but Sean Driscoll met his stare quite frankly.

"Well, Michael, Padraig," he said, softly, "there we have it, neat and clear. What do we think our landlord's promises of gratitude might be worth? And how frightened ought we to be of his threats, even if he has made a pact with the Devil?"

For a few seconds, neither of the others spoke, but then Michael MacBride said: "Well, Sean, it seems to me that there's no sin or crime in recovering stolen goods, or in helping a man to do it, on behalf of his poor sister."

"Aye," said Padraig Reilly. "Surely even an English jury could see that, if they had the evidence before them. If not, there's no justice at all in this godforsaken world."

"That's not the point," said Mathieu, swiftly. "The point is that it might not have the effects you expect, that it will certainly do harm but might not do any good...."

But for once, he had been too honest.

"*Might*, you say?" Sean Driscoll challenged him. "Do you mean to say that you don't know for sure?"

Mathieu tried to backtrack. "It's never been tried," he said, weakly, "but all the indications are...there's always a rate of attrition...until I can find a way of multiplying the agent...."

He knew that he was losing. Even if he could explain the delicacy of the logic, it wouldn't be enough. They had justice on their minds, and retribution. The calculus of probability couldn't be applied in meticulous isolation.

Suddenly, Sir Julian leapt for the gun, trying to take Thomas Deangate by surprise, and perhaps thinking that Deangate would not shoot him while he wanted to leech his blood. Perhaps he was right about that, but the hypothesis went untested, because Sean Driscoll intercepted the baronet and stopped his bound. MacBride and Reilly instantly launched themselves forward to help him. Between the three of them, they immobilized the baronet, and then looked at one another, realizing that they had now crossed the metaphorical line to which their landlord had referred. They had come too far now to turn back.

They did not seem regretful, so far as Mathieu could tell. In fact, they seemed proud, like men who had just exerted their courage fully, in a just cause.

Perhaps strangely, given his turbulent character, Sir Julian did not put up much of a fight thereafter. The three Irishmen, having subdued him easily, trussed him up and secured him to the chair—after which he did not struggle, seemingly accepting the inevitability of his fate. The baronet seemed to see the awful logic of the situation as clearly as Mathieu did, and to feel the weight of its narrative propriety just as forcefully; he seemed resigned, at least for the moment, to the fact that his hubristic defiance of natural destiny had finally been called to account, and that Nemesis had abruptly descended upon him.

But Mathieu knew that that resignation was based on a premise that might be false. Templeforth did not know, in any precise sense, what was about to happen to him. He was thinking of it merely as a loss of his stolen advantages, a return to his "true" appearance as a man of fifty-nine. For the moment, he was capitulating with superior forces, reserving his vengeance for later, and doubtless thinking that he would have time and opportunity to make it terrible.

Mathieu was not at all sure that the cost to be baronet would be as cheap as that, but he did not make any attempt at physical resistance either. Nor did he entertain the notion of trying to cheat his oppressors, by substituting some other procedure for the one they were demanding that he carry out. He was still determined, though, to make one last effort to explain the true situation—and he could see that Driscoll, at least, was as hungry for an explanation of what was going on as he was to see some result. Even Thomas Deangate, who desperately wanted to see a miracle performed, was man enough to want to know exactly what had been done to his sister, and how and why. In Mathieu's estimation, too, the sailor was fully entitled to know exactly how and why his passionately-desired miracle might fail to materialize.

Before he began the preparatory work, however, Sir Julian whispered in his ear: "I have your money in my pocket, Mathieu. I'll get you more—as much as you need. We'll begin again, when this setback is behind us. We'll set everything to rights. This won't stop us." The baronet's voice was quivering with desperation, eager for reassurance.

Mathieu refrained from telling his patron, bluntly, that it wasn't as simple as that. It might be best, he thought if Sir Julian continued to believe, for as long as possible, that he could very easily be restored to his present condition once this little "setback" had been put behind them.

Before he began his general explanation, though, Mathieu instructed Michael MacBride to make a large pot of tea, and asked Sean Driscoll to send Padraig Reilly out to the night-stalls in Goldhawk Road, in search of bread, meat pies and oil for the lamps.

Thomas Deangate had set his ugly sister down on a kitchen chair, positioned so that she could see every detail of what happened to Sir Julian Templeforth. Mathieu noticed that she was staring, not at her brother, whom she did not seem conspicuously pleased to see, but at him, with an expression that was puzzled, but not hostile. She was not looking at him with the glare of someone in search of revenge, but of someone appealing for help. The image of the face that she had had before—the face that she had had when he had used her body—was still before him, and he felt an overwhelming surge of emotion in which pity and guilt were compounded.

He went to her, and put his hand on her shoulder. "Don't be afraid, Caroline. I won't hurt you. I'm not at all sure that I can do what your brother wants me to do, but I certainly won't hurt you, and I'll do everything I can to help you get better, no matter how long it might take."

She, at least, seemed to trust him, although she had no more reason to do so than anyone else, and perhaps even less. She looked up at him, and nodded her head slightly. He wished that he could be sure that what he had just told her was really true in every detail.

He turned his attention to the baronet. "I'm sorry, Sir Julian," he said, "but I'll make you the same promise. Whatever the effects are, I'll do my very best to repair them."

He did not see the same innocent trust in Sir Julian's eyes that he had seen in the girl's—but there was nevertheless a certain confidence there, a conviction that Mathieu would do his best to repair any damage done, and that his skill and his method would be equal to he task.

The baronet groaned when the needles were inserted into his veins, and his eyes bulged with a certain unsuppressable horror as he watched the blood begin to flow through the filtration apparatus, knowing as he did what was flowing away with it. He watched the golden droplets begin to ooze into the collection tube with a fascination very different from the one with which Judy Lee had watched.

Once the extraction and filtration of Sir Julian Templeforth's blood was under way, Mathieu was able to step back. The slowness of the process gave him the opportunity to offer a detailed commentary on what was happening, and the historical background to his research. The explanation he had earlier given to the uncomprehending Judy Lee now served him as a useful rehearsal, and his audience seemed to be following his account of his initial ambitions and the discovery of the filter well enough, in spite of the unfamiliarity to the jargon.

Mathieu broke off his discourse when Reilly returned with the goods that he had been sent to buy. While the others set about making a frugal meal, Mathieu refilled the lamp that had gone out and lit it, bringing the room some way back from the dismal gloom that had set in. He topped up the other lamp, and turned up its flame, but the illumination the lamps provided, even at their maximum effect, had an ocher tinge that did not make the assembled apparatus seem any less sinister.

Afterwards, he continued his account of the logic he had employed in deducing from the principle of natural selection that most of the invisible organisms living within the microcosm of the human body must be benign, working to the advantage of the health, longevity and reproduction of their universe.

"So that," said Sean Driscoll," pointing at the collecting tube that was slowly filling with golden fluid decanted from the absorbing gel, "really is an elixir of long life…and youth? And what you're saying, is that the physical appearances we associate with youthfulness and virility are actually the product of germs resident within us?"

"No," Mathieu said. "What I'm saying is that it is to the advantage of some of our indwelling micro-organisms to enhance or augment those aspects of youth and virility that facilitate human reproduction. I don't claim that any of these attributes is the creation of the passengers within our personal universes, but I do believe that there are biological agents dwelling within us that assist in the amplification of our reproductive capacities, without actually creating anything, perhaps by virtue of a kind of catalysis. The effect is at its maximum when our reproductive capacity is at its peak, and it tails off drastically once that capacity begins to dwindle."

Driscoll seemed to be trying hard to grasp the argument in all its intricacy, even though he had obvious difficulty grasping such concepts as catalysis. "So the symptoms of old age—wrinkles, the thinking of the skin, thinning hair and so on, come about because these benign germs are no longer active?"

"In a way, yes. It varies from person to person, of course, every person being a distinct universe with respect to the invisible organisms within, but in general, as the catalytic contribution of the golden fluid dwindles, the organism's ability to repair and maintain the appearances of virility and sexual attractiveness becomes less effective. Men become less handsome, women less pretty."

"It's a bacillus of beauty!" Driscoll said, catching a straw of enlightenment.

"Not a bacillus, strictly speaking, and there might well be more at stake in physiological terms than our ready-made but rather shallow concept of *beauty* usually embraces—but yes, in simple terms, I'm referring a biological agent that promotes sexual attractiveness. What I took from Miss Deangate some months ago and gave to Sir Julian isn't youth, *per se*, but a means of assisting alluring appearance. As you observed before, I've contrived to turn a man who was exceptionally plain in his prime into a man who is exceptionally handsome at an age when that is very rare—although not as rare in men than women, because make virility tends to last longer than the female capacity for successful childbirth."

At that point in the argument, Mathieu thought, every eye in the room should have turned to Sir Julian, who was still outrageously handsome in spite of his pallor and the fact that he was slumped in his chair, exhausted by the extended circulation of his blood. In fact, his uninvited guests looked in another direction entirely: at Caroline Deangate. Instead of wanting to appreciate the glory of Mathieu's achievement, they were intent on examining its cost.

Mathieu could remember quite clearly now thinking that Caroline Deangate had been too beautiful to be a common whore. Even at the time, the thought had seemed rather paradoxical, given that it had been that very observation that had led him to treat her as a common whore, as well as stealing her blood, rather than refusing her quasi-automatic attempt at seduction, as he had with Judy Lee. He also remembered now that she had seemed quite healthy—unusually, for someone in her profession. Cormack had obviously found the Bethnal Green flesh-market uncommonly well-stocked that day.

Now, she was ugly: not disfigured, or leprous, and certainly not possessed of any kind of Medusal mask, but she was definitely lacking in the conventional aspects of sexual attraction. Her cheeks and chin were slack and dull; her complexion was gray; her hair was thin and lusterless; her lips were thin and pale; her teeth were colorless. Even her eyes, which still held a certain desperate gleam, were watery and sullen. Hers was not the ruined face of a victim of vitriolization, by any means, but it was a face that she might well have been ashamed to show to anyone who had formerly known and loved her. She had surely been proud of her beauty, and its unnaturally rapid fading must have come as a profound shock to her.

The result of that rapid fading, that theft of her precious catalyst, was what the Irishmen and Thomas Deangate chose to look at, now that Mathieu had confirmed and explained what they had already seen for themselves. Instead of admiring the magnificent work of scientific art that was Sir Julian Templeforth, they preferred to disgust themselves by staring at the girl—one of many girls who had chosen freely to trade their beauty away, at a certain market price, in order to further the cause of progress.

In time, as he had insisted so frequently to Sir Julian and all his other patients, Mathieu hoped that he would be able to pay them all back—if they could only survive the ravages of disease and deprivation long enough. Once he had discovered a means of reproducing the agent *in vitro*, he hoped to be in a position to banish ugliness from the world once and for all: to make every human being alive, and all those yet to be born, as beautiful as it was possible for them to be, in the context of nature's fundamental provision.

What a gift to humankind that will be! he thought Was there any gift more desperately desired, more desperately needed? All that he required was time....

Except, of course, that—as he had also scrupulously pointed out—the arithmetic of the transaction was not as simple as that.

Thomas Deangate pointed at the golden fluid in the collecting tube—the alchemical catalyst—and then the residuum of the blood he had taken from Judy Lee. "But when you've given her that, mixed with the blood, she'll be as lovely as she was before."

Mathieu tensed his body. "No," he said, "I fear that she won't. It's not impossible, but it's highly unlikely."

"Why not?" the seaman demanded, sharply.

"For one thing," Mathieu said, "there's always a rate of attrition. Every transfer, ever filtration, reduces the effect of the agent, either by reducing the quantity of viable organisms or impairing their potency in some fashion. That attrition is compounded by the change of environment. As I said, from the point of view of their indwelling microbes, every individual human body is a universe, and the organisms that involve within it are unique to that universe. They follow parallel patterns of evolution toward similar effects, but every human individual is different. Some randomly-selected pairs are more similar than others, but it's not a simple matter of close kinship.

"When golden fluid from one individual is introduced into another, there's a necessary process of adaptation; sometimes the adaptation is easy, sometimes difficult—but it's never perfect. The mortality of the transplanted agent is increased. In short, the effect of the initial transplantation on Sir Julian was temporary. To maintain the effect, he needed another, and then another—and the repetition exerted an attrition effect of its own. The duration of the effect is becoming shorter with every treatment.

"In the same way, replacing the amount of fluid taken from Caroline won't restore the full effect of what was taken from her. It wouldn't, even if it were the filtrate taken from her own blood. Because it isn't...well, to be honest, any effect is likely to be both partial and temporary...for the present."

"For the present?" Thomas Deangate queried, hoarsely.

"Until I can find a means of inducing the agent to maintain and augment its own effect, to enable it to reproduce itself, in a Petri dish to begin with, and then, hopefully, within a new host body, an alien universe. Then, there will be no limit to what the effects of the catalyst might be. But to reach that point, I need to work on the problem, and to work on the problem I need blood...and money."

"But to get back to the point," said Sean Driscoll, "You're saying that the stuff you've just taken out of Sir Julian probably won't do the girl much good, in the long run?"

"Yes."

"And its effect would be reduced even if you put it back into Sir Julian right away?"

"Yes—but not to anything like the same extent. Putting it back into Sir Julian is by far and away the best chance of obtaining the maximum possible effect, though. In the interests of my patient, that's what I advise. If you force me to inject it into Caroline...you must take responsibility for the effects, or lack of them, on both parties."

"The man is a vampire," said Driscoll, flatly. "And you're his instrument. There are some who'd say that you're both only fit for the gallows."

"Are you one of them, Mr. Driscoll?" Mathieu asked, thinking that he had reached the crucial question.

"I haven't made up my mind yet," the Irishman replied, bluntly—but there was another thought he wanted to follow up "But we're talking in terms of probabilities and chances, aren't we? You really don't know how much of an effect that yellow fluid might have on the girl, or how long it might last?"

"No," Mathieu admitted. "The experiment is one I haven't yet tried—but those I have tried, although their effects have been variable, don't give me any grounds for optimism."

"Any chance is better than none," said Thomas Deangate, stubbornly, "Whatever chance she has, she's entitled to try it."

Sir Julian made as if to interrupt and make his own contribution to the debate, but Sean Driscoll cut him off with a gesture.

"You don't seem to me to be the same kind of man as *him*," the Irishman said to Mathieu, indicating his landlord. "He was born a vampire, sucking the blood from his tenants, at least metaphorically. But you… how do you sleep at night, Dr. Galmier?"

Mathieu shook his head. "I don't." he said, simply. "But what other means do I have of repairing the damage I've already done than to see it through?"

"You could give it up," Driscoll said.

"Not before he's given Caroline back whatever he can of what he stole from her," said Thomas Deangate.

"And not before he's given me back what you've just forced him to steal from me," Sir Julian Templeforth put in, "else you'll all suffer. My servants are already late bringing my carriage. When they get here, believe me, there'll be hell to pay."

The three Irishmen exchanged glances. They knew that time was pressing—but then they looked at Thomas Deangate, tacitly deferring to him, and to the girl whose beauty had been stolen.

"If you don't do it," Driscoll said to Mathieu, "the sailor will. Better that it be done by a skilled hand, if it has to be done, don't you think?"

"I've already seen you prepare a syringe to inject into the dandy," Deangate reminded him.

Mathieu bowed to the inevitability. He drew a liter of Caroline Deangate's blood, mingled it with the golden fluid and agitated the mixture briefly in the water bath. He could feel Sir Julian's angry gaze upon him, but the baronet did not utter any threats, He knew that he could not send Mathieu to Hell, or offer him any violence, while he had such a desperate need of him on earth.

Afterwards, if the nightmare ever ended, things might well be different.

VII

Driscoll had untied the cords binding Sir Julian Templeforth to the chair that was set beside the filtration apparatus, and had cut the string that secured his arms and legs. He was free to get up and move away, had he so wished, but he remained where he was, seemingly utterly dispirited, but perhaps only putting on a show of seeming harmless while he bided his time. In the meantime, Mathieu bandaged Caroline Deangate's arm with all due expedition.

The representatives of Sir Julian's tenants' association might have entered into negotiations while they had their adversary at something of a disadvantage, but Driscoll made no attempt to do so. It was presumably not his sense of fairness that prevented him, but his sense of now being involved in something of an altogether different order of importance. There would, Mathieu presumed, be abundant opportunity for the other kind of business later—at least, he hoped so.

Thomas Deangate was now the man who felt most urgency to talk, perhaps because the revolver had begun to weigh very heavily upon his hand and he had become fearful of the possibility that he might eventually be led to fire it.

"Why *him*, of all people?" he said, to Mathieu, waving the weapon's barrel vaguely in Sir Julian's direction.

"We met, quite by chance, in Paris," Mathieu told him. "He was there pursuing an *amour*—a genuine affection, not some whoring expedition. He was in love, but his feelings were not reciprocated. He had felt the burden of his plain looks for a long time, for he had a secret image of himself as a dashing cavalier, which his swordsmanship supported well enough but his face could not. He was referred to me by a mutual acquaintance who knew of my work at the Institut, with no more initial ambition than the hope that I might cure his pustulent complexion. He was a very willing subject for experimentation, and was very enthusiastic at that time to pledge his entire fortune to anyone who could offer him a chance of becoming the kind of man he had always longed to be. Since he has actually became that kind of man, alas, his attitude to his fortune and its conservation has changed somewhat."

Mathieu observed Sean Driscoll nodding sagely, although Sir Julian was scowling.

"It seems to me," Michael MacBride observed, "that you might have found a female employer far more generous and far more grateful. There's no shortage of tales of rich old women ready and eager to bathe in the blood of virgins to renew their beauty."

"Indeed," croaked Sir Julian. "Had he stayed in Paris, Sarah Bernhardt might have been only too pleased to employ him, now that she is in her forties, and Liane de Pougy would have been fighting to reach his door—but you could not stay in Paris, could you, my friend? You had provided too much fuel to rumors of vampirism and diabolism, and there were deaths that would, in time, have been laid at your door. I was a godsend then, was I not? And your career in London has not been so spotless that you could present yourself at the palace, pleading for an interview with the Queen, no matter how great her need for your talents might be."

"Deaths?" queried Sean Driscolll. "What deaths?"

"I'm no murderer," Mathieu retorted, quietly. He added an almost reflexive lie: "Those who died were victims of accidental injuries, and perhaps their own innate infections."

Caroline Deangate looked up at that, and stared at him as if he had leveled some terrible insult against her, but she said nothing.

"But it doesn't trouble you," her brother said, in her stead, "to leech the beauty from innocent maids to feed some petty Anglo-Irish aristocrat with the appetites and delusions of a French dandy?"

Mathieu ignored the insult to his nationality, and thought it imprudent to point out the blatant inaccuracy of the term "maid" in this context. "One must go to the best available source," he said, grimly. "My hope and intention has always been to increase the natural supply of the agent a thousand- or a million-fold, and eventually to render it irrelevant, so that anyone and everyone might benefit from the knowledge and the artifice. Sir Julian was as much a means to that end as your sister was."

"Well now," Sean Driscoll put in, "it seems to me, on that reckoning, that Mr. Deangate might have been doing you a favor just now, by increasing the range of your experiments. I'm right in thinking, am I not, that the likely result of what you've done is that Sir Julian will revert to his natural appearance in the course of the next few days…or hours?"

Mathieu, still thinking that it was necessary to play for time as well as to be hopeful, said: "Yes, that's correct."

"And now you've finally stopped messing about with your flasks and potions, and returned what you've stolen to my sister's veins," Thomas Deangate insisted, stubbornly, "she'll recover the looks she had before the *Hallowmas* left Tilbury last year."

Mathieu saw no point in repeating his cautions again. "I sincerely I hope so," he said, "and it's an experiment I haven't yet attempted, so I can't deny the possibility." Now that the critical point had been passed, he thought, perhaps his sole concern ought to be getting out of the house in one piece, with no pursuit, in order to get to Rockley Road as soon as possible—and after that, Bordeaux. In a sense, he had no other options left…but he still had a duty to his patient.

"I need to go outside," Sir Julian stated, meaning that he needed to visit the privy in the back yard. He was not asking for permission—merely explaining what he intended, in case Driscoll's men moved to stop him. No one did—but when the baronet had gone through the door Driscoll nodded to MacBride, instructing him to follow and keep Sir Julian in sight.

While Mathieu began tidying up his materials, with the mechanical patience of a automaton, he heard his patron go out, and then come back in a few minutes later. He judged by the consequent pattern of noises that Sir Julian had gone to the kitchen sink to wash his hands.

There was a shaving-mirror on the kitchen wall, next to the sink. Exactly what Sir Julian would see therein in, if he looked into it at all, Mathieu could not guess, but he felt the pressure of time upon his weary shoulders. The clock in the hall chimed ten, each chime seeming to add a further blow to his exhaustion. He pricked up his ears, half-expecting to hear the rumble of carriage-wheels drawing up in the street outside, but there was no such noise to be heard at present. Cormack was very late indeed; he was by no means strict in his punctuality when his master was not actually with him, but he would have been risking disciplinary action even had the visit been a routine one. Doubtless he would have some plausible excuse, though.

"How are you feeling, Caroline," Mathieu said, with scrupulous politeness. "You're not feeling any ill-effects from the infusion?"

The girl was obviously still frightened, but she was also hopeful, doubtless encouraged by her brother's seeming control of the situation. She had returned to Mathieu's house in the hope that he might be willing and able to help her in her present distress, without actually realizing that he had been the cause of it, but she had heard enough now to understand, at least vaguely, that he had stolen her beauty somehow, and that the injection she had received might return it to her. The operation had seemed alarming to her, but the promised result…

"I feel very strange," she said.

"Don't worry," her brother said. "We'll go home to Mother now."

"Mother?" That thought seemed to alarm her all over again. She had not been home for some time. There were things that Thomas Deangate might not know, Mathieu thought, things that she might not want him to know. On the other hand, given the somewhat fearful fashion in which Caroline was looking at her brother, there might be things that he knew only too well. "No, Tom," she said, quietly, after a pause. "I don't live there any more."

"You ought to stay here a little longer," Mathieu told her. "You too, Mr. Deangate—just to make sure that everything's all right." He thought abut advising Sean Driscoll to take Sir Julian away for their planned meeting, but decided against it. In any case, he presumed, Sir Julian would not consent to leave, at least until Cormack brought the carriage— the carriage that surely must have suffered an authentic accident, to be so late in arriving—and it was probably for the best that he stay, in spite of what might happen.

"Why wouldn't everything be all right?" asked Thomas Deangate, sharply. "If anything happens to her…" He made a significant gesture with the gun.

Mathieu believed the threat, but it had all gone too far. The die was cast. Whatever was going to happen would happen. He was more worried about Sir Julian than Caroline. The effect on him might well be more rapid, and more drastic…and the consequent response more explosive. At least Tom Deangate had the gun.

Caroline was looking up at him. He knew by her expression that she remembered—not just the first extraction of her blood, but its prelude. Perhaps that ought to have made her hate or despise him, but there was no hatred in her gaze, and there did not seem to be any resentment or accusation there. In fact, her eyes seemed to be appealing to him. Perhaps, he thought, it was just automatic professional seduction—but he could not believe that. In the midst of confusion, she still trusted him. Perhaps that fact that he been attracted to her before, had been seduced by her body, actually made her expect more of him now, increasing her trust rather than decreasing it.

"It's all right, Caroline," he said. "I'll look after you, as best I can. Don't be afraid."

She nodded, imperceptibly. Again, he wondered why she was looking to him for the reassurance she needed and not to her brother. He thought back to the moment she had recognized him, and blurted out his name. Had she been glad to see him? Not nearly as glad, he concluded, on reflection, as the seaman had been to see her—and perhaps there had been more alarm in her exclamation than any other emotion.

Mathieu turned off the gas to through whose flame he had carefully passed his hollow needle back and forth in order to sterilize them. In between times it had warmed the bath of water in which he had placed the blood-extracts, but that was redundant now. He stoked up the furnace that fed steam to the autoclave, which would eventually serve to sterilize the more substantial items of his equipment, and he paused, waiting for Sir Julian to return from the kitchen.

The baronet came back in, and cast a hostile glance around, while lending an ear to the sounds of the streets outside, doubtless cursing Cormack silently with the full range of his extensive vocabulary.

Carefully, Mathieu examined Caroline again, taking her pulse, inspecting her eyes and taking her body temperature, and trying to soothe her anxieties with the gentle pressure of his hand. Everything seemed normal. In his best bedside manner voice, he said: "I think she's stable now, Mr. Deangate, but please don't upset her. Take her wherever she wants to go, for now. Be patient with her, and all will be well." *For a while*, he thought.

He was still holding the girl's hand, and he felt its tension increase as he spoke. She did not want to go with her brother, he thought, but did not dare to say so.

"That's good," said Sean Driscoll. "Now, perhaps, we can get on to our business, Sir Julian. There's a public house…"

Mathieu took the risk of interrupting him. "Actually, Mr. Driscoll, given that Sir Julian has that nasty cut on his cheek, it will probably be best if he stays here rather than accompanying you to a public house, or even returning to Holland Park, even when Cormack finally arrives, in order that I can keep him under observation. I have only the one bed, which I'll gladly surrender to Sir Julian, but you're welcome to share my vigil if you wish."

"Vigil be damned," Sir Julian said, less hotly than he would probably have liked. "I'm going home—and you're coming with me, Galmier. You've got what you wanted, Mr. Deangate, and I'll thank you to hand my revolver back now, if you don't mind."

Sir Julian stuck out his hand, as if he had every expectation of receiving the weapon—but Thomas Deangate, fearful of what the baronet might do with the weapon if he took possession of it, did not surrender it.

It was during that moment of tense hesitation that Mathieu heard the belated sound of Sir Julian's carriage arriving to collect him. Cormack would be in the box, he knew, and there would likely be a footman behind, as well as a coachman. If it came to a fight now, the odds would have shifted very significantly—and Sean Driscoll's expression showed that he understood that.

Mathieu saw Sir Julian take manifest courage from that realization, and the baronet drew himself up to his full height as he turned away from the recalcitrant Deangate to meet his unruly tenant's eyes.

Templeforth opened his mouth, perhaps intending to tell Driscoll and his companions that he would not meet with them now, or anywhere in England, and that they must return to Ireland to air their grievances to his steward, or perhaps merely intending to threaten to send him to Hell again.

Driscoll was already opening his mouth too, presumably to protest that anticipated instruction—but neither man contrived to utter a word, because Driscoll's eyes suddenly betrayed astonishment, and Sir Julian read that astonishment with all the alacrity that dire anxiety could induce. He also began to tremble, as if subject to a myriad of small convulsions.

Merde! Mathieu thought. *One hour might have made all the difference. Just one hour more, and I might have had Sir Julian on his own. Now...*

Sir Julian had to fight to stay on his feet, because he was shivering badly, perhaps suffering slight quasi-epileptic convulsions, but he managed to do it, albeit by clinging on to a workbench with both hands and holding his arms as rigid as he could; he was a strong-willed man, and he did not want to show weakness before his tenants. Had he not been gripping the bench he might have raised his hands to his face, but as things were the arching of his spine caused him to tip he head slightly backwards and expose his face fully to the light. For a full minute, he shook spasmodically from head to toe.

In the meantime, his face, racked my muscular tics and nervous shocks, had begun to change. Sean Driscoll and everyone else could see it plainly—and the baronet, although his eyes were doubtless having difficulty focusing, could read what was happening in their expressions.

This metamorphosis was not the relatively slow and gradual transformation that overtook the girls who had sold their looks for a guinea. This was more reminiscent of a lycanthropic change of form, as brutal as it was sudden. It was not simply that Sir Julian's complexion became dull, or his features slack, or that his face acquired any of the other trivial stigmata that marked Mathieu's young victims; this was a tortuous, twisting, quasi-epileptic transfiguration, which erased the face that was no longer quite that of an angel with a single merciless sweep, and in a matter of little more than a minute and a half, substituted a face that seemed entirely that of a demon.

Mathieu was amazed. He had feared that the transformation might be rapid, and had feared that rather than simply returning to his former plainness, Sir Julian would suffer a loss parallel to the kind of loss that his victims had suffered, but he had not expected the phenomenon to strike with such sudden violence, or to proceed to such a drastic extent. Indeed, he had never dreamed that such a drastic transformation might be possible. Clearly, the multiple transfusions of golden fluid that Sir

Julian had received from different sources had brought his innate population to a state of stress, and the sudden removal of a part of his fluid had triggered a catastrophic collapse of the remainder, with truly horrible effects.

Common ugliness, Mathieu knew, really was mere plainness—a purely negative phenomenon, a mere absence—but the total absence of human beauty was no mere featurelessness. When a human face became a *tabula rasa*, because of a catastrophic disruption of one or more of its populations of internal commensals, it apparently exposed the pre-human animal: the species of beast that humankind had been before human beings and their microcosmic passengers had begun their long collaborative evolution towards naturally-selected sexual attractiveness. Sir Julian might have been ugly, as Sean Driscoll had alleged, when he was thirty-and-one years old, but he became a great deal uglier than that now that the removal of so many of the benevolent passengers from his personal microcosm had precipitated a massive discordance of their internal collaboration.

Mathieu could not help the commonplace phrase "as ugly as sin" popping into his mind, and thinking that whatever sin Sir Julian Templefoth was now as ugly as must have been a mortal sin indeed: a blackness of the soul hardly imaginable, even in a man such as him.

Mathieu's mind was racing, his thoughts crowding one another and competing for the focus of his attention. According to Charles Darwin's bolder acolytes, he knew—and all the serious evolutionists in France—human beings were close kin to the great apes, to gorillas, orangutans and chimpanzees, but the apish creature that Sir Julian now became did not seen to him to have the majesty of a gorilla or the amicability of a chimpanzee. His features were by no means as hairy or flaccid as an orangutan's, and he was not only still recognizably human, but still recognizable, in a weirdly suggestive fashion, as a caricature of his old unhandsome self, but the ghastly pallor of his glabrous skin only seemed to added an extra dimension to its quasi-simian horror.

It occurred to Mathieu—and must have occurred to Driscoll too—that had Sir Julian not been clad in his typical elegant costume, presumably carrying documents adequate for identification in his wallet, he might have a great deal of trouble henceforth persuading anyone, including his own servants, that he really was Sir Julian Templeforth.

The scientific element of Mathieu's consciousness thought: *What a specimen! What a subject for research!* But that was not the dominant element of his character, at least for the moment.

It was presumably impossible for anyone to judge what thoughts might have sprung into the baronet's mind, but the resultant action was obvious enough. The subhuman Sir Julian, seemingly fully recovered from his temporary epilepsy, suddenly reached out and snatched the revolver rudely from Thomas Deangate's reluctant hand, and did his best to cover everyone as he backed through the door of the laboratory and headed along the corridor—not aiming for the front door, it seemed, but for the kitchen.

Mathieu waited, holding his breath, for the scream that might accompany Sir Julian's first sight of himself in the shaving-mirror, almost prepared to pray that he might hear a shot immediately afterwards as the once-handsome man proved incapable of tolerating the notion of what he had become.

There was no shot. Sir Julian Templeforth, it seemed, still had faith in Mathieu Galmier, and in the possibility that what had just been undone might be repaired, with the aid of an abundant quantity of young blood.

Thomas Deangate, meanwhile, was staring at his sister, obviously expecting a similarly abrupt transformation that might transform her into a living angel. Nothing of the sort happened, or seemed likely to happen any time soon.

"Go!" said Mathieu, to anyone and everyone who could hear him. "For the love of God, go away! Leave me to do what I can for Sir Julian!"

No one moved to obey, but he received support from an unexpected direction when Sir Julian appeared in the doorway again, brandishing the pistol wildly, and screaming "Get out!" at anyone and everyone—except, presumably, Mathieu. The words were hardly distinguishable; clear speech was a trifle difficult for the baronet at present.

Mathieu assumed that it was simply some absent-minded mechanical response that made Thomas Deangate reach for the shelf where he had deposited his knife. He felt certain that the seaman was merely collecting his property before departing, and surely meant no harm to anyone—but Deangate had already thrown a scalpel at Sir Julian, and had cut him badly in the face: a wound that Sir Julian had felt as a profound insult as well as a source of pain.

Perhaps misreading Deangate's intention, or perhaps not caring what that intention was, in his state of horrified excitement, the baronet fired the gun.

Unimaginably ugly he might be, and hardly capable of comprehensible speech, but the baronet's hand and eye were sound. The shot struck Deangate in the side of the head, and the sailor collapsed, his skull perforated and his brain pulverized—but he was a tall man, and a long-limbed one, and he did not fold up as neatly as he might have done. While his sister screamed, his convulsively-extended arms struck out in both directions, violently upsetting numerous items of glassware, including the bath full of lukewarm water, the furnace and the autoclave, and one of the oil-lamps. A flood of flame gushed across the table-top.

What the intentions of the three Irishmen might have been, Mathieu could not be sure. Driscoll, at least, probably tried to disarm the baronet in a spirit of pure altruism. The others also moved toward him, albeit more probably driven by an instinct of self-preservation than any rational plan. Whatever the truth of the matter, there was an obvious threat of a brawl, and the threat was immediately realized.

Sir Julian, no matter what strain his lightning transformation had put on his muscles and his metabolism, was strong, and he was furious. He fired the revolver again, and again. Mathieu ducked swiftly, but he did not close his eyes, and felt like a coiled spring, ready to leap into action as soon as an opportunity to act presented itself.

Driscoll went down, and Reilly too. Understandably, neither of them was at all careful about the way that he sprawled as he fell.

Broken glass flew everywhere, and the initial river of flame was scattered into half a dozen tributaries. The cluttered laboratory began to fill with acrid, cloying smoke.

VIII

Mathieu could not have said, afterwards, with his hand on his heart, that he kept his presence of mind. Indeed, he had no clear memory of exactly what he had thought, or of formulating any of the intentions behind his action.

What he actually did, however, was heroic, after a fashion. He made haste to seize Caroline Deangate, plucking her thin frame out of the chair as if she weighed nothing at all, and, keeping his head down, he ran for the door, cradling her like a babe-in-arms. He hurdled Sean Driscoll's body, and cannoned into the still-upright baronet head first, deliberately butting him in the lower ribs with the full force of his impetus. In spite of the considerable difference in bulk there was between them, the subhuman gunman did not have sufficient equilibrium to maintain his stance or to make Mathieu rebound. The creature that had been Sir Julian Templeforth fell back, and his head smashed into the door lintel. Then he fell like a stone, firing his weapon one last time.

The last bullet missed Michael MacBride by quite some distance, but the latter did not even notice that he had been at risk. He was on his knees beside Padraig Reilly, trying to pick him up as Mathieu had picked up Caroline, but having great difficulty doing it; Reilly was too heavy.

Somehow, Mathieu got his burden through the doorway without tripping over anyone, living or dead, and without even bumping Caroline's head against the doorpost. Once in the corridor, he was in the clear.

He turned left, went through the kitchen and out of the back door. He crossed the yard in two strides and kicked the rickety back gate off its hinges rather than troubling to lift the latch.

No one had followed him, but he did not pause. In the grip of panic, desperately in need of hectic action, he ran, and he did not stop running until he reached the bushes in Ravenscourt Park, where he swiftly took shelter, collapsing in the leaf-litter, exhausted, panting hard in what suddenly seemed the enormously difficult task of recovering his breath.

While absorbed in that painful physical restoration, he could not even make the effort to think, but once his body had finally attained an equilibrium, and his lungs could draw in air with a regular rhythm, his mind began to function again, and he endeavored to grasp the situation, to find a basis for rational action.

Caroline Deangate was still in shock. "Tom," she murmured, in a voice that seemed strangely dispassionate. "I've killed Tom." Seemingly, it had not occurred to her as yet to attempt to blame anyone but herself for the train of events that her arrival in Mathieu's lodgings had set in motion. She had arrived on the scene late, and events had moved with a rapid precipitation thereafter. She had probably missed too much of what had happened beforehand to make any sense of the explanations that Mathieu had tried to offer, or of what had happened to her. She had simply deferred her power of decision to others.

Not only was the poor child not blaming him for what had happened, Mathieu realized, she was actually clinging to him desperately, begging for his protection with her hands, if not her voice.

Somewhat to his surprise, Mathieu realized that he really did not care at all about the three men who had been shot, or the two he had just left behind in the burning house—but he did feel terribly guilty about Caroline Deangate. That was not because he had responded to the demand made of him to restore her beauty, even though he had every reason to believe that the transfusion would only have a feeble effect, nor even because he had stolen that beauty in the first place, when she had unwittingly sold it to Cormack for a derisory price. He felt guilty, most of all, because he had taken personal advantage of that beauty, to satisfy his physical desire, when he had known full well that he was about to destroy it.

That, he thought, had been a sacrilege, and he cursed himself for having given in to the temptation. Although the debt that he had contracted to her was the theft itself, which had probably damaged her permanently and irreparably—one of many symbols marked in red in his moral account book—the discomfort it caused him was multiplied in acuity by that extra crime, even though it had caused her no harm and no distress.

His hands tried, awkwardly, to respond to the demands of hers, with a grip that he hoped might reassure her, and would at least inform her that she was not alone. In the meantime, he tried to evaluate the threats and possibilities inherent in the situation.

He made a rapid estimate of the amount of flammable material that had been contained in his laboratory, and the time it would take for a fire engine to reach the burning building. Everything, he thought, would have been thoroughly consumed before the fire could be brought under control. There would probably have been nothing that Cormack, and any other servants who might have been with him, would have been able to do, even if the butler had been the kind of man to run into a burning building, blinded by smoke, without a voice calling for help to guide him.

MacBride, he assumed, might well have escaped, if he had had sense enough to abandon his dead friend in time. If he had gone through the front door, he might have run into Cormack, but it seemed unlikely that he had paused to offer any explanation of what has happened, let alone that he had remained or returned to the scene in order identify the four charred bodies that would be presumably pulled from the ruins tomorrow or the day after. In all probability, therefore, what had happened in the house would remain a permanent mystery to any investigators.

He made some rapid corollary calculations, in spite of what experience had taught him about the unreliability of simple arithmetic.

"For all that anyone knows," he said, aloud, addressing himself although he probably would not have voiced the thoughts had the girl not been there to supply an apparent audience, "I'm numbered among the dead. The coachman had parked the carriage outside the front door, on the assumption that Sir Julian was inside, so they'll probably take it for granted that the baronet is among the dead, even if his wallet doesn't survive the blaze, but if he's badly burned, they'll readily assume that he died as handsome as he went in. Will they ever be able to put names to any of the others? Probably not—and they might not even try very hard. It might be days before the seaman is registered as missing, and it's highly unlikely that they'll be able to connect him to the house. So…"

If only, he thought, Sir Julian had handed over the money he had brought! He could really use that now. But it might not matter overmuch, since he had another recourse ready to hand. At the moment, the idea of a quiet château in the south of France seemed like a hint of paradise. That had to be his objective now.

But first, he had to take care of Caroline Deangate. He could not simply abandon her. That would be too atrocious. "I'd better get you home to Stepney first," he murmured, unthinkingly.

The girl had not been listening to his monologue, or only listening distractedly, until the pronounced the word *Stepney*. Then she reacted. Her grip on his arms tightened, painfully.

"No!" she said. "I can't! I won't!"

Mathieu did not know what to read into that reaction, but he remembered having guessed previously that the change in her appearance could not have been the only reason for the disappearance from home that had sent Thomas Deangate searching for her. He knew that he could not simply abandon her. He had abandoned so many of his victims, one by one, as if they had not mattered in the least—but the sequence had been broken now, and the list of what he had done had been added up to form an enormity. It seemed bizarre to him now that he had ever been able to avoid thinking of the steady accumulation of that total, and that he had been able to keep it locked away for so long in some closed compartment of his conscience.

The grip on his arms slackened, and the hand that was holding his left arm let go. By the not-so-distant light of a street-lamp in Paddenswick Road, Mathieu could see that Caroline was touching her face with tentative fingers, perhaps wondering if and when it might be begin to return to its former magnificence. Her other hand was still holding his right arm, but it was no longer gripping it desperately.

"There's hope yet," he told her. "Destruction is easy, and restitution is hard, but sometimes…"

He left it there. In a fairer world, he thought, there would be a balance in such matters, but Nature's notion of compensation was by no means egalitarian. The owl's delight in making each of its nightly meals was a poor recompense for the agony of the mouse that had to die to provide it.

But he realized that he had misread her gesture. She had only been touching her face to make sure of its solidity, to confirm that she was still alive, and whole. She was collecting herself, making an effort to cast aside her panic and bewilderment.

Caroline looked up at him, and her pale face caught the light of the street-lamp. Mathieu was sure that the gratitude in her gaze was sincere. Foolish it might be, but it was spontaneous. Nor was it the gaze of a child; she had begun to pull herself together, and her maturity was beginning to show through again. She was probably no more than eighteen, but she was certainly no Judy Lee, and she was making a deliberate effort not to be childish now, to be an adult.

"I'm sorry, Doctor," she said. "I'm being silly. Thank you."

Caught off guard, he couldn't help saying: "For what?"

She seemed surprised. "For saving my life. If you hadn't picked me up…" She stopped then, perhaps because she didn't want to think about the possibility that she might have died in the fire, but perhaps also because she did not want to think about the dead brother she had left behind to burn.

When he made no response, she added: "But you've lost everything, haven't you? Your house, your work…"

He had no idea what to say to that, so he simply shook his head.

She was still trying to work things out, in an adult fashion. After a long pause, she said: "What happened to that man was what happened to me, wasn't it, only far worse? And it was because of what you did, bleeding me?"

"Yes, it was," Mathieu said, steeling himself for her reaction to that admission.

It was not what he expected. "But it was an accident, wasn't it?" she said. "You didn't mean to hurt me…or him?"

If only that were true! he thought.

He took a deep breath, and said: "In the beginning, I just wanted to help people to be more beautiful. That's what everyone wants, after all. I wanted to find something more fundamental, more precious, than cosmetics or adornments. I thought I had…but it went wrong. I really was trying to fix it…but I just made things worse. I'm truly sorry, but I did hurt you, knowingly…and now your brother's dead. You have every reason to hate me."

Contrary to popular advertisement, the confession did not seem to have been good for his soul. He did not feel as if a burden had been lifted. He simply felt sick.

"But you were trying to put it right," Caroline Deangate said—which was true, after a fashion.

"If only I could," he murmured.

The grip of her hand tightened again, but not desperately. Now, she was trying to reassure him. She wasn't foolish enough to think that, simply because he was a doctor, he could do anything, but she couldn't believe him guilty of malevolence.

"Why can't you?" she asked, looking down and moving her bandaged arm, as if to restore circulation that inaction had made sluggish.

To some extent, he thought, she was trying to catch up, to begin, belatedly, to make sense of the explanations that she'd heard, but hadn't been able to follow. She wanted to understand her own situation. But to some extent, too, she was trying to encourage him, to rally his morale.

"Beauty is a delicate and costly prize," he told her. "If it weren't, millions of years of natural selection would have made it a far more commonplace commodity than it is. I was stupid to think that its secret could be so easily mastered."

"But you did make that man handsome," she said. "You do have the secret."

"I had a means," Mathieu admitted. "But the increase in Sir Julian's seductiveness was hard-won. It required a kind of continual predation similar to the nightly hunt that sustains an owl in the ceaseless struggle for existence. I didn't realize that in advance, just as I didn't realize immediately that the girls' blood wouldn't renew the golden fluid—but when I did, I just kept on going. I thought…"

"What?" she prompted.

"That if I went on, I could find a way to fix it."

Again she moved her bandaged arm, and this time she let go of him in order to palpate the bandage. "But you don't think this will work?"

He felt a strong urge to try yet again to explain: to talk about the inefficiency of the process of extraction and filtration, the rate of attrition of the golden solution, the problem of the agent's instability and fragility. He wanted to try to explain his most recent deduction: that every strain of the golden substance, being the product of a single human microcosm, was to some degree unique, and could not help competing against others of its kind. He wanted to explain to her that although the introduction of the alien strains of the agent of into Sir Julian's microcosm had produced the desired effect, to begin with, their introduction into his organism had been far from unproblematic, that his original native strain had probably been gradually obliterated by the sequence of invasions, and that the removal of a substantial fraction of the warring factions that remained to him had resulted in a rapid and total collapse of his internal equilibrium. But what would be the point? Did he possess anything more than a mere illusion of understanding himself?

"I really don't know," he told her, in a whisper. "But if it does work, the credit will be due to your own microcosm, not to my method."

She didn't bother to ask him what the word *microcosm* meant. Instead, she said: "I need to get better."

He recovered something of his beside manner. "Yes, he said. "You need to get better, and you will. Over the next few days, you will get better. Just rest, and eat and sleep a well as you can. Is there anywhere you can go—anywhere I can take you?"

She shook her head. For the moment, she didn't want him to take her anywhere. She wanted him to stay with her, to protect her. She wanted his help. But what help could he give her, given that his own house was in the process of burning down, with his own protector lying dead inside it?

"Poor Tom," the girl murmured, in a different tone now that she was no longer bewildered and semi-delirious. "That bastard killed Tom…and the two Irishmen," She had evidently stopped blaming herself.

"Yes, he did," Mathieu agreed. "The strain was too much. He went berserk. He might have killed us all, if he'd had time. But you and I got away. We're alive—and while we're alive, hope is alive too. But we need to act. We can't stay here. If there's nowhere for you to go, you'll have to stay with me…at least for now. Can you stand up?"

Caroline Deangate nodded her head, and demonstrated that she could. Mathieu did the same, and they peered over the bushes into the darkness of the park. It seemed deserted. Mathieu took a moment to get his bearings, but realized that Goldhawk Road was only a short distance away. Bordeaux was much further, and the Château de Valcoeur doubtless further still, but he had a brief sensation that fate was smiling on him. At least he had a direction in which to go, and an objective in mind.

He put out his hand so that Caroline might take it freely, if it was her desire that he give her the continued benefit of his protection. She took the hand readily enough. In spite of everything, she was ready to accept Mathieu's offer of succor, to put her trust in his knowledge and his capability, if not his ambition and his dreams.

"I won't abandon you, Caroline," he told her. "You're my patient, and my subject. If you'll allow me to do it, I need to find a way to give back what I stole from you, permanently, even if it takes a long time. We mustn't despair, you and I. We have work to do. Come with me."

He had not taken three strides, however, when a shadow loomed up out of a further clump of bushes and moved to block their path toward the gate of the park.

"Forgive me, sir," said Michael MacBride, with a respect that seemed almost farcical, in the circumstances, "but there's something you need to know, and it might be best if we were to stick together, for we might need one another's testimony—and this young woman's too, if she's capable of giving any."

"What?" demanded Mathieu, baldly.

"Sir Julian's butler helped me to pull him out of the house, sir. Padraig was dead, but the landlord was only stunned. He's alive. He might have had difficulty having himself recognized, but I convinced the butler that it was him. I'd like to think that he'd be grateful to me for pulling him out, when he wakes up, but that might be foolish optimism."

"Did you tell Cormack what had happened?" Mathieu asked, anxious.

"I told him that Sir Julian had shot three men in the house with the gun he was still clutching, but I didn't go into detail. For all the butler knows, at present, you were one of them. I didn't mention the girl at all. But it doesn't matter what I said. When Sir Julian comes round he'll be free to make up his own story, and I fear that he might not be the kind of man to take blame that he can possibly lay elsewhere."

"You think he'll accuse me?"

"No, sir, but I think he might try to lay the blame on Sean and Padraig, and me too. If he thinks you're alive—which he will, if he can remember who he shot—he'll need you to try to restore his looks, but he promised to send the rest of us to hell, and I fear that he might not be the man to let go of a promise like that. Together, though, we can at least cast doubt on his account. We'll never get him convicted of murder in an English court, but at least we can get ourselves acquitted…provided that we stick together."

"Damn!" said Mathieu, quietly. "Yes, obviously, Mr. MacBride, we need to stick together…but it might be better not to risk arrest at all." He thought rapidly. "Do you have a wife, Michael?"

"No, sir. Sean brought Padraig and myself over the water because we had no hostages to fortune. He was afraid of reprisals, even if things went smoothly."

"So you have no need to go back to Ireland?"

"I don't think I can, sir. Even if Sir Julian can't have me convicted of any crime, he has other ways of sending me to Hell."

"And Caroline doesn't want to return to Stepney. Look, Michael, I can't make any promises, but there's a chance I can get all three of us out of this, if you'd care to come with me swiftly as far as Rockley Road. The Valcoeurs might cut and run when I explain what's happened, but if they really do imagine themselves as modern Rosicrucians…will you trust me?"

MacBride laughed. "What alternative do I have, sir?"

Mathieu did not bother to ask Caroline. She had already run out of alternatives.

"Come this way," he said. He felt a sudden sense of urgency. If Sir Julian was alive, even if he were in no condition to think straight for the moment, there was a possibility of almost-immediate pursuit, and who knew what the baronet might tell the police about what had happened in the house? Perhaps he would think it politic to say nothing at all, and perhaps he did not know, as yet, that anyone but MacBride had survived the fire…but while so many possibilities were in suspense, he thought it best to make haste. It was not only his own fate that he had to think about now, but Caroline Deangate's. She was his patient. Michael MacBride, technically, was not, but Mathieu did not want to abandon him either, to the mercy of his landlord and English justice.

Mercifully, Rockley Road was only a few hundred yards away. Mathieu and MacBride had to lend Caroline a little assistance, but her legs did not let her down, and she seemed to gain in strength while they walked, as if the sensation that she now had a destination were invigorating.

"Wait here," said Mathieu, in the lobby of the Brook Green Hotel, when the bell-boy came back down to confirm that Monsieur and Mademoiselle de Valcoeur would see him. He ran up the stairs, knocked on the door and went in.

"I'm truly sorry," he said, before Philippe or Myrtille could speak, "but something has happened that might change your attitude to the possibility of taking me into your employ, and I need to explain."

Rapidly, without taking the seat that was offered to him, he gave them a brief summary of the night's events. The brother and sister remained standing too, listening to him with attention but without alarm. He was surprised that so many events could be condensed into such a brief narrative, but the whole story only required a few minutes to tell

Mathieu concluded by saying: "I have no idea what my situation is with regard to Sir Julian now, but I fear that MacBride might be correct in anticipating that he'll extract what revenge he can on him, and perhaps Caroline as well. I don't feel that I can abandon them. In all probability, everything I possess has been destroyed, and if I fall into Sir Julian's hands, no matter how desperately he needs my services, I dare not expect generous treatment from him. I realize that this is not what you expected or hoped of me, but that is now my situation. Can you help me?"

Only then did he pause. The brother and the sister did not seem shocked or appalled. Indeed, they actually seemed perversely pleased. Mathieu felt a tremendous surge of relief.

"Of course we can help you," said Myrtille de Valcoeur, immediately taking charge, with the easy entitlement of an elder sibling. "Philippe, get a cab and go to the port immediately. Book passage on the first available steamer to France—anywhere in France. Take whatever berths are available, for the six of us. I'll have Isabelle start packing immediately and make all the necessary arrangements with the hotel—but first I need to see your protégés, Dr. Galmier. We'll all go downstairs together."

They did that, and Myrtille de Valcoeur introduced herself to Michael MacBride and Caroline Deangate.

"I understand that you might be in danger," she said to them both. "Are you willing to go to France to escape it?"

"Certainly," said MacBride.

Caroline simply nodded her head.

"Good. Are you wiling to enter my family's service, Mr. MacBride? I hope you won't find it any more onerous than laboring the fields in Ireland."

"Yes, Mam'zelle," said MacBride, without hesitation.

"Caroline," said the Frenchwoman then, addressing the girl, "are you willing to place yourself under Dr. Galmier's guardianship?"

Caroline presumably knew what guardianship implied, and could probably have replied, whether it was true or not, that she did not need a guardian, but she was no more in a mood for quibbling than MacBride had been; she nodded her head decisively.

"Good," sad Myrtille de Valcoeur. "Please come upstairs. We'll have to wait, I fear—all night, at least, and perhaps much of the day as well, but we'll make ourselves as comfortable as possible in the meantime. This time tomorrow, hopefully, we'll be at sea…and after that, the future is ours. So far as Sir Julian Templeforth is concerned, you'll have vanished into thin air."

Mathieu felt a pang of conscience as he thought about Sir Julian's reaction to the disappearance of the one man who might be able to ameliorate his plight, but he quelled it.

What alternative do I have? he asked himself—and for the moment, he could not think of any.

IX

In fact, they were at sea well before noon, aboard the *S.S. Pendark*, a British merchant ship bound for Madrid that was due to call in at Cherbourg and Bordeaux. Philippe had only been able to reserve two cabins, each with two bunks, but Michael MacBride had been given a hammock in the crew's quarters, and Myrtille's maid, Isabelle, expressed her perfect contentment with the floor of the siblings' cabin. Caroline retreated to her bunk almost immediately, lack of sleep and the pace of events having hastened the onset of seasickness, and Myrtille commissioned Isabelle to maintain a vigil over her while she and Philippe took Mathieu up on deck in order to begin the explanations that they had not had time to give him the day before.

Once the ship was out of the Thames estuary the water became a trifle rough, and, although it was not raining, there was a keen wind that kept most of the vessel's small complement of passengers away from the deck. Even so, Myrtille had no difficulty in guiding the three of them to a relatively sheltered covert where there was a bench of sorts on which all three of them could sit, with Mathieu in the middle.

It was Myrtille who took the lead in the discourse as well, but Mathieu did not want to turn his back on Philippe, so he contended himself with staring out at sea rather than looking her in the face as she spoke.

First of all, she produced a package wrapped in silk, which, when unwrapped, proved to be the miniature that Mathieu had seen on the mantelpiece of the hotel room the first time he had visited the Valcoeurs. At close range, its antiquity was obvious.

"An ancestor?" Mathieu enquired.

"No," said Myrtille. "It's supposedly a portrait of la Belle Paule, a famous Toulousan beauty of the sixteenth century."

"Supposedly?"

"The date of the picture suggests that the artist could never have seen la Belle Paule in her youth. It's possible that he derived the image from a more famous portrait that still hangs in the Capitole, but more likely that he simply attributed the name to a hypothetical image of ideal female beauty, the woman in question having been held up as a incarnation of that ideal in a once-famous treatise by Gabriel de Minuit."

Mathieu thought that the artist had not been able to live up to his ambition of capturing the ideal of female beauty—but he knew the painter was by no means alone in that.

"The task is inherently difficult," Myrtille added, "but it has long been something of a preoccupation in the region of my birth. Have you ever heard of Clémence Isaure?"

"No," Mathieu admitted.

"She was the legendary founder of the Consistori del Gay Saber, the oldest literary society in the world, which was an attempt to preserve something on the verge of extinction: the lyric poetry of the troubadours. She supposedly instituted the annual floral games, competitions in Occitan poetry, which still exist. There are multiple paintings representing Clémence Isaure, all of which are, like this miniature, attempts to synthesize an ideal of female beauty. Clémence herself is a kind of legendary copy of the archetypal lady of courtly romance, representations of whom were often passed off as images of the Virgin Mary, in order to reconcile them with the Church."

"There's nothing unusual about that," Mathieu pointed out. "The ancient Greek sculptors produced countless images of the goddess Aphrodite, with the same intention."

"Indeed—but in France, the tradition has particularly deep roots in the Occitan region. Nowadays, the floral games are purely a literary festival, but at their supposed origin, in the fourteenth century, they were strongly infused with mysticism—a secret mysticism that was partly a residuum of the Catharist heresies stamped out a century earlier by the so-called Albigensian crusade, and partly a continuation of more ancient traditions. That extirpation was so successful that few Albigensian documents survive, and most accounts of their beliefs and practices are based on the calumnies of their enemies. Anything that survived the crusade was driven underground, only becoming manifest in disguised and symbolic form. The Consistori del Gay Saber may well have been a secret society for some time before surfacing in a carefully sanitized appearance.

"No one can now be sure, obviously, but the idea persists that there has long been a continuity between various secret societies maintaining an esoteric tradition, and various common threads connecting them. Numerous modern historians, trying to patch together that hidden history, have tried to identify such a thread of continuity between the mystical ideas of the Cathars, the Consistori del Gay Saber, and the Fraternity of the Rose-Cross. As you said yourself when you saw the design on the mantelpiece when you first visited our hotel, almost all of that is fiction, a kind of scholarly fantasy, because it could not be otherwise—but within that fantasy, or at least within its symbolism, a truth is hidden. The details professed by various contemporary occult sects and societies are all invented, but the essential quest they are trying to pursue is very old, and very important."

"I don't deny that," said Mathieu, "but I can't see what it has to do with my work, which is purely scientific."

"Don't be disingenuous, Mathieu," said Myrtille de Valcoeur. "You know perfectly well that your work is not, and cannot be, *purely* scientific. You might be using scientific means and scientific method, as Philippe is, but you know perfectly well that its essential goal is alchemical: that it's a quest for a kind of essence—the essence of beauty. Like the artists who tried to embody that essence in images of Aphrodite, la Belle Paule and Clémence Isaure, you're dealing with a fundamental esthetic principle. How could that ever be purely scientific?"

"All right," Mathieu conceded. "I admit that I've even described my fluid serum—the agent that transmits human beauty—as alchemical gold, because of its color."

"It might be a better alchemical analogy to think of it as the azoth," Myrtile told him. "That's the agent of transformation, sometimes vulgarly considered as a solvent or a medicament, but actually more fundamental than that—the ultimate catalyst, to employ Philippe's preferred jargon. Mother doesn't entirely approve of my describing the agent in her potions as the azoth, but she has no better name for it."

"Your mother is an alchemist?"

"Yes, and a Rosicrucian, although the rose in our symbolism is red, the color of blood, not white. That does not mean, however, that we are not aiming at a kid of purity, because our notion of perfect beauty has moral connotations that go far beyond superficial appearance. Our ancestors thought of their endeavor not as a matter of sexual attractiveness but as an alchemical quest for the soul of blood, and the blood of the soul. Philippe does not like that jargon at all, and my mother and I have different interpretations too, but you'll have abundant opportunity to question all three of us as to matters of detail. For now I'm trying to explain the basis of our present work: the exploration of the relationship between blood and beauty. For Mother and me, Philippe's science, and yours, is one means to that end. For us—and, we think, for you too—there is far more at stake in your work than enabling vain men like Sir Julian Templeforth, or vain women, to maintain their seductive qualities for the purposes of ostentation and vulgar debauchery. You have higher aims than that, as we do. Is that not so?"

"Yes, evidently," said Mathieu, "but I'm not all sure that my higher ambitions are the same as those of the fictitious Fraternity of the Rose-

Cross, or whatever might have been the purpose of the Albigensian mystics and the founders of the floral games, in spite of the apparent preoccupation of the latter with the ideal of beauty."

"Indeed," said Myrtille. "That is why I am trying to help you out of your uncertainty, to achieve a greater clarity. You are aware, I suppose, that the legal ban on blood transfusions that was recently repealed in France, permitting your experimentation to go ahead, was never universally observed within the profession?"

"I'm aware of rumors," Mathieu admitted, "as well as reports of such work outside France as James Blundell's, but whether the ban prevented all experimentation or not, it certainly prohibited almost all publication."

"Quite so—and that is by no means a new phenomenon. Oppression and persecution have never stamped out enquiry, but they have been far more successful in stamping out reportage. That is why there has always been an occult tradition, incapable of publication, but not of covert transmission."

"You're telling me that there's an occult tradition of experiments in blood transfusion?"

"I am—and one that is far older than you probably suppose. The legendary record is necessarily sparse and disguised, but you're doubtless familiar with the story that Joseph of Arimathea brought the Holy Grail to the south of France in the first century, and various other stories associating that Grail with the region, especially with the Albigensians."

"And you think that legendry is associated with blood transfusion?"

"Of course. It is, at any rate, manifestly associated with sanguinary mysticism, with the attribution to blood, in some circumstances, of special supernatural properties of regeneration and transformation. The blood in question was often identified with the blood of Christ, for the same reason that images of the troubadours' ideal lady were often identified with the Virgin Mary, but you must be able to imagine a different decoding, more closely akin to your own discoveries. In which case, you can understand, can you not, why modern inheritors of that tradition might be exceedingly interested in the filter that you have discovered, apparently capable of extracting a fluid serum from human blood. That serum is new, obviously, in the precise form that you have developed, but there are historical analogues.

"In the same way, your employment of Pravaz syringes, their associated apparatus, and modern sterile technique, is new in detail, but not without precedent. Might I point out, too, that details of your filter have not been published, nor have details of the blood-typing system that your colleagues at the Pasteur Institut are already employing in assessing compatibility. Doubtless they will be published in the future, but for a few more years, at least, and perhaps decades, the knowledge will remain esoteric, the clotting factors known only to professionals, and your gel filter, for the time being, known only to you."

Mathieu was still lingering on the fundamental notion, and could not help laboring the point. "And you're claiming that, although there's no exoteric documentation of it, there's a tradition of alchemical experimentation with blood that goes back centuries, which is directly relevant to my research?"

"Yes. Although, we naturally think that it is your research that is relevant to the tradition, rather than the other way around. The point is, however, that we can give you access to the ideas and findings of that occult tradition. To what extent that might aid and guide your future research, we can't be sure as yet, but we're convinced, obviously, of the possibility of a reciprocal benefit."

"I see. But in the centuries of research in question, no one has yet discovered an elixir of youth, or a potion of beauty?"

"In fact, they have—several, in fact. But as you've discovered yourself, such discoveries usually bring inconvenient snags and awkward costs. All of them have been imperfect in some way, and all of them have exposed their inventors and users to danger. Attempts to maintain secrecy have always led, inevitably, to calumny and distortion, and frequently to persecution—a pattern with which you are in the process of becoming familiar. The ordeal that you have undergone is, I fear, not at all original. Indeed, it's something of a tradition itself, almost a cliché. And the accusation that you have cast evil spells is not entirely unjustified, it seems, given that you have now taken one of your victims under your wing, at least while you retain the hope of lifting the spell."

"Touché," Mathieu conceded. "But if I'm now reading the hidden meaning of legendry more accurately, the cliché in question includes analogues of Sir Julian Templeforth as well as persecuted alchemists. That legacy hardly suggests that vanity and debauchery have played no part in the secret history to which you refer."

"Of course—how could it be otherwise? But the legendry also gives abundant evidence of the long existence of scholars possessed of higher ambitions—the followers of the Rose Cross, in the broadest sense of that symbolism: dedication to the two ideals of virtue and beauty, and the association of the two."

Mathieu looked at Philippe and Myrtille, in turn. In a curious sense, he would have liked to have been able to doubt them, to suspect that they could no more live up to that ideal than he had been able to do. In fact, he found it all too plausible, judging by appearances, that they were, in fact virtuous, and that they really were lovers of beauty in a sense that went beyond mere lust.

"I fear," he said, dully, "that I haven't lived up to those ideals myself."

"Few people can, with complete consistency," Philippe observed. "The point is to aspire to do so, and sincerely to repent one's failures."

Mathieu laughed briefly. "That I seem to have been able to do, at least recently," he conceded.

"And also to be able to go forward," Myrtille added. "To persist in striving toward perfection, even if its attainment comes to seem impossible."

Mathieu did not reply to that recommendation. Comment seemed superfluous, given that he was here. The subsidiary clause was, however, worrying, especially in juxtaposition with the claim that previous alchemists had made discoveries akin to his own. If every single one had failed to perfect his discovery, what chance did he have of success, even with the aid of fungal gel and Pravaz syringes? What if every quest for the ideal of beauty were somehow doomed by ironic Destiny to end in the parody of human being that Sir Julian Templeforth now was? What if poor Caroline, perhaps after a temporary improvement, had further depths of degeneration yet to plumb?

"You seem disheartened, Dr. Galmier," Myrtille observed. "There really is no need. The path of progress is a thorny one, as I said before, but it does lead upwards. What you have already achieved is a step forward—a smaller one that you hoped, certainly, but a step nevertheless."

"At what cost?" Mathieu asked, quietly. "And at what further cost will any future steps be taken. How do you procure…raw material…for your own experiments, assuming that it has not been safely restricted to the library? Not by relieving innocent whores of their meager heritage of pulchritude, I presume?"

Myrtille did not react to the application of the adjective "innocent" to the noun "whores," nor to the vulgarity of the noun itself.

"No," she said, "we do not use prostitutes. Our donors are fully-informed volunteers, but their individual donations are far less copious than yours. They have long been moderate in their effect, but that is an effect of a lack of refinement in processing and delivery that Philippe is working hard to redress. With Mother's permission, Philippe will be able to give you a demonstration of his methods, from the initial donation to the ultimate administration, when we arrive at the château. We shall then be able to combine our experience with yours, with a view to refining our various methods—but that will take time, I fear. Steamships have the reputation of being rapid, but the pace of this one is a trifle leaden, and we shall not be putting into Cherbourg until past midnight. We should leave reasonably early in the morning, after unloading and loading, but the journey to Boulogne will then be a tedious one, and will not be completed in a single day. Traveling overland from Cherbourg to Boulogne would not involve any significant saving of time, given the layout of the railway network, so we shall simply have to be patient."

"That should not be a problem," Mathieu said, dryly. "Two or three days' rest will be welcome—although poor Caroline might think otherwise, if her seasickness persists."

"She's fortunate to have a doctor on hand," said Myrtille, with no hint of sarcasm. "You'll be able to monitor her progress carefully."

"Yes, I shall," said Mathieu, in an equally neutral tone. "In fact, perhaps I ought to check on her now, to see whether I need to draw some laudanum from the ship's pharmacy. It will be a long night if the poor child cannot sleep."

With that, he took his leave, politely, and went down to the cabin.

* * * *

Isabelle was sitting with Caroline, but she was grateful to be given leave to go.

Mathieu sat down on the floor so that his head was level with the lower bunk.

"How are you feeling?" he asked his patient.

"Better, thank you," Caroline said. "Isabelle gave me some kaolin and morphia, which has quieted my stomach. She offered me some porridge too, but I don't feel capable of eating yet."

"You ought to try, when you can," Mathieu told her. "You'll need nourishment. I'll try to obtain something a little more appetizing than porridge, though. Tomorrow, the fare should be better, when we've taken on supplies at Cherbourg."

"I'm sorry to be such a poor patient," she said, "but I've never been to sea before. Tom would think me a terrible weakling." Her eyes misted over slightly, but either she had no more tears to spare, or she was not as regretful regarding her brother's death as she might have been.

"I'm truly sorry for everything that has happened to you, Caroline," Mathieu said, quietly. "I'm responsible for all of it, and I can never make it up to you, but I'll do what little I can. I've just had a long talk with the Valcoeurs. I think you'll be safe, and perhaps happy, on their estate."

"You saved my life," Caroline observed.

"Having first imperiled it."

"Not really. And even if you did, the saving makes up for a lot, I think. Not that the life of a cheap whore is worth a lot, I suppose."

Mathieu blushed. "I'm truly sorry about that, too," he said. "I should never…"

"Oh, don't worry about *that*," she said. "Compared with that fat but-ler, who complained about my lack of expertise, you were…well, a wel-come relief. I hadn't been on the game long, but long enough to know what pigs most men are. Far better to be someone's ward, and better yours than anyone else who's paid to screw me, believe me."

Mathieu started. "That's not what I understand by guardianship," he assured her. "I won't…" He stopped as he saw the expression on her face, which was by no means one of gratitude.

"It's all right," she said, sadly. "I understand. You don't want me now. Not unless this works." She raised her bandaged arm slightly.

Mathieu blushed again. "That's not why," he said. "It just wouldn't be right. To me, guardian means guardian—and I'm sure that's what Myrtille meant, too."

"Are you? It didn't seem so to me—but no matter. Whatever you want, Doctor. You don't need to feel bad about anything. You had to do what you had to do, just as I had. It's rotten world. At least neither of us is trying to make it any worse than it already is, unlike that fat butler and the fellow you turned into a monster. Pity you didn't kill *him*."

"I didn't mean to turn him into a monster," said Mathieu. "If only it hadn't happened as rapidly…another hour, and you and Tom would have been away and clear."

"And he's have taken me home," Caroline said, pensively. "Wouldn't have taken no for an answer, even if…he wouldn't have understood, you see. Or he would, which would have been worse. Better here, quite frankly.…"

Mathieu thought about asking for details of exactly what was that Tom Deangate might or might not have understood, but decided that there had to be safer subjects of conversation. He inspected her face carefully, intending at first to do it just for show—but when he looked closely, he saw distinct signs of change in the texture of the skin. The complexion was still very pale, understandably, but the lips were fuller and the eyes brighter.

"What is it?" she asked, seeing his reaction but being unable to eval-uate it.

"I think the injection is beginning to take effect," he said. "You really must try to eat something this evening, to give your metabolism a boost. Drink some wine, too, when you can."

"I'm really getting better?"

"I think so." He did not add that the effect might only be temporary. Professional optimism seemed required.

"I knew you could do it," she said. "And then you'll…" She paused, and then resumed: "Look, Doctor, I didn't want to be a whore. I don't know any whore who did. To tell the truth, I didn't want to be a wife either, to get beaten just the same and treated like a dog just the same. What the whores I know want, mostly, is for someone to love them, and most of them are so desperate for that that they'll convince themselves that some bastard who beats them, takes their money and treats them worse than a dog is only doing it because he loves them. Well, I don't want that either. What I want, is to be treated decently, and if that's what you mean by being a guardian, them what I want is a guardian. But if you do that, I'll probably end up loving you, and then I'll feel bad if you don't want to screw me. I know it's all topsy-turvy, and I'm sorry, but you'd better be warned: if you treat me nicely…and you've already made a start…I might get stuck on you…so be careful. And now I feel sick again, so hand me the bucket."

Mathieu had no idea what to make of that, but he handed her the bucket. She retched a few times, but she had nothing to bring up except a trickle of sticky clay.

Afterwards, she seemed calmer. "You don't get seasick, then?" she said.

"No. I was born in Brittany, not far from Brest. I went sailing a good deal as a child. This lump of iron is as steady as a rock by comparison—and almost as slow, unfortunately. On the other hand, she can keep plugging on through calms and tempest with the same steady tread, so she's more reliable. On a day like today, though, with a wind that's just brisk enough, one of those Breton yachts could run rings round her."

"You had a happy childhood, then?"

"Very."

"Heard about those. Read about them, too—I can read, you know. Not completely stupid—been to Sunday school. Don't hold with God, though. You?"

"I don't trouble him, and he doesn't trouble me. That caused some friction with my former employer. He liked God and hated Darwin. I like Darwin and couldn't care less about God. But we got along, until…"

"Until what?"

"Until my work began to generate bad feeling and bad publicity. Two patients died—it wasn't my fault, but they were in my care, and my treatment had been…well, unorthodox. There was talk of pursuit, a tribunal. Pasteur cut me adrift then. The Institut couldn't afford a scandal, he said. That's when Templeforth stepped in."

"Like a vulture."

"Perhaps—but I was grateful to him at the time, and if I'd been able to give him permanence in his new appearance, he'd doubtless have been my friend for life. He's hot-tempered, and a rake, but he's not such an evil man, fundamentally. It wasn't to be, though."

"But the Valcoeurs seem nicer by far…very respectable, Isabelle says. Their mother's a Marquise, but she's a cripple and has to be carried around the house. Myrtille's very pretty, and Philippe's very handsome—a rogue with the girls, apparently, but charming. Isabelle says that the Marquise is a little crazy, but as mild as milk. Everyone loves her, apparently. She's the one who sent them to fetch you. Fancies herself a great scholar, even though she's a woman. Philippe messes about with blood, much the way you do. There are secret rituals, Isabelle says."

Isabelle had obviously said a great deal while passing the bucket. "What sort of rituals?" Mathieu asked, interested.

"She doesn't know—they're secret. She's not a member of the society, yet, but she says it's just a matter of time. Her blood's as good's anyone's, she says."

"What else did she tell you?"

"Not much. Myrtille disapproves of Philippe's womanizing. She's a virgin, according to Isabelle, although she must be thirty, and she has no intention of marrying. Eyewash, if you ask me. She's a sly one, that's all."

"Did she say anything more about the Marquise de Valcoeur?" Mathieu asked, thinking about the mother's scholarly credentials.

"Looks younger than she is—you'd be able to guess why better than me. Always reading or writing, letters to Paris, Germany, England. A slut and a half in her day, apparently, but quiet now—for lack of opportunity, not appetite, Isabelle says. Mind you, it takes a slut and a half to know a slut and a half, if you want my opinion. Poor Michael better watch out—she'll have him for breakfast." She stopped suddenly, and her wan cheeks colored with the faintest of blushes. "Pardon me," she said.

"Its all right," he assured her. "I'm a doctor. People have to tell me the things they can't confess to their priest. I might be shy, but I don't shock easily."

She looked him in the face, but more curiously than brazenly. "If you mostly tend to whores," she commented, "I guess you have to look at a lot of nasty things."

"They're no worse than wives, for the most part," he observed. "But I've worked in Paris for most of my life—the new Babylon. London women tend to have more bruises, though."

"I can believe that. The whores in Paris have nicer underwear, it's said."

"That's true," Mathieu admitted. "Better perfume, as well."

"Well," she said. "When you dump me, leave me there. Got to be better than Bethnal Green. Make me pretty first, though."

"I'm not going to abandon you, Caroline. Trust me. Can you write as well as read?"

"Yes. Bad speller, though. Why?"

"When you come of age and I can't be your guardian any more, you can be my secretary."

She thought about that for a moment or two, and then said: "Good. I'd like that. I'll practice the spelling. And you'll have to dress me nicely, if I'm your secretary—nothing with a low neck, obviously, but neat and tasteful. I'd like that."

"I'm glad the idea pleases you. We seem to have come a long way in one day."

"Oh, I've gone further than that in an hour, not all of it flat on my back—but I wasn't seasick then. Talking's good. I feel better—maybe I will be able to eat something in a little while. Got a mirror?"

Mathieu shook his head. "I'll try to find one. I'll get you a better lamp before I go, though; this candle's about to die. Do you need anything else?"

"Lots, but you can get them one at a time…unless you're as strapped for cash as I am, in which case, I'd best do without."

"Philippe's given me a little money, but he says that he'll go ashore at Cherbourg while the ship's loading and unloading, to make the most necessary purchases on our behalf. I'll give him a list."

"You aren't going ashore yourself?"

"No. We won't be docking until after midnight. I could do with a good night's sleep—it's a while since I had one."

"Me too."

Mathieu rose to his feet. "I'll get the lamp. Do you want me to fetch Isabelle to sit with you while I'm gone?"

"No—I can reach the bucket myself, if I have to. Anyway, I feel much better. Thank you, Doctor."

"I haven't done anything."

He was about to leave, but she caught his hand. "You've talked to me like a human being," she said, "for longer than anyone has done for as long as I remember. That's not nothing, and it's done me more good than a dose of laudanum."

"Good," he said. "I'll repeat the prescription when I can."

X

At the evening meal, Mathieu met up with Michael MacBride. Neither of them had been granted places on the Captain's narrow table, being too far down the status hierarchy of the *Pendark*'s brief passenger list, but neither of them took the slur to heart. "It won't be too uncomfortable in the crew quarters, I hope?" Michael said to the Irishman.

"No, sir. I've slept in a hammock many a time, and a good percentage of the crew is Irish. Former canal-diggers and railway laborers, mostly. Navvies to the navy, in a manner of speaking. We have tales to swap—we'll get along just fine. How's the girl?"

"Seasick—but getting better, in more ways than one."

"I'm glad. Mam'zelle de Valcoeur's been telling me what kinds of duties I might have at her château. Sounds like easy work, although I can't really judge. Lots of vines, apparently, and no potatoes. Looking after horses, too—I can do that. The girls are very pretty, she says, but she's told me to beware of her little maid. Breaks hearts, she says—but I can stand that, and the little darling's promised to help me learn French. All in all, the Château de Valcoeur sounds like one step from paradise to me, but we'll see."

"Mademoiselle de Valcoeur gave me an explanation of sorts of what they expect of me, but it was short on detail. They'll have plenty of time to fill the picture in before we get to Bordeaux. Will you go ashore in Cherbourg?"

"Have to. Philippe needs me to carry stuff. Got to get clean clothes for you and the girl, apparently, and other necessities. There wasn't time in London, with doing everything in such a hurry, and there won't be another chance until Bordeaux. I'll get some sleep before we dock, though. It's no trouble. Will you be you staying with your patient?"

"Yes. I'm sorry for the way things worked out, Michael. This must be a terrible wrench for you."

MacBride shrugged. "Could have been a lot worse," he said. "It's Mrs. Driscoll and Sean's boys I feel sorry for. It's hard for widows, when you have a landlord like Templeforth, even when he isn't bearing a grudge. Should I have left him to burn, do you think, sir?"

Mathieu considered the question for a moment, and then said: "No.

You did the right thing. And he's not really a monster. I don't think he'll persecute the widow and children of a man he's shot in a fit of rage. I don't say that he'll be generous, but he's surely not completely malevolent."

MacBride seemed to weigh the question up, and then said: "Sean knew him way back when, and thought it was worth coming to see him. He thought we had a chance of making him see sense, if we could only talk to him face to face, so he can't be all bad. I hope you're right, sir—and I want to thank you for looking out for me. You didn't have to do that, and you seem to have helped me land on my feet. If you ever have need of me out there, you can rely on me."

"Thank you. We met in rather unfortunate circumstances, but I hope we can be friends." MacBride was looking at him oddly. "What's the matter?" he asked.

"Nothing, sir. I was just trying to imagine an English doctor saying that he wanted to be friends with an Irish peasant. Couldn't manage it—but they say the French are gentlemen, and real men as well. Might be true."

"I was born and raised in a small coastal town. We passed for solid bourgeois there, but when I went to Paris to study, the natives thought I was a peasant through and through. As a doctor, I've mostly dealt with poor folk—if I hadn't worked at the Institut, I certainly wouldn't have been able to live on my fees. I feel a world apart from old aristocrats like the Valcoeurs, no matter how many Revolutions we've had since eighty-nine."

"Ours is still to come, alas," said MacBride. "I hope I might live to see it, though, and if it arrives while I'm in France, I'll be on the boat home, working my passage if I have to. I guess I'm a week-kneed rebel, though, else I'd be headed there now."

"I'm a weak-kneed Anarchist myself," said Mathieu. "Come the day…but until then, I have quieter battles to fight, and I wish they had fewer casualties."

"You'll look after Caroline, though, come what may?"

"Yes, I will—come what may. Speaking of which, I'd better take her some food and a little liquor, to help her sleep. With luck, tomorrow she'll be as right as rain…and perhaps looking much prettier." He stood up, and offered his hand to be shaken.

The Irishman took it. "Good luck, sir," he said, softly, and watched him draw away.

Mathieu nodded politely to his new employers, who were at the captain's table, before he made his way to the galley.

Caroline sat up on her bunk when he came in.

"Can you eat?" he asked. "I've got soup, and soft bread, candied fruit and some sherry."

She nodded her head, albeit with determination rather than eagerness, but once he had set the tray down, she seemed to warm to the task. She ate most of the food he'd brought, and drank all of the liquor. Afterwards, he took the tray away, and the bucket, but he brought the bucket back once it had been washed out, assuming that they would need it even if she didn't bring back the food she had just eaten. Fortunately, she showed no sign of doing so.

"Is it dark outside now?" she said him.

"Yes," he told her. "It's been dark for some time. It's getting late."

"It's funny not being able to tell. I thought ship's cabins had portholes"

"Some do—but the better passengers always get the choice of those."

"But you're a doctor—or is it me that's bringing you down?"

"No. I'm a French doctor, and this is an English ship."

She seemed slightly puzzled, although she could hardly have lived eighteen years in London without hearing vulgar abuse heaped on the French. Obviously, she had assumed that the antipathy ought not to extend to physicians.

"I was on the same table as MacBride," he told her. "He seems happy enough. Isabelle's going to teach him to speak French, apparently."

"So she said. I asked her if she'd teach me, but she just laughed and said she'd leave that to you. You have a better accent, she said."

"It's kind of her to say so. Most Parisians think it's barbaric."

"Really? Mine's considered awful in Mayfair, but a bit stuck-up in Stepney. Sometimes, you can't win. But I'm not sure she really meant your accent. She's a sly one. Will you teach me to speak French?"

"Yes, of course. You'll have to be fluent, if you're going to be my secretary."

"Right—I hadn't thought of that. I'm a slow learner, though—you might get impatient."

"I'm a doctor; I don't get impatient. Quite the contrary, in fact."

It took her a second or two, but then she smiled broadly—not at the weak joke, but at the fact that he'd made it. "What's French for doctor?" she asked.

"Docteur."

"Oh. Is it all as easy as that?"

"Malheureusment, non."

"Come again?"

"Unfortunately, no."

She looked at him quizzically, for a moment or two, and then said:

"Oh, I get it. Renewing the prescription, right?"

"What prescription?"

"Talking to me like a human being. You're being a doctor, Docteur."

He laughed. "No," he said. "I'm being a human being." Then he paused for thought, and said: "But not quite the way I was before. The weight is lifting. You did that—you and MacBride. I feel that I've been forgiven—as if I'd been to confession for the first time in years…which I have, in a way. Oh, by the way…"

He took a small shaving mirror out of his pocket and handed it to her. He lifted up the lantern whose candle was lighting the cabin, while she inspected her face for some time. She seemed disappointed.

"I look awful," she said.

"Just a little pale. Comes of being sick all day. You seem a lot better now, though. A good constitution—some people are seasick for days on end."

She looked at him quizzically again, not sure whether he was deliberately misunderstanding what she meant.

"It is better," he assured her. "Give it time. Tomorrow, with luck, you'll see a real difference."

"It's all right," she said, shaking her head. "It doesn't seem to matter as much now as it did before. Being pretty's not everything…even has its downside. But Isabelle says the girls in Valcoeur are pretty. I don't want…but then, it doesn't really matter, does it? There are worse things than being plain."

"Yes there are—but I'll do my best to help you to be pretty again. Philippe has tricks of his own, apparently. If he and I put our heads together, we might make the breakthrough I've been hoping for."

She looked into the mirror again. "But if you don't…," she began.

"You'll still be my secretary."

She studied him, carefully, for some time, as if trying to summon up courage to say something.

In the end, she said: "You're my doctor, right?"

"Of course."

"Can I ask you for another prescription, then?"

"I though we were already talking like human beings."

"We are. I mean, *another* prescription."

"What do you need?" he asked, warily.

"Oh, not that. What I'd like, if you wouldn't mind, is for you to put your arms around me and hold me for a little while. Not for long. You can screw me if you want, obviously, but that's not what I'm asking for. What I'd like is just to be held for a little while. Just held. It's a stupid narrow bunk, I know, and it won't be very comfortable for you, but if you could do that for me, I think it would make me feel a lot better. A lot better."

"I can do that," Mathieu said. "For as long as you like."

The bunks were very narrow, but Caroline was thin and Mathieu not unduly robust, and it was possible to lie together, both fully dressed, with her back to his breast and his arms folded around her body protectively. She seemed perfectly content with that.

After a while, thinking that she had fallen asleep, Mathieu detached himself gently, maneuvered his body over hers, blew out the candle in the lantern, and then eased himself into the top bunk.

He had only been there for a few minutes, however, when she climbed up and assumed the same position beside him. She didn't say a word. When he put his arms around her, though, he could feel her heart beating in her chest, with anxious rapidity.

Mathieu did not protest. Her presence did not seem burdensome, and in fact, he felt that he might be receiving as much comfort from her presence as she was from his.

Eventually, her heartbeat slowed down, and assumed a steady, unhurried rhythm.

Exhausted as he was, it did not take long for him to fall asleep.

* * * *

He was woken up by an ear-splitting scream. He would have sat bolt upright if he could, but the space between the upper bunk and the low ceiling did not permit that, and because the room was now illuminated by an oil-lamp held aloft, he was able to see the ceiling in time to avoid smashing his head into it.

He remained in an awkward slanting position, peering over Caroline's head. He felt her body pressing into his urgently, as if trying to fuse with it. Her head was below the plank that provided the bunk with a side of sorts, as if she were trying to burrow far enough into the meager mattress, in order to be unable to see what she had beheld so horribly.

Mathieu did not have to ask what had frightened her. As he blinked in order to adjust his eyes to the light, the reason became all too obvious.

Standing in the narrow cabin, holding the oil-lamp above his head, and staring him in the face, was a creature more reminiscent of a beast than a human being, but whose naked face Mathieu had not the slightest difficulty in recognizing as that of Sir Julian Templeforth.

"I apologize for coming in so unceremoniously," said Sir Julian, speaking with a slight lisp but articulating his words more clearly than he had immediately after the transformation, "but the door wasn't locked, and I wanted to be quiet. I'm sorry that I frightened the girl, but it is partly your fault, is it not, that I'm such a hideous sight?"

Mathieu tried to speak, but barely managed to formulate the word: "How…?"

"Child's play," said Sir Julian negligently, "although the chase proved somewhat frustrating. I didn't have a chance to tell you the evening before last, that I had asked Reilly to follow you when you left my house the night before, in order to make sure that the man in the park wasn't on your trail. Imagine my surprise when he told me about your visit to the hotel in Rockley Road. A morning visit and a small bribe told me the name and place or origin of the people you had visited, and I went to consult a royalist refugee from Bordeaux in their regard. He wasn't able to tell me much, but he did mention that the Valcoeur family had long had a reputation for secret magical practices, of a sanguinary nature, and that the family of the present Marquise had a similar reputation—which seemed significant, in view of the fact that they had come all the way to England in search of you, and that you had somehow forgotten to mention when you saw me that they had contacted you.

"Unfortunately, by the time I had recovered consciousness after banging my head in your house the following evening, time had moved on considerably, and I felt very weak, presumably as an after-effect of the fit I had when I nearly collapsed in your laboratory. Cormack and I then had to deal with some awkward questions from a horribly bourgeois police inspector from Scotland Yard. By the time Cormack was able to ferry me to Rockley Road, you had left the hotel. It didn't take long to discover where the cab had taken you and the name and itinerary of the ship on which you had booked passage, but it had just sailed when we reached the dock. We headed for Victoria at full tilt and caught a train to the south coast, after telegraphing ahead to charter a fast yacht. I slept through the train journey, but that, a steak and a bottle of wine at least gave me the energy to press on.

"I calculated that we could reach Cherbourg well ahead of the rust-bucket in which you were traveling, and so it proved. I have, alas, been relegated to a hammock in the crew quarters, there being no cabin available, but Cormack and I have both seen service in India, so that will be scant inconvenience, and another day at sea will help me get a little more of my strength back. You really shouldn't have run away, Doctor, abandoning your patient when he needed you most, but what's done is done. Now, though, I need to ask you a favor."

Mathieu was still completely lost in astonishment, but he managed to focus his mind sufficiently to ask: "What did you tell the police?"

Sir Julian might have grimaced, but it was difficult to tell. "The truth, I fear. What else could I do?"

"The truth?" Mathieu stammered.

The hideous eyes wrinkled slightly. "Did you really think that I would lay a false accusation against someone else? Considering that you have known me for a long time, now, you really don't know me at all, do you? I told the police that I had shot three men in self defense, after they had threatened my life and yours. I kept your role to a minimum, obviously, but I had no alternative but to tell them what threats had been made against me, and carried out. I fear that you might have a more difficult time than me, if the police ever get round to questioning you—and the fact that you ran away will hardly count in your favor. But as I say, what's done is done, and we simply have to move forward."

Caroline stirred in Mathieu's arms, but did not raise her head.

"This girl is under my protection," Mathieu said. "If you or your butler try to harm her..."

Sir Julian might have seemed startled and offended, but it was still impossible to read his bestial features with any degree of accuracy.

"Harm her?" he objected. "Nothing is further from my mind. As for Cormack, I don't believe that he has ever done anything in her regard that you have not done yourself—although I can see that the two of you have become better acquainted in the interim."

Mathieu felt a flush of fury. "That's correct," he snapped. "And as I say, any insult offered to her is offered to me, and will be considered as such."

"Of course," said Sir Julian "But there really is no need for either of you to be anxious—and no reason for Mr. MacBride to worry, either. He might be an unruly tenant, but he helped Cormack pull me out of a burning building, and I owe him a great debt for that. I can hardly blame him for thinking the worst of me, I suppose, in the circumstances, but again, I'm disappointed in you."

"I watched you shoot three people!" Mathieu protested. "And whatever you told the police, it was *not* in self defense!"

"I believe that you'd find, in the unlikely event that the matter ever came to court, that it was," said Sir Julian, his lisping voice still scrupulously level. "But at the risk of becomingly tediously repetitive, what's done is done. I'm not here to justify myself, but merely to ask you for the favor I mentioned."

"What favor?"

"I'd like you to introduce me to the Valcoeurs this morning, once they go up on deck, and I'd like you to argue, forcefully, that whatever they want you to do for them, your first duty is to me, as a patient in dire need. I have no wish to impede their projects, of course, but I do want to be treated in parallel. I would like you to make that necessity clear to your new associates, as you are surely honor bound to do."

Mathieu felt utterly trapped by the strength of the argument, and knew that it must be obvious.

"I'm delighted to see, by the way," Sir Julian added, "that I have every reason to be confident, and that your work is progressing well in spite of the unplanned interruptions." His eyes drilled into Mathieu's, evidently curious to see his reaction.

Mathieu felt strangely guilty about disappointing him, but he had no idea what the baronet might mean.

Sir Julian nodded, as if an unasked question had been answered. "Let me assure you once again, Dr. Galmier," he said, "that I have no hostile intentions toward anyone aboard this ship. I'm truly sorry for my unprepossessing appearance, which I shall keep carefully hidden from now on, but I thought that I really ought to appear before you in such a way that you can judge the effect of your handiwork, and the magnitude of the task before you. There really is no need for you or the young lady to be frightened, but I'll leave you now, since my presence appears to be distressing her. You know where to find me when you've had a chance to warn the Valcoeurs of my presence and are ready to make the formal introduction. Again, I'm sorry for disturbing you."

And he left, taking the oil-lamp with him and closing the cabin door behind him.

Caroline turned over, and threw her arms around his neck. "Thank you," she said. Although it was now pitch dark, he knew that she was weeping, because he could feel the tears on her cheeks.

"I didn't do anything," muttered Mathieu, gruffly. "You heard him— he has no intention of hurting either of us."

The young woman eased herself over the plank at the edge of the bunk and let herself down to the floor. "So he says," she said. "But ugly or handsome, men like him can't be trusted. He needs you now, but if ever he thinks he doesn't, or that you can't help him…he'll do you a bad turn, and me too."

"Can you find the lantern?" Mathieu asked.

"Found it," she said, "but the candle inside is just a puddle of congealed wax. Might be light outside—shall we take a look?"

"Give me a minute to collect myself," Mathieu said. "That was quite a shock…and it complicates the situation considerably…although he is right. He's my patient, and I can't abandon him, all the more so as I'm responsible for his condition."

As he spoke, Mathieu eased his way gingerly to the floor of the cabin. Before he could suggest going up on deck in order to discover what time it was, however, there was a knock on the door.

He groped for the handle and found it. When he opened the door, light came in; it was only pale candlelight, not as bright as Sir Julian Templeforth's lamp, but it was very welcome. Again he blinked, in order to help his eyes adjust, but he heard a sharp intake of breath before he managed it.

The man standing in the doorway was Michael MacBride, who was balancing a candle-tray, more than a trifle awkwardly, on his head, while he held a bulky parcel trapped under his left arm and his right hand was clutching a bucket whose contents were emitting water vapor.

The sight was a trifle comical, and the farcical effect was enhanced by the expression of amazement on the Irishman's face. He set the bucket down on the cabin floor, threw the parcel on the lower bunk, snatched the precariously balanced candle from his cranium, and uttered a faint wordless exclamation.

Only then did Mathieu realize what he was looking at, and why he was so startled. He realized, too, what Sir Julian Templeforth had meant by his cryptic congratulations.

When the candle had gone out the previous evening and Caroline Deangate had lain down in the bottom bunk, she had been almost as plain as a young woman of her age could be without any particular deformation. She was no longer plain. In fact, she had not only recovered her former good looks, but actually seemed more beautiful than Mathieu remember her. He was certain that his memory was clear, and that, pretty as she had been then, Caroline had not been as strikingly beautiful as she was now. Her dark hair was unkempt and unwashed, but had nevertheless recovered a certain natural gloss. Her face was very pale, but not in the least pasty, and there was no slackness in the flesh of the cheeks and chin. Her complexion was silky, her nose and mouth perfectly formed and her eyes a marvelous shade of royal blue, with a gaze that was positively magnetic.

I shouldn't be surprised, Mathieu told himself. *I've seen Sir Julian's looks improve dramatically half a dozen times, sometimes overnight.* Nevertheless, he *was* surprised. Sir Julian's transformations had been far more modest in scope, although the one of which he was now in need would be even more drastic, if it proved to be possible.

"What is it?" asked Caroline, frightened. "What's wrong?"

"Nothing," Mathieu hastened to assure her. "It's just that the treatment has worked—better than I expected, in fact...."

"I can't find the mirror!" she complained, looking round.

"There's one in the parcel," MacBride was quick to say, "along with clean clothes for you both and various other toilet accessories—including soap. Sorry about the bucket, but on a ship you have to make do. At least there's no shortage of hot water on a steamer...." He suddenly cut himself off. "But there's bad news, sir."

"I know," said Mathieu. "Sir Julian's already been here."

"Ah," said MacBride. "He assures me that he means none of us any harm…but to be honest, sir, I wouldn't trust him as far as I could throw that lumpen butler of his."

"In all fairness," Mathieu observed, "if he really did admit to the police that he shot your friends and Tom Deangate, then he has no reason to want to harm any of us, and every interest in facilitating the progress of my work."

"Aye," said MacBride, dubiously. "Maybe."

Caroline had unwrapped the parcel and was rummaging through its contents. She pulled out a small toilet bag, and extracted both a bar of soap and a small hand mirror similar to the one that Mathieu had brought her. She snatched the candle-tray from McBride's hand in order to illuminate her face and inspect it.

She uttered a tremendous sigh of relief. Then her gaze took on a slight hint of suspicion. "But that's not what I looked like before," she said. "I could be a different person…another different person."

"It's really you," Mathieu assured her, "And I'm delighted to see it." *But how long will it last?* he couldn't help thinking,.

He saw Caroline wipe away some residual tears—but he was surprised to see that her face was still troubled. The initial surge of relief having passed, she was obviously being assailed now by different anxieties."

"Well, sir," said MacBride. "I'd better leave you to clean yourselves up a little while the water's still hot. I hope the clothes fit. Doubtless I'll see you on deck later."

"Doubtless," said Mathieu, still watching Caroline.

When the door was closed, she immediately began to strip off her clothes, before grabbing the soap again, and a soft sponge. She was stark naked in a matter of seconds.

"I can leave…" Mathieu began.

"Don't!" she said sharply. Then, confusedly, she said: "I don't want you to leave me alone. I'm sorry."

"It's all right," he said, and carefully turned his back while she completed her ablutions. Then she handed the soap and sponge to Mathieu, dried herself off with a towel that had also been in the parcel, and started sorting through the clothes that McBride had brought.

"Your turn," she said, absent-mindedly.

Mathieu stripped down to his underwear.

Caroline looked at him curiously. "It's nothing I haven't seen before," she remarked. "But here—I'll turn my back like you did."

Mathieu thought he must be blushing from the roots of his hair to his toes, but she did indeed keep her back studiously turned while he washed himself thoroughly, dried himself, and located some clean underwear in the untidy pile on the bunk.

While he finished dressing, feeling a great deal better now that he was clean and wearing clean linen, Caroline studied herself in the mirror, carefully angling the candle.

"Thank you," she said, again, when he had finished.

"Thank your brother," Mathieu murmured. "He forced me to do it. I didn't even think it would work."

"But it was your…what did you call it? An agent?"

"I thought of it as alchemical gold," Mathieu admitted, "but apparently that's wrong. In alchemical jargon, according to Myrtille de Valcoeur, it's the azoth—and they've known about it for centuries. They just didn't have the filter."

"Gold," she murmured. "I prefer that. It won't last, though—that's what you told Tom, isn't it?"

"I really don't know," Mathieu told her. He went on, reluctantly: "But if Sir Julian's experience is a reliable guide…it might not?" He saw a fearful expression cross her face. "No," he was quick to add. "What happened to him won't happen to you. It's just that the effect might fade gradually…unless I can find a way of stabilizing it. The Valcoeurs think they might be able to help with that, but…"

"But…?"

"They're modern-day alchemists. It's not a science that has ever produced much, especially in its mystical aspects. Myrtille's blathering about the soul of blood doesn't fill we with confidence. But still, if they can give me a place to work, and time…"

"And a supply of whores," she added, bluntly.

"They say that won't be necessary. They say they have a supply of willing donors."

"I was a *willing donor*," Caroline observed, quietly.

"You were tricked, and abused…and for my part in that, I truly am sorry. It's unforgivable, I know, but…"

"It's not," she countered, pensively. "And I'm not saying that because I'm pretty again. I forgave you…some time ago."

"That's kind of you," he said, "but I really don't deserve it. Even if I can stabilize it…well. I can't undo what I've done."

She stood up abruptly. "I need some air," she said. "I don't feel queasy any more. But…"

"But…?"

"You might think I'm a terrible coward," she said, "but I really don't want to be left on my own. I don't want to be a nuisance, but…please don't leave me alone."

"I won't," he promised.

XI

The sky was heavy with cloud, so the daylight was by no means bright, but it seemed very welcome to Mathieu. There was a breeze, and the air seemed clean and healthy. The Valcoeurs were already on deck, sitting on the same bench as the previous day. They both stood up as Mathieu and Caroline approached, their attitudes primed for politeness—but as soon as they saw Caroline's face at close range that attitude changed.

After a few tokenistic salutations Myrtille de Valcoeur took Caroline by the arm and moved her toward the rail, where the light was better, She inspected her face very carefully, touching the chin, cheeks and forehead with her delicate fingers, in a fashion that made Caroline look toward Mathieu with an expression of appeal; but as soon as he took a step toward her, Myrtille released her and turned toward him.

"Remarkable," the Frenchwoman said. "I've never seen a transformation like it. Your discovery really has overtaken, in a single step, hundreds of years of patient enquiry." She turned back to Caroline. "I apologize for my rudeness, my dear, but you cannot understand what significance this discovery has for us. Forgive me, please." Her gaze scanned the younger woman from head to toe. "The clothes are a very approximate fit, I fear, and hardly becoming, but we shall be able to do better when we reach Bordeaux tomorrow morning. Tell me, can you feel the azoth working within you? By azoth I mean...."

"I know what you mean, Mademoiselle," said Caroline, having moved closer to Mathieu, as if his physical presence radiated a protective aura. "Yes, I could feel it inside me all night long. I could feel myself... growing. Not in size, obviously, but...becoming stronger. Not more solid, because it seemed to be flowing...but not in my veins. Like a warmth in my body, especially in my head and in my heart. Yesterday, I felt terribly sick, but all that has gone. I've never felt better. But..."

She stopped.

Myrtille wanted to hear the reservation, but Caroline simple shook her head and said: "I don't know."

Mathieu felt that it was time to interrupt.

"I have some bad news, I'm afraid," he said.

"Sir Julian Templeforth is aboard," Philippe put in, promptly.

"You know?"

"We're aboard a ship," Philippe observed. "News doesn't have far to travel "Will his presence be a problem, do you think?"

"He came to see me, to ask me to introduce him to you formally. He's anxious to make some provision to resume treatment…all the more so since he's seen the transformation in Caroline."

Philippe looked at his sister. "We shall be vey happy to welcome him as a guest at the château," she said. "He will be a valuable…experimental subject. Had events not moved so rapidly in London, we might well have entered into communication with him there, in the hope of coming to a mutually satisfactory collaborative arrangement."

"Mr. MacBride thinks him untrustworthy," Mathieu felt obliged to put in.

"So do I," Caroline put in.

"You know him better than any of us, Doctor," Myrtille observed. "What do you think?"

"I think that he's an arrogant, violent, lustful egotist…but that he can be ostentatiously polite when he deems that to be the best way of achieving his ends. For the moment, it is. It wouldn't be in his interest to offend any of us. I shall feel more comfortable working on his treatment in France than I did in England, where he considered himself the absolute master of the endeavor."

Myrtille nodded, and then looked away briefly as she caught sight of MacBride coming along the deck. The Irishman bowed to her and Philippe and nodded briefly to Mathieu, but his attention was obviously focused on Caroline. "You look beautiful, Miss," he said. "I'm glad to see that you're feeling better today."

"Would you be kind enough, Monsieur MacBride," said Myrtille, "to inform Sir Julian that we shall be glad to meet him as soon as it's convenient."

MacBride bowed again. "Mam'zelle," he said. But before he turned away, he looked at Caroline again, and then at Mathieu. Mathieu could not interpret his gaze at all.

When the Irishman had gone, Mathieu felt the gazes of Philip and Myrtille weighing upon him too. Myrtille's, in particular, alternated between him and Caroline. Mathieu wondered how Pygmalion might have felt, when he first exhibited Galatea.

But it's not set in stone, he reminded himself. *It's fluid, and mercurial. It could vanish as swiftly as it was produced. I'm not in control. I'm dabbling with forces that I don't really understand, which really do seem more alchemical than chemical.* And he suddenly felt a great pity for Caroline, who seemed delighted, now, by the admiration that she was attracting, but who probably only had a vague consciousness of the awful fragility of her condition.

Caroline moved closer to him them, to make actual contact with him, as a strange figure moved along the deck toward them, accompanied by Michael MacBride.

In the privacy of the cabin, Sir Julian Templeforth had revealed his face nakedly, but on deck, in the daylight, where there were sailors working, he obviously thought it best to hide. He was wearing a garment reminiscent of a monk's cowl, but he was not content simply to hide his features in the shadow. He was wearing a black silken mask, of the kind sometimes worn by Parisians during Mardi Gras, which covered his whole face, save for the eye-holes.

Feeling slightly ridiculous, Mathieu introduced the baronet to Myrtille and Philippe de Valcoeur in a formal manner.

"And now the cast of our little drama is complete," Sir Julian observed, speaking English, although Mathieu knew hat he could make himself understood in French. "The Beauty, the Beast and the Good Fairy who is to complete my transformation into a handsome Prince." His languid hand vaguely indicated Caroline, himself and Mathieu, in turn. "And I believe," he added, "that we shall have the perfect setting, in one of the ancient châteaux of the land of Oc, fortunate enough to have survived the Albigensian crusade."

"Your history is slightly at fault, alas, Sir Julian," said Myrtille, dryly, replying in perfectly fluent English. "The original château was pillaged and destroyed by Simon de Montfort's troops, although most of the valley's inhabitants were fortunately able to take refuge in the forest. The one in which we live now has been restored and extended to such an extent that it must be reckoned an entirely different edifice."

"I stand corrected," said Sir Julian. "And I apologize for my ancestor."

"You're descended from Simon de Montfort?" Philippe asked.

"A trifle indirectly, via his younger son, who became Earl of Leicester and led the second Barons' revolt, becoming, for a while, the effective ruler of England. Nowadays, a baronetcy is a meaningless title, but there was a time when my ancestors really were knights, in the true sense of the word."

Mathieu had no idea whether or not that was pure invention, but guessed that Sir Julian was attempting to judge the effect of his claim on the Valcoeurs. In the lands devastated by the Albigensian crusade, he knew, the name of Simon de Montfort was still reviled, after six centuries and more.

Neither of the Valcoeurs showed any evident reaction. "I shall be glad to introduce you to my mother, Sir Julian," Philippe said. "The decision is hers of course but I am sure that you will be welcome to stay at the château for as long as you wish, while Dr. Galmier continues to treat you."

"I look forward to meeting the Marquise," said Sir Julian. "And seeing the château, obviously. I dare say that it will be a much more comfortable environment for Dr. Galmier to work than the laboratory that I was able to equip for him in London. And with you as a collaborator, Dr. de Valcoeur, I'm sure that he will find solutions to the problems that plagued his research in Paris and London in no time at all."

"I hope so," said Philippe.

"He is so very close," Sir Julian continued, in a light tone that seemed ill-fitting to his rather sinister costume. "I wish that you could have seen me as I was three days ago, a true testimony to the magical power of his golden fluid. Still, we have the young lady before us, who offers striking testimony to the ability of aristocratic blood to simulate a plebeian soul...remarkable testimony, in fact, since Dr. Galmier seemed far from convinced that it would have such an effect. Or were you merely lying, Doctor, in the valiant hope of dissuading the young lady's brother and the Irish rebels from obliging you to bleed me dry?"

"I wasn't lying, Sir Julian," Mathieu said. "On the basis of the transfusions carried out previously, I didn't think that the injection of the... azoth derived from your blood into Miss Deangate's veins would be adequate to restore her to her...former condition."

"Because you'd tried before, with other...girls who came to you for help? But those must have been far smaller does—and must have employed golden fluid conserved from their own donations. The cases are not similar."

"True," Mathieu admitted. "But all my experiments have indicated that every transfusion involves an attrition, that the depletion suffered by a donor was not transferred with arithmetical accuracy to the recipient. My hope that the agent might be able to renew and reinvigorate itself, with the appropriate stimulus, had so far proved unfounded."

"And now?" the baronet was quick to interject, with a gesture of the hand in Caroline's direction. "That certainly seems to me to be *renewal and reinvigoration*."

Once again, all eyes were fixed on Caroline, who tilted her head toward Mathieu as if to hide in his shadow.

"Yes, it does," said Mathieu. "And if I can identify the cause..." He paused, and then started again: "My initial hypothesis to account for the gradual decline of the fluid's effect in your body, Sir Julian, was that the organisms making up the fluid had difficulty adapting to the environment of your body and began to decline as soon as they were introduced, slowly at first but with increasing rapidity. The problem got worse after repeated donations, because, I suspected, the mixture of fluids from different sources might be causing awkward interreactions. I feared that those reactions could only become more harmful if I reintroduced the cocktail of fluids from your body into Caroline's. The initial effect on your own system was, indeed, catastrophic. Although I only removed a fraction of the fluid from your circulatory system, the remainder obviously suffered an immediate and drastic loss of effect. In Caroline's case, however, there has evidently been a swift adaptation and a positive interaction. If that can be understood, and replicated..."

He left the implication hanging, not sure how to spell it out precisely.

The man in the mask turned to Philippe. "And what's your opinion, Dr. de Valcoeur?" he said. "Do you have anything to add to Dr. Galmier's attempted explanations?"

"We cannot draw any conclusions without further experimentation," Philippe said scrupulously.

The mask prevented a clear sight of the precise direction of the baronet's gaze, but Mathieu felt sure that it was alternating between Philippe and Myrtille.

"That's the doctor speaking," said Templeforth. "What about the alchemist? If what Galmier has filtered out of human blood really is the mysterious azoth, why does it seem to be having such a powerful influence on the face of a—forgive the expression—cheap harlot, when it seemed unexpectedly feeble in the body of a hereditary knight?"

Mathieu put his arm round Caroline, as if to defend her against the slur.

"That is a very interesting question, Sir Julian," Myrtille de Valcoeur put in. "There were illuminati in the past, it is true, who wanted to believe that the azoth has an innate morality, but I suspect that they would not have approved of its preference in the present case. The evidence of history, as well as that of science, certainly suggests that the azoth does not discriminate between good and evil in any simple sense while distributing its rewards, but I am personally convinced that factors that Philippe would call psychological have a vital importance in understanding the effects of Dr. Galmier's golden fluid."

Sir Julian shrugged his shoulders slightly. "Perhaps I am a bad man," he murmured, "but I really cannot see that an East End whore has any better claim to the moral high ground."

"As I say," Myrtille persisted, her voice perfectly level, "the mysterious workings of the fluid require much more careful consideration, philosophically as well as experimentally. In any case, its transfers and its interactions cannot to be seen in terms of arithmetical subtraction and addition. The reality is far more complicated than that, in what, if I you will forgive me, I shall call spiritual terms. We cannot draw any conclusions without further investigation, but in the course of that investigation, we will surely have to think beyond the materialistic rationality that Dr. Galmier has so far been able to bring to bear on the question."

"There are magicians, spiritualists and Theosophists a-plenty in London," said Sir Julian, "and Rosicrucians too, who all lay claim to being custodians of occult knowledge and power, but one thing I've noticed is that, with the exception of a few young mediums employed as mere instruments by mesmerist pimps, they're all as ugly as sin. Have you ever met Madame Blavatsky?"

"As a matter of fact, I have," said Myrtille, untroubled, "and I can understand perfectly why you looked to the researchers of the Pasteur Institut rather than to any of Sâr Peladan's followers and imitators for practical results. My mother made exactly the same decision, else we would not be here—but the fact remains that if we are to formulate a theory to account for Dr. Galmier's results, especially the latest, we probably will not find it in terms of hypothetical microbes and Mr. Spencer's brutal struggle for existence."

"You're right, of course, Mademoiselle," said Sir Julian, his tone weakening, perhaps for more than one reason, "and I'm delighted to find you collaborating with my friend, enriching his experience with yours. It gives me hope, even if my ancestry, in your view, might disqualify me from the rewards of drinking from the Holy Grail, metaphorically speaking, while elevating…well, I take back the terms I used a moment ago, carelessly. Whatever Miss Deangate might have been in the past, her body is clearly a temple of Aphrodite now, which Dr. Galmier is fully justified in coveting so jealously, and if the young lady helps to provide the means to restore my own blooming health, I shall be eternally grateful to her."

"You shot Tom," said Caroline bluntly, as if that rendered all his flowery rhetoric irrelevant—as, Mathieu thought, it probably did.

"Yes," said Sir Julian. "I did do that—and an apology would doubtless seem insufficient. I shall just have to do without your forgiveness, child—and yours too, Mr. MacBride, for having shot your friends. But still, you did not let me die when you had the chance, and Dr. Galmier will not let me remain as I am if he has a chance to restore me to what I was. If that makes you better men than I am, so be it. But without my intervention, remember, Dr. Galmier would be in prison now, and the curtain would have been firmly brought down on transfusion research, at least in Paris. As Mademoiselle Valcoeur says, the azoth does not appear to discriminate between good and evil in any simple sense, and progress is certainly not entirely the prerogative of the virtuous. I look forward, Monsieur and Mademoiselle, to meeting the Marquise your mother, in the hope that she will grant me hospitality. In the meantime, my odd appearance is beginning to attract unwelcome attention, and I think it might be politic for the Beast to hide for a while and leave the deck to the Beauty."

And with that, he bowed and withdrew.

Mathieu looked around, and saw that the group they formed had indeed become the center of surreptitious attention for everyone else on deck, although he was not at all sure that it was the baronet's bizarre figure that had attracted that attention, rather than Caroline's pulchritude.

"What a remarkable man," said Myrtille de Valcoeur, pensively. "One can almost feel the wrath seething beneath that surface, behind that mask." She looked at Caroline. "You're right to mistrust him, my dear—there's more to his hatred than mere resentment of the fact than the extract of his blood seems to be doing you more good than it did him…but that's all the more reason for delivering him from his predicament, if we can."

"He frightens me," said Caroline.

"And in that," opined Myrtille, "I'm sure that your instinct is correct. But we shall not allow him to harm you, shall we, Dr. Galmier."

"If he has any such design," said Michael MacBride, quietly, "he'll have to go over my dead body. I was a fool to pull him out of that burning house."

"No, you were not," said Myrtille. "As he said himself, you're a better man than he is. There may be a design in all this, and if there is, he has his part to play. Might I have a word with you in private, Mademoiselle Deangate?"

Startled by the request, Caroline immediately looked up at Mathieu."

"He won't lose sight of you," Myrtille said, "and I'll be brief—but it really is important that what I say is for your ears only, for the time being."

She took Caroline by the arm, gently, and drew her away along the deck in the direction of the ship's prow. As she had promised, she did not remove her from Mathieu's line of sight, but the two of them were well out of earshot when she drew her to the rail and started whispering in her ear.

"What's that about, do you think?" MacBride asked Mathieu, although his eyes were fixed on Philippe.

The latter seemed just as puzzled as Mathieu was himself, but he understood that both his companions were looking at him for some sort of explanation.

"My sister does not always confide in me," he said, "especially in what she considers to be matters of purely female concern. She and my mother…well, suffice it to say that her family and my father's have long grown accustomed to habits of secrecy. Miss Deangate, I presume, has not—but there is a universal sisterhood that might prevent her telling any of us whatever Mytille is confiding to her."

So far as Mathieu could tell, whatever Myrtille was saying was not making Caroline feel at all comfortable, even though she nodded her head several times, meekly.

Afterwards, Mathieu was careful to take Caroline aside, but as Philippe had predicted, her only response to his question regarding what Myrtille had said to her was a flat: "I can't say."

"I don't think we have any reason to be frightened," Mathieu told her. "Even if Sir Julian does dislike us both, he has every interest in no harm coming to us."

"I've been frightened by worse men than him" sad Caroline, dismissively, "and almost as ugly. In Stepney, hate is in the air. You get used to it. I did ask the lady what was going to happen to me when we get to where we're going, though. She says that I'm welcome to stay at her château permanently, if I want, and that I'll never have to sell myself again."

"That's good," said Mathieu.

"She says that you can stay there permanently too, if you want."

"I'd already gathered that," Mathieu agreed.

"Will she marry you, do you think?"

Mathieu looked at her in surprise. "What on earth makes you think that?" he asked.

"Because people like her do marry people like you, don't they?"

Mathieu laughed, uneasily. "Actually, no," he said. "She's an aristocrat, and I'm a mere bourgeois. Not that it's relevant, given that neither us has the slightest romantic intention. She gives the impression, very strongly, of having higher spiritual ambitions."

"Yes," said Caroline, in a low voice. "I suppose she does." She emphasized the feminine pronoun slightly. Mathieu was all too well aware, in her company, of his failure to match such high ideals.

He was uncomfortably aware, too, that he could no longer look at her without feeling a lust that he had not felt the previous day, before her transformation, and was ashamed of himself for it, even though he understood the logic of it very clearly. Was not his entire argument regarding the nature of the golden fluid the notion that it was in the Darwinian interest of benign microbial commensals within the human microcosm to enhance their hosts' sexual attractiveness, in the cause of their own reproduction? Given that the fluid was proving far more effective in Caroline's body than he had anticipated or hoped, how could he avoid feeling the physiological response that it was designed to induce?

Understanding his response, however, did not help him to solve the moral question of what he ought to do about it—or ought *not* to do about it—given that he had formally accepted the young woman's guardianship.

"You don't seem entirely delighted with the idea of taking up permanent residence at the Château de Valcoeur," Mathieu observed to Caroline. "Compared with Stepney, it will surely seem like paradise."

She shrugged. "Haven't seen it yet," she said. "Might be, might not."

"Well. I promise you that I'll do everything possible to get rid of Sir Julian as soon as possible. He won't want to stay there anyway—and once the serpent is out of Eden…. In the meantime, MacBride's won't be the only dead body he'll have to pass over if he tries to hurt you."

"You don't have to take any risks just to stop me getting raped, Doctor," she said, softly. "I've been raped before."

"All the more reason…," Mathieu began.

"Not by you," she was quick to say, "nor even that slimy butler. Not the point, anyway. I don't want you to take any risks on my behalf. It wouldn't be worth it. What MacBride said was just a manner of speaking, but you…you might actually mean it. And you shouldn't. I don't want you to."

Nonplussed, Mathieu sought for the best objection, but she did not give him the chance to formulate it. "Last night," she said. "You held me. Nobody ever held me like that before, or at all—not out of kindness, anyway. I've never been more grateful for anything in my life, but… well, I don't know…but don't ever put yourself in harm's way for my sake. I don't want that."

"You're wrong not to want it," Mathieu said, quietly. "You ought to want it. And if you want me to hold you again, you'll be right to want that too."

But have I the right to want it? he asked himself, silently. He saw MacBride hovering, hesitating to approach and interrupt, and he beckoned to him.

"I've promised Mam'zelle de Valcoeur to keep an eye on Templeforth and Cormack," the Irishman said. "She has the right instincts, that one. I wanted to make you the same promise. It's my fault he's still alive, so it's up to me to make sure nothing bad comes of it."

"I really don't think that's there's any need to worry," Mathieu said. "Not for the time being—and if I can succeed in restoring Sir Julian's appearance when we reach the château, he'll surely have to set off for

Ireland right way, in order to defend his interests there. With luck, neither of us will see him again for some time."

"But that's another thing, sir," the Irishman said, uneasily. "He's in a bad way, I admit—but if the price of making him handsome again is the blood of young maids like Miss Caroline, given that he'll be even more of a danger to other maids once his vanity is given free rein again…I'm not sure that I can be a party to that. Mam'zelle de Valcoeur can say all she likes about the willingness of her tenants to donate blood for her brother's experiments, but I know exactly what a tenant's willingness amounts to. I've accepted to be her servant, and I'm glad of the opportunity, but there's a limit to what I'll do in service, and if Mam'zelle's tenants are in as dire need of organization as the folk back home…well, I'm no Sean Driscoll, but I know where my heart will be. If that's treachery, then so be it. I think you're a good man, sir, even though you've done bad things, and I hope you think like me now. You've taken Miss Caroline under your wing, after all. She might not be the only one in need of your protection."

Mathieu felt the full weight of that accusation, and the full responsibility of that optimism. "I'll do my best, Michael," he said. "I really will. But I've come too far simply to stop. If I need more blood in order to complete my work…"

"You can have mine," Caroline put in.

Both men looked at her in frank amazement.

"Why not?" she said. "If it means I won't be pretty any more, so what? It might not last anyway. It's the least I can do."

"I don't want…," Mathieu began—but she was ready for that.

"You're wrong not to want it," she retorted, almost triumphantly. "You ought to want it."

"No, he's not," said Michael MacBride. "You can have mine, Doctor, although I'm not pretty so it might not be any use, but please don't take hers."

Bewildered, Mathieu put his hand to his forehead. "I need to consult the Valcoeurs," he said. "Caroline, would you mind staying with Michael for a while?"

"Yes, I would," she said. "You promised. Anyway, I don't want Myrtille de Valcoeur whispering in your ear—I know what comes of that. She's very kind, but…well, she's still a witch. Don't let her put a spell on you."

Giving up on the possibility of making sense of that strange admonition, Mathieu gave in, and took Caroline with him back to the bench where Philippe and Myrtille de Valcoeur were still enjoying the fresh air, in spite of the gray cloud.

"I wonder, Monsieur de Valcoeur," he said to Philippe, "if you'd mind giving me a few more details of the way that you collect blood for your experiments. I don't have any high ground from which to judge, but I developed qualms in London with regard to the way that I was obtaining my supply, and I'd like to ease them if I can."

Philippe glanced at Myrtille, who said: "He's been taking to Mc-Bride." She immediately turned to Mathieu. "I don't disapprove of his anxieties, Dr. Galmier, or yours. I agree that there are certain compromises that need to be made in order to continue work of this kind, and I won't stoop to the simple argument that the end justifies the means. The people of the community whose effective ruler and high priestess my mother is might, from your viewpoint, be deluded, and exploited, but for what it may be worth, they do not see the matter in that way. For centuries, they have participated in what they consider to be religious rituals involving donations of blood, and for centuries, there has always been an occult purpose—more than one occult purpose, in fact—behind these rituals. We are not devil-worshipers and we do not practice any kind of murder, but my family, on both my father's and my mother's side, have been involved for a thousand years in a quest for a more perfect form of association and an authentic spiritual enlightenment.

"You see human beauty in Darwinian terms, as an enhancement of sexual attractiveness, an inducement to reproduction. We do not. We see it as an end in itself, as a kind of perfection, as a reflection of the soul. We do not see the love of beauty merely as a disguised and embellished form of lust. I tried to begin that explanation when I showed you the miniature supposedly representing la Belle Paule and spoke to you about the legend of Clémence Isaure, but any such discussion can only lay groundwork. You cannot begin to understand until you see the reality. In the meantime, we only ask you to be patient. If, when you understand, you do not want to collaborate with us, that will be your choice, and we will respect it, but I have every confidence that you will come to see matters as we do. I have the same confidence that Mr. MacBride's anxieties will be laid to rest. Caroline knows that I am not in a position to say the same of her own fears, but she understands why I am not."

"I don't," said Mathieu, bluntly, even though he knew that he was being deliberately sidetracked.

"It's not necessary that you understand that. It's only necessary that you be patient. The journey to Bordeaux will be tedious, I fear, and the subsequent journey overland even more so, but not endless. At least the journey overland will have better scenery, and we shall be able to eat and sleep in inns that are a little more comfortable than the *Pendark*'s disgusting cabins. When we eventually reach Valcoeur…well, once you've seen Mother, I hope you'll begin to understand."

XII

The ship continued its slow progress southwards, initially under sullen skies but eventually under brighter ones, without running into any violent storms. Sir Julian Templeforth kept a low profile; he did not appear on deck again and did not come to the dining room for the evening meal.

Caroline not only maintained her appearance as the day gradually brightened, but seemed, to Mathieu at least, to become even more beautiful, becoming extraordinarily striking. Few of the mariners had noticed her when she first boarded the ship, however, and none had seen her while she was in her cabin suffering from seasickness, so the extent of her metamorphosis was not generally appreciated, although her presence aboard the ship during the final phase of its journey certainly attracted a great deal of comment. Mathieu found himself the objective of many glances of naked envy, it being generally assumed about the vessel that Caroline was his mistress.

Mathieu managed to have a long and more detailed conversation with Philippe regarding some of the transfusion experiments he had carried out and those he hoped to carry out with the aid of Mathieu's filter, but Philippe remained coy about certain aspects of his work that he had inherited from previous generations of occult research, saying that his mother, the Marquise, would be far better able to explain that. He did, however, reassure Mathieu's by means of his insistence that the abundance of available donors meant that only small quantities of blood needed to be taken from each one at any one time.

"The filtration of the golden fluid might still have deleterious effects," said Mathieu, dubiously.

"We shall be careful," Philippe promised. "It will be necessary, in any case, to treat Sir Julian."

"If I can," Mathieu. "I really don't know whether any infusion of golden fluid will suffice to restore the condition he desires, and if the fluid comes from a dozen different donors, I've no way of knowing what kind of complex interreactions might take place, or what effect they might have on the recipient."

"Mother might be able to give you some vague indication on the basis of her precious archives," Philippe said, dubiously, "but she's a

trifle secretive even with me. She says that she doesn't want to preju-
dice my expectations, but I sometimes think that it's mere force of habit.
Myrtille has been initiated into more of the mysteries, but she appears to
be acquiring the same caution, even though she and Mother have their
differences."

Mathieu made no attempt to follow up those intriguing hints, esti-
mating that there would probably be time enough when he eventually
reached the Château de Valcoeur.

He also found time in the afternoon to begin teaching Caroline the
rudiments of the French language, while they sat together on the deck.
She did not seem to have been unduly modest in saying that she was a
slow learner, but there was no faulting her determination. She seemed to
have become remarkable intense, but his attempts to find out what was
troubling her came to nothing.

Her insistence on not being separated from him continued, but he
did not think that it was a specific fear of Sir Julian Templeforth and
Cormack; the environment of the ship was entirely alien to her, and the
attention she attracted increased her nervousness. She seemed to feel
that there was a unique security, or at least a unique reassurance, in his
protection.

He knew that the insistence in question might soon become problematic, and had little or no idea what effect it would have on him as time
went by. He felt that he had an obligation to her that he had to honor to
the fullness of his ability, but he had no clear idea of what that ought to
entail, or what she might expect or demand of him in the longer term,
especially if, or when, her seemingly-supernatural beauty began to fade
again, as the fluid that he had injected into her veins began to lose its
force. He could not tell how rapid the likely deterioration would be, how
far it would go, or what her response to the eventual circumstance might
be.

He continued to curse himself for ever having started this experiments, for ever having involved himself with Sir Julian Templeforth, and
for continuing to take blood from prostitutes even when he became fully
aware of the toll that it was taking of its donors, but Sir Julian's laconic
judgment that what was done was done and that one could only move
forward from the present situation kept coming back to haunt him.

When the evening meal was concluded and Mathieu and Caroline
retired to their meager cabin with the lantern, Mathieu asked her whether
he would like him to hold her for a while again, as he had on the previous
night. If she was surprised or offended that he did not want to make love
to her, she did not show it, and she simply said that she would, indeed
like him to hold her. It seemed to him that there were a great many pro-

vocative or ironic remarks that she might have made, but she appeared to have become very guarded and very docile, and it occurred to him that she must have even less idea than he had as to how their peculiar relationship might progress, what she might expect or demand of him, and what he might expect or demand of her. For the time being, she seemed to have settled, as he had, for seeing out the rest of the journey to their immediate destination.

He could not resist asking her once again, as they lay together to he lower bunk, what Myrtille de Valcoeur had said to her, what the Frenchwoman's cryptic remark about being unable to settle her anxieties meant, and why she had referred to Myrtille as a witch, but Caroline simply said that she had been asked not to reveal what had been said to her, and that it was perfectly obvious that Myrtille was a witch.

Mathieu had asked MacBride to attempt to obtain some clarification about that particular mystery from the usually voluble Isabelle, but he reported that she did not seem to know anything about it. He added that when he attempted to interrogate her about the mysterious blood rituals of the Château de Valcoeur she had fallen silent, apparently respecting a stern command of secrecy.

The *Pendark* reached Bordeaux not long after dawn, and The Valcoeurs immediately set off with MacBride and Isabelle on a further shopping expedition, leaving Mathieu and Caroline to wait in a harborside café. Sir Julian and Cormack set forth on business of their own, visiting the telegraph office before going to a bank. Neither party was gone for long, and when they returned the Valcoeurs had hired a four-seater carriage for themselves, Mathieu and Caroline, while Isabelle sat beside the coachman and MacBride took the position of postillion. Sir Julian and Cormack had hired their own two-seater carriage, in order to travel in convoy with the larger vehicle.

As the Valcoeurs had promised, the scenery was far more spectacular and delightful than the tedious aspect of the sea, but the further away from Bordeaux the two vehicles went, the poorer the roads became. While they were following the Garonne along the road to Toulouse the highway was well-maintained, but when they turned away from it in the late afternoon of the first day of the journey, the jolting became far more noticeable. Although the territory was by no means mountainous, one they had left the Garonne valley there were hills a-plenty, which forced the road to wind around their contours, between the slopes of vineyards. They changed horses three times in the course of the day, which caused further delays. It was a great relief eventually to halt at an inn for a late meal and to spend the night.

Caroline insisted on sharing a room, and even a bed, with Mathieu.

Although he assured her of her security, she still did not want to be alone, and the continued proximity of Sir Julian and Cormack gave her a ready excuse, even if it was not the whole reason for her fear. Mathieu had found self-restraint becoming increasingly difficult, but he still wanted to take his role as guardian seriously, and was reluctant to commit what seemed to him to be a violation of his promise of protection.

She accepted his decision, but did not seem happy about it, and was subdued and sulky during the second day of the journey, which began to seem exceedingly tedious—a tedium not relieved by further interruptions to change horses at way stations where the Valcoeurs were obviously well-known, but where Sir Julian's mysterious attire and Caroline's beauty both attracted embarrassing attention.

The second overnight stay was to be the last; Philippe assured them that they would reach the château the following day, provided that the carriages did not suffer any accident. Again, Caroline insisted on sharing Mathieu's room, and seemed insulted by his reluctance, although he could not tell whether her dominant emotion was annoyance, frustration or mere puzzlement.

"You'll have your own room when we reach the château," he told her, a trifle uneasily, looking at the bed, which, without being capacious, was large enough to hold two people far more comfortably than the bunks in the cabin on the *Pendark*.

"I've asked Mademoiselle de Valcoeur about that," Caroline told him, in a neutral tone. "She says that I can share your room, if I wish—and if you'll permit it, obviously." She looked at him, tacitly asking the question of whether he would.

"Mademoiselle de Valcoeur presumably thinks that you're my mistress," he muttered.

"Perhaps," said Caroline, "and perhaps not. Everyone else does, I think. Why am I not?"

Mathieu hesitated, and eventually said: "It wouldn't be right."

"It wouldn't be wrong," she countered, the attempted boldness of her voice undermined by a certain nervous tremor. "You want to, and I want to, so why wouldn't it be right? I know you can. Is it just because I'm a whore? You didn't object before. Or is it because you don't think of me as a whore any longer, and you've only ever slept with whores?

The last question was too close to the mark for comfort. After another pause, Mathieu said: "Are you really so frightened that you need me to hold you every night?"

It was her turn to hesitate. She sat down on the bed, and reached up to start unbuttoning her dress, but she changed her mind. Instead, she looked up at him, as if mustering every vestige of her courage. Eventually, she said: "No. That's not the reason. And that's not what I want. Can I tell you what I do want—or, rather, why I want it?"

He sat down on the bed beside her, as if to reassure her, but in fact to make himself more comfortable. He met her eyes as steadily as he could, and said: "Go on."

"I've been screwed a lot," she said, her voice firmer now that her decision was made. "Since I was a little girl. More often than not I was a…willing donor, but even then, it was something done to me, not something I did. I…took myself away. I was never really *there*. It was never something I *did*, as I say, always something that was *done to me*. Well, this time, I want to be there. I want to be doing it, not having it done to me. And I want to be there with you, and do it with you, because you're the only person I've ever wanted to be there with, to *do* it with. I suppose it's a lot to ask, but this might be my last chance, so I wanted to. We've done it before, I know, but that was like every other time—it was just something done to me. I want it to be different, this time, if you will. Anyway, that's what I want, and why. If you don't want to, you don't have to. If you tell me I have to go, I'll go."

Mathieu thought about that. He realized that for Caroline, what she was asking represented what Sir Julian Templeforth might have called her personal progress. She thought of it as a way of moving forward. Could he deny her that? Would it not be cruel even to suggest that he might? And would it not be perverse, given his own desire?

"No," he admitted, finally. "I don't want you to go." He knew that it sounded like a concession, and he didn't want it to sound like that, so he added, swiftly: "It might seem absurd, but I'm not sure that when we did it before, I was *really there*. I was answering a physical urge, a kind of itch. I was just using you. I'm not sure that it's ever been any different, although I've sometimes tried to persuade myself that it was. But if we do it again…when we do it again…it won't be the same. I know you now. I've held you in my arms…and I'm sure I got as much comfort out of that as you did, because, to tell the truth, I was just as scared."

Still looking him in the eyes, she said: "No, you weren't. Believe me." Then she uttered a deep sigh. "So I *am* your mistress, then."

"Yes, you are," he agreed.

"And?"

He nodded his head. "And," he agreed, presuming that she would take the right inference.

Presumably, she did, but she didn't fling her arms around him, or resume undressing immediately. "It's all right," she said, slowly. "You don't have to say you love me. No one who ever did ever meant it, so I wouldn't believe it if you did. I know that nothing can some of it, in the end. I know that it probably won't last long. I just want to be with you while I can."

Mathieu stared at her, examining her beautiful face. He did not find any difficulty at all, at that moment, in thinking that it was something more than mere physiological bait, that it was a kind of ideal in its own right.

"And you're not going to say that you love me?" he queried, eventually.

She blushed and lowered her eyes. "No," she said.

"Because you think I wouldn't believe you?"

"I don't see how you could. I don't know if I can believe myself. I don't know whether what I'm feeling is love. How can I? People talk about it all the time, but I don't believe any one them can ever know what they mean, let alone mean what they say. So no, I don't think you'd believe me, and I can't say that you'd be wrong. I just know that I want to be with you, more than I've ever wanted anything before, and more than I ever thought it was possible to want anything. I can't promise you that it will last, because I don't know whether I can trust my feelings, but what I feel is that I want it to last for as long as it can, for as long as you'll have me. I know I'm worthless, and that you probably won't want me for long, but while you do, that's what I want."

Her courage gave out, and she lowered her eyes. He put his arms around her.

"You're not worthless," he said. "You're…"

She stopped him.

"Don't make any promises you might regret," she said. "I don't want that."

He hesitated, and then said: "I once thought I was a benefactor of humankind, or at least a doctor, a good man," he said. "Now, I don't. I see myself sowing harm and misery wherever I go, and everything I try to do to make things better…goes wrong. I wish I could promise you that what my treatment has done for you will be permanent, but I'm afraid… well, perhaps you're right to claim that you've been more scared that I can ever know, or can ever be, but believe me, my fears aren't trivial. Sometimes, I think I'm accursed."

She looked up at him again, this time in frank surprise. "I don't believe that," she said. She touched her face. "As for this, let it fade. That's not why I…why I feel about you the way I do, why I want you the way I do. I'm glad I've got it for now, if it helps you want me. But what you've given me is worth far more to me that a pretty face. Nobody ever…well, I suppose I haven't seen a lot of kindness in my life. You were kind. I probably didn't stand a chance. As soon as you held me the way you did, and even before that, I was bound to…well, I won't say fall in love, because that makes it sound like just another thing that happened to me, and it wasn't. This is something I'm doing for myself, something that's really me."

A thought occurred to him. "That's what Myrtille de Valcoeur whispered to you on the deck, isn't it?" he guessed. "She read it in your gaze. That's why you called her a witch."

Caroline shook her head. "I wasn't surprised that she saw it," she said. "I was just surprised that you couldn't."

Mathieu was momentarily puzzled. "Then why…?" he began, and then he jumped to the further conclusion. "She told you that that's why the treatment is working so well, didn't she?" he guessed. "That's why she was so curious about the way you felt. She thinks that the mysterious interaction that defied my calculations of probability was caused by your falling in love with me…or your deciding to love me."

Her admission was a mere nod of the head.

"And you think that if you can't keep on…."

She didn't give him the change to finish. "No, I don't," she said. "If that was all it took to make sure that the effect doesn't fade, there wouldn't be a problem, because no matter what happens, I don't think I'll ever stop loving you. But I know that it might fade anyway, because the *agent* isn't strong enough. I didn't need her to tell me that, and I didn't need her to tell me that it wouldn't be my fault if it does fade, that it wouldn't be because I didn't love you enough. She thought I thought that, but I didn't. Satisfied, now?"

"And that's why she couldn't settle your anxieties. I see. You could have told me."

"No," she said, "I couldn't. Because if I had, you'd have told me that it wasn't true that what I felt about you had anything to do with my becoming pretty again…and I didn't want to hear you say that."

After a pause, Mathieu said: "I don't know whether it's true or not. It might be. It's not as if there's any lack of evidence. Love does often seem to make people more beautiful…and lack of it certainly makes them uglier. It's too simple an answer, though. There are too many obvious exceptions. Sir Julian isn't one, I admit, but…well, there are too many exceptions."

"So now you know what the witch told me," she said. "But it doesn't alter anything, does it? I'm still your mistress. It's what every man wants, isn't it? A mistress who's besotted with him, without him having to care about her in his turn…no, forget I said that. I'm not accusing you of not caring about me. I know you care. That's obvious."

"But you wouldn't believe me if I said I loved you?"

"No. Caring is one thing. Loving…well, you couldn't…or shouldn't."

"Why not?"

"Because people like you can't love people like me—or if they do, it's bad for them. You need to love someone like Myrtille—not her, if she can't love you back, but someone like her. Respectable. Honest. Not… spoiled."

"Just because you had to sleep with men for money, it doesn't mean that you're spoiled."

She laughed, briefly. "You have no idea, Doctor…no idea. But I can be your mistress, until the time comes when you find a wife and have to get rid of me, because she won't be able to tolerate another woman loving you. I think I always will, but that's not really a bad thing, for you or for me."

When he made no response to that, she looked pensive for a few moments, and then said: "Is that why you haven't screwed me these last few days? Because you were afraid that if you did, you might start to love me?"

He mimicked her brief laugh. "That's not the way the psychology works," he said. "I was doomed that first night. No matter how hard I pretended that I was only doing it for you, I knew full well that I didn't want to let go of you. It must have become obvious by now…at least to Myrtille de Valcoeur, if not to you."

Caroline tilted her head slightly, as if assessing him to see whether he had become any better looking of late. "She did say that the effect wouldn't have been so pronounced if the feeling wasn't mutual," she admitted. "I didn't believe her."

"Will you believe me if I tell you now that it is?"

"No, because you couldn't possibly feel the way about me that I feel about you—but I'll believe that you didn't want to let go of me, because I felt that, and I can't help being glad about it, even though I know that, in the end, it will be bad for you."

"I don't believe that."

"I'm glad about that, too, even though I know you're wrong. I want you to believe the opposite, with all your heart, at least for a while, although it's selfish of me."

"That's too complicated," Mathieu told her.

"Yes, it is, she agreed. It's really quite simple, and we really shouldn't be wasting time talking." Again, she started unbuttoning her dress. Mathieu had to withdraw his arms to give her room to do it.

"It is simple," he said, more to himself than to her. "You want me and I want you. What more is there to say, or to wish for?"

She had pulled the dress off, and he reached out to put his arms around her again. She moved into them. "To say, nothing," she murmured, seemingly wanting to have the last word. "To wish for...you have no idea, my darling doctor—no idea."

* * * *

The following morning, when they boarded the four-seater to complete the last stage of their journey. Myrtille de Valcoeur sat down facing Mathieu. She looked at Caroline, and then at him, and then back at Caroline, before reaching out with a gloved hand to touch Caroline gently on the knee, through the light gray fabric of her skirt. Mathieu understood by the gesture that Myrtille had not, in fact, assumed that Caroline was already his mistress, in the full sense of the word, but that her piercing gaze had had no difficulty detecting that she was now.

He looked out of the window, trying hard to suppress a blush. Myrtille did not say a word, but she seemed strangely satisfied, as if some machination that she had concocted had taken a further step.

They had been on the road for more than half an hour, and the conversation had not risen above the banal, when Myrtille suddenly said to Mathieu, in French: "How much do you know about the three seventeenth-century documents on which modern Rosicrucian organizations are based?"

"Almost nothing," Mathieu said, in the same language. "And when I invited you to tell me more, on the boat, you said that it was a task best left to your mother."

"And so it is, at least with the first two documents, which are broadly in line with the pervious heritage. The third is an allegory laden with Biblical symbolism, and appears to be a contemporary transfiguration of a much older story, which embellishes and distorts it considerably. Mother can give you the details. Its title is *The Chymical Wedding of Christian Rosenkreutz*—slightly misleading, in that Rosenkreutz is not the one who gets married, but merely a guest invited to a wedding, in the aftermath of which he's knighted. It describes the stages of a journey analogous to the path of spiritual enlightenment—but the ending is missing and the intended meaning gnomic."

"And what relevance does it have to my project?"

"Perhaps none—but the notion of a chymical, or alchemical, marriage might refer to a combination of two factors necessary to the reproduction, or fructification, of the azoth. Your system of filtration extracts or purifies the principle, but its activation might require a second component. In your world-view, of course, that would be a biological component of some kind, in ours a spiritual one, the soul of the blood—but in either case, a stimulus, or perhaps a catalyst. At any rate, the point of the story, either in the seventeenth century version or the original, appears to be that the wedding isn't the end of the story, and not the objective of the journey, but a means to a further end, that of the distribution of wellbeing: a difficult mission in which few succeed. and even Christian Rosenkreutz, for all his virtues, seems likely to fail."

"You're suggesting that even if I find the missing piece of the puzzle, and figure out how to enable the golden fluid to maintain and renew itself, that I might still fail in some further objective?"

"I'm suggesting that things might be far more complicated than they seem, and that if we *are* working out a design, the objective of the design might not be clear, as yet."

"Not *Amor omnia vincit*, then?"

"Perhaps not—but it does help, I suspect…provided that you remember that it's a stage on the journey, not the end."

"Thank you for the advice. I'll bear it in mind."

Mathieu glanced at Caroline, whose language lessons had been completely inadequate to permit her to follow the conversation, and who seemed resentful of the fact that Myrtille had spoken in French in order to exclude her from understanding, and that he had followed her lead. Then he glanced at Philippe, who seemed utterly disinterested, deliberately unconcerned with weddings, alchemical or otherwise.

The roads were now almost deserted, save for the occasional cart drawn by a weary Percheron; they no longer crossed the path of any vehicle similar to their own or Templeforth's. Peasants leading donkeys or mules could occasionally be seen, but all were on foot; MacBride was the only mounted man they encountered once the sun began to decline from the zenith.

By the time they finally came within sight of the Château de Valcoeur, perched on a hilltop, the sun was already low in the western sky, and the oblique rays of light cast the long shadows of trees around over its walls. It was not the fortified dwelling that Mathieu had imagined; it had no crenellated towers, and no ramparts. Its only tower bore a close resemblance to a belfry, although it had no clock-face, and Mathieu doubted that it contained a bell, and was more akin to a watch-tower.

There was a sizeable hamlet in the valley below, extended along the banks of a broad stream, but the absence of a church prevented it from qualifying, strictly speaking, as a village. The valley had fields of wheat and rye as well as vegetable-plots and the inevitable vineyards. Everything seemed somnolent, although dusk had not yet fallen even on the valley floor. No heavy farm machinery was visible; there was nothing obvious to link the scene to the nineteenth century. The road to the château was, however, in better condition than some they had recently traveled.

"It has been suggested that it warrants the description 'the middle of nowhere' better than anywhere else in France," Philippe observed, in English, "but we prefer to think of it as the heart of the nation that might have been, but for Simon de Montfort and his murderous bandits. There are compensations in remoteness, however, for scholars. Obtaining equipment can be challenging, but endeavor is undisturbed." He looked at Caroline, who was watching him, and added: "You'll find it very different from London, Mademoiselle."

"Good," she said.

As they drove through the hamlet, people came to their doorsteps to watch them go past. Many of them waved. Children ran to the roadside to get a closer view.

Myrtille waved a gloved hand in the direction of a group of young women who had gathered, seemingly to discuss the unusual convoy.

"I told you that the girls here are pretty," she sad. "The domain includes half a dozen hamlets like this one, scattered over an area that would take more than a day to circle around on foot. The forests are full of animals, but we don't hunt, so they don't fear us."

"A true Eden," Mathieu commented.

XIII

Philippe Valcoeur's first concern when they arrived at the château was to give Mathieu and Sir Julian Templeforth a brief tour of his laboratory. It was a great deal more capacious than the cramped room in the house in London, and had a proportionately greater quantity of standard apparatus, with a particular emphasis on equipment to facilitate the extraction and replacement of blood.

Mathieu pronounced it satisfactory after barely a glance, but reminded his host and his patient that the first and most important obstacle to the application of his process would be the manufacture of the filter used to extract the golden fluid from the blood while circulating outside the body. Because the raw material of the filter was alive and easy to grow *in vitro* with the aid of a standard nutritive substrate, supply ought not to be a problem once he had set up a growth facility, and the fungal spores of an appropriate species were easy enough to obtain, but processing the initial batch of fungal hyphae to produce the gel was a more delicate operation.

"If I work around the clock," he informed them, "with the aid of two competent laboratory assistants, I should have enough gel to begin processing blood in three days. At that point a supply of blood will become necessary, and I'll be able to draw up a schedule for preliminary experimentation."

"Damn preliminary experimentation," said Sir Julian, speaking from behind his black mask. "You'll start with me, and you'll work as fast as you can. Where could you ever find a better specimen to demonstrate your alchemical prowess?"

As he spoke, his mask turned toward Caroline Deangate, who was still by Mathieu's side, as if to remind those present of the other spectacular specimen demonstrative of Mathieu's wizardly, and that there was a hint of vanity in his claim to constitute a better one—provided, of course, that the treatment worked.

Mathieu did not want to embark upon a discussion of the reasons why it might not work, or why it might not be as successful as Caroline's treatment. Nor did Sir Julian, who had avoided any such discussion on the ship and during the journey overland; in his view, it was not a matter of weighing risks and probabilities couched in careful scientific terms: it was a matter of an all-or-nothing bet, staked on the only card he had to play. He was still suffering some physical side-effects of the fit he had suffered during his abrupt metamorphosis, and Mathieu would have liked to give him longer to return to full fitness, but the baronet wanted the result as quickly as possible, and he wanted Mathieu to do his utmost to produce it. He did not even want to contemplate the possibility of failure.

Mathieu made no objection to the baronet's insistence on being the first recipient of the renewed treatment, but merely looked to Philippe for confirmation that his part of the operation could be slotted into the timetable he had laid down.

"You'll have all the blood you need," Philippe confirmed, "and reassurance, too, that the extraction will do no harm…provided that Mother consents."

"Why should she not?" growled Sir Julian.

"I'll take you to see her now," was Philippe's only reply.

He led them through the lamplit corridors and staircases of the ancient edifice to a room in what seemed to be the opposite corner of the main building, on the first floor. The room into which he took them was far smaller than the laboratory—little larger, in fact, than the bedroom that had been allocated to Mathieu and Caroline—and had a lower ceiling, Mathieu judged that it must be brightly illuminated in the mornings, for it had two large ogival windows facing east and south. At present, because it was pitch dark outside, it was illuminated by half a dozen wax candles disposed in brackets of candlesticks, although there as also a tall bronze oil-lamp that was not lit.

The room was, in fact, a bedroom, because it had a curtained alcove opposite the east-facing window, but it as also a work-room, for it had a large leather-topped desk, and with the exception of the chimney breast, on which four portraits hung, two by two, almost all of the wall space was covered with shelving, most of which accommodated books and manuscripts in what seemed to Mathieu to be a state of casual confusion.

There was no fire in the grate, but three armchairs had nevertheless been arranged in an arc around the hearth, and the arc was extended by a wheelchair, in which the Marquise de Valcoeur was sitting, with a blanket covering the lower part of her body.

"Forgive me for not getting up," she said to her visitors, even before Philippe had introduced them each by name, "but I haven't had the use of my legs for twenty years. I'm a terrible inconvenience to my family and servants, as you can imagine."

When Sir Julian was introduced, and bowed, she indicated the seat furthest from her own, and with the same automatic authority she directed Mathieu to take the next seat along. Before inviting Caroline to sit down, however, she extended an arm toward her. She did not have to beckon to make the command to come closer evident, and Caroline obeyed without hesitation.

The Marquise took her hand, very gently, and Caroline inclined slightly in response, so that the older woman could examine her face at close range.

Mathieu knew that the Marquise must be in her late forties, at least, if she had married young, and might well be in her fifties, but he was impressed by the remarkable beauty of her face. It was a mature beauty rather than a youthful beauty, and it did not give a false impression, but it was striking nevertheless. It was not, however, an assertive or arrogant beauty; it gave no impression of vanity, as the face that Mathieu had gifted to Sir Julian Templeforth had. It was a quiet, almost saintly beauty, which seemed to radiate kindness and virtue.

"You're very beautiful, my dear," the Marquise said to Caroline, continuing to look at her, smiling, rather than glancing sideways at Mathieu to deflect any of the credit. "Please sit here, beside me."

Caroline sat down. Only then did Mathieu and Sir Julian take the seats indicated to them.

"I want to thank you all for coming," she said to them, as if all three had responded to personal invitations. "It means a great deal to me to have this opportunity to see the furtherance of an exceedingly ancient endeavor that is finally about emerge from the darkness of ignorance into the light of science. Please, Sir Julian, would you mind removing your hood and mask? I do not want to importune you, but I would like to see your face."

Templeforth took off his mask, and pushed back the hood of his cape, to reveal his features.

"There, Madame," he said, with a contrived note of levity. "The study in contrasts is complete. The epitome of human ugliness, to set beside the standard of perfect beauty—but remember, I beg you, that it was the cauldron of my blood that produced the magical potion that transformed the…young lady."

The Marquise looked at him, albeit at a greater distance than she had looked at Caroline, with a similar fascination.

Eventually, she said: "A study in contrasts, as you say, Sir Julian. Quite remarkable. The cauldron of your blood…how very apt. But I sincerely hope that Dr. Galmier will be able to rectify the harm he has inflicted…was forced to inflict, if the account my daughter has given me of the incident is accurate."

Because there was a hint of enquiry about the last observation, Mathieu thought it might be necessary to offer an excuse, but Sir Julian got in ahead of him. "I do not hold it against the doctor that he capitulated to the threat," he said. "He is what he is—and he was trying to save the situation as best he could."

The scorn in the remark was sufficient to sting Mathieu. "Tom Deangate was also trying to save the situation as best he could," he remarked. "And succeeded in saving it…for which you shot him in the head."

"I did," the baronet agreed, looking at Mathieu with narrowed eyes, as if his ugliness were a provocation, "and my rebel tenant and my door-keeper's nephew with him. That was ill-tempered, I admit, and also caused the fire that might have cost me my life, or at last destroyed any hope of my redemption from these Hellish stigmata. I am a sinner, reckless and unrepentant to boot. I am also at your mercy. If you were to decide, in the name of justice, that I wear these stigmata until death…"

He turned toward the Marquise to add: "But Dr. Galmier is a man of science, not an avenging angel, and he would make every effort to restore me, simply to demonstrate that it could be done, even if he were not mortally afraid of me. Your children, I think, are of the same opinion, but I know that the final verdict rests with you, Madame. You have an exceedingly kind face, but I'm aware that appearances can sometimes be deceptive."

He stopped at that, issuing no further justification and to further plea, seemingly content to await the judgment. Mathieu could not help feeling a certain admiration for the bravado of the declaration.

"I would not dream of opposing Dr. Galmier's attempts to redeem his own sins," Madame de Valcoeur said, silkily. "The state of his soul and conscience are exceedingly precious to me. My children and I will give him every possible assistance to fulfill his obligations to all his patients. You are a welcome guest here, Sir Julian, and I hope fervently that your sojourn will be a rewarding one. Would you be kind enough to leave us now, so that I can speak of Dr. Galmier and Mademoiselle Deangate in private?"

The baronet replaced his mask and took his leave with the utmost politeness, without managing to dissimulate completely the satisfaction he felt in having acquired the assurances he wanted.

Mathieu had the feeling that he ought to offer some kind of apology for having brought Sir Julian to Valcoeur, and for ever having involved himself with him in the first place, but the Marquise raised her hand slightly, bidding him not to speak, for the moment, and focused her attention on Caroline again.

"I'm truly sorry for your loss, my dear," she said, "but you do understand, I know, that nothing will bring your brother back. Hatred and a desire for revenge merely cause further damage—and, in fact, constitute further damage."

Caroline shook her head slightly to signify her confusion. Very faintly, and sadly, she said: "I wished him dead so many times."

Mathieu knew that she was not talking about Sir Julian.

The Marquise reached out and took Caroline's hand again. "My life has been exceedingly comfortable, my dear," she said, in a tone that was almost regretful. "For me, virtue has always been ridiculously easy—although not everyone would agree with the notion of virtue that I had before my accident. At any rate, I am the last person in the world competent to judge or advise those who have faced much sterner challenges. Dr. Galmier is doubtless better placed to judge than I am in your regard, as you are in his, but I will say this: yours is a beauty of which you have absolutely no reason to be ashamed."

She returned her attention to Mathieu then. "I am going to tell you things, Dr. Galmier," she said, softly, "in a fashion that might test your credulity, even though you must have guessed most of them already. I merely ask for your patience and your indulgence. I shall not apologize for not having sought you out sooner, for I always strive to find a design in things, and prefer to believe that you have arrived here at the right time and in the right circumstances, no matter how uncomfortable those circumstances seem to you. You have undergone an ordeal of sorts, as people marked for great accomplishments very often do, but you are aware, I think, that it is trivial compared to the ordeal that this poor child has undergone. I have nothing to ask of you in that regard, but I think you understand how much she stands in need of whatever love you can give her, and how much benefit she might obtain from it.

"My daughter has told you something of the symbolism of the Rose Cross, I believe, although I dare say that her account has been a trifle unsympathetic, as she considers that symbolism to have been disastrously cheapened by its recent popularization. I take her point, but I think there is a certain cowardice in abandoning symbols merely because others have made them seem slightly ridiculous. Even the farce of Christian Rosenkreutz is not without an underlying good intention, which should not do its modern adherents any harm. At least they will not suffer the fate of the Albigensians. Did Sir Julian tell you that he is descended from Simon de Montfort?"

"Yes," said Mathieu. "But I didn't believe him. I thought was simply a provocation."

"Perhaps it is, but it might well be true, if the available genealogies can be trusted—and that too, if one sees designs, might be part of the design. The tradition to which my ancestors have long adhered, however, antedates the Albigensian crusade by a long interval of time. Its origins predate history, and nothing remains of the foundations of its thought but myth and legend, but that is the case for all traditions; it could not be otherwise. The troubadours, the story of the Holy Grail, even the Roman Bacchanal, are all mere side-branches of an older conviction. The Christians, naturally, have tried to claim the cross of the Rose Cross as their own, but its antedates the tragic death of Christ by a length of time now incalculable. You're doubtless familiar with many other employments of the symbol, including those invented by science and mathematics, but you understanding that in essence, it simply symbolized intersection, the productive and transformative encounter. The more elaborate element of the collective symbol is the rose—red in our version, although later users have substituted a white one. As a matter of interest, Doctor, how would you interpret that symbol?"

"As a flower, the rose provides a definitive symbol of beauty," Mathieu said, "and I presume yours is red to declare an association with blood. But long before Linnaeus's system of classification, it was recognized that the flower is the sexual part of the plant, the organ of its reproduction, and we now recognize that its visual beauty and scent have been designed by natural selection to attract the insects necessary to collaborate in pollination and hence complete the process of reproduction. That complicates the notion of beauty considerably."

"It does," the Marquise agreed, serenely. "And that complication is not unconnected with the complications that it has in our tradition, which do not see beauty as mere appearance but as something intimately connected with the soul, albeit in somewhat mysterious ways. Caroline, would you care to remind Dr. Galmier of the most important element that his analysis omitted?"

Caroline seemed startled to be asked, but had no hesitation in replying: "The thorns?"

"Thank you. As you see, Mathieu, a mind not focused by science or fine art automatically associates the image of the rose with the flower's covert associate—the instrument of the defense of its beauty against predators. There are many beautiful flowers, of course, that do not have that association, but the symbol of beauty that seems, as you put it, definitive, inevitably carries that corollary. And the definitive characteristic of a thorn is that it draws blood."

"True," admitted Mathieu. "The Pravaz syringe and the lancet are, in essence, merely technological sophistications of a thorn...as the sewing needle was before them, and the dagger too. The rose cross, then, in your interpretation, is fundamentally concerned with the drawing of blood, not merely its color?"

"The notion that the essence of life is contained in the blood is very old. When Christopher Wren attempted experiments with blood transfusion, in the hope of contriving a means of rejuvenation and the prolongation of life, he was by no means the first, but merely one of the first to undertake his endeavor under the formal aegis of science rather than that of religion or magic. The drinking of blood and the sharing of blood are involved in countless rituals whose origins are lost in the darkness of time…but it seems likely that they have always excited horror as well as avid attraction. The oldest documents of history inform us of that unease, including the prohibitions of *Leviticus* and the legal suppression of the Bacchanal by the Roman Republic in the second century before Christ.

"It has always been a matter of routine for such practices to lead to persecution, and to be driven underground, to be practiced in secrecy—but they have usually persisted, in spite of that persecution. And where the suppression has been successful, the cost of that success has sometimes been the replacement of the literal by the symbolic, as in the Christian mass, and such mythological corollaries as the legend of the Grail. There is an essential ambivalence in that long history and prehistory, just as there is in the inherent symbolism of the rose cross."

She paused, waiting for an endorsement.

"It's arguable that the psychology has shifted of late," Mathieu observed. "Two centuries of blood-letting by physicians has made some contribution to demystifying medical trafficking with blood. My own experience has not been entirely fortunate, but I have always told my patients that in the next century, blood transfusion will become standard medical practice. Blood replacement is already becoming common in surgery, and my former colleagues at the Pasteur Institut are in the process of developing a classification of blood types that will permit safer and more elaborate replacements in that context, which will save many lives."

"And will that same change of attitude allow your procedure to become similarly routine?" the Marquise asked. "Will it initiate a traffic in youth and beauty, that will allow the rich and powerful to steal those privileges from the poor, and secure a monopoly by means of predation?"

"That isn't my objective!" Mathieu protested.

"No," said the Marquise, "but it might nevertheless be the consequence, as Sir Julian's example must have reminded you—painfully, if my daughter has judged you correctly. And by virtue of that awareness, and that pain, you ought to be in a position to appreciate the predicament of the magicians of the remote past who developed methods of the transmission of beauty that, although far more primitive than yours, did have a similar effect…and similar costs."

"But it couldn't work," Mathieu protested, albeit a trifle feebly. "I can understand the psychological basis of superstitions that attributed powers of rejuvenation and life extension to the drinking of blood, or the application of blood to the skin, the inevitable development of complex rituals and recipes in the hope of finding a formula that might contribute that effect—but the fact remains that it couldn't work. Without the filter, the refinement of the gel…"

He stopped, realizing the limits of his argument. The fungus from which his gel as derived was a common species, found virtually everywhere that humans made bread, and although the process of refinement and chemical transformation to which he subjected the hyphae was complex, it was not impossible that far more primitive treatments, either of the fungus in isolation or, more likely, crude cultures grown on bread or animal fat, might have produced a paste capable of extracting a measure of the golden liquid from blood, doubtless with countless impurities, but nevertheless capable of some limited action, even via such crude means as ingestion or external application. He could not declare it impossible that magical or alchemical dabbling might have produced a crude analogue of his process.

And as soon as he had admitted that, the problem that he had just allowed the Marquise to pose, and which he had always carefully avoided addressing on his own behalf, became pertinent. If a magician or alchemist had come into possession of such a secret, what attitude would he have been likely to have taken his discovery and how would he have been likely to employ it?

"You live in a materialistic era, Dr. Galmier," said the Marquise, "a period when the initial impulse of scientists making discoveries is to publish them, whether in quest of personal glory or in respect of a perceived duty to increase the sum of general human knowledge. But that is a recent attitude. For much of human history, the instinct of scholar making discoveries has been to maintain secrecy, to confide them selectively, with the utmost precaution, either in quest of the particular personal glory of knowing secrets unknown to other men, or in respect of a perceived duty to maintain the elitism of wisdom and capability. You doubtless consider the replacement of the earlier attitude by the modern one as a matter of social and intellectual progress, and perhaps it is—but you must be aware of a contemporary school of thought that regrets the fact that the monks who made such discoveries as eau-de-vie and gunpowder released them, so that their fellows could make whatever destructive use of them they wished.

"It does not matter whether you or I approve of the attitude and conduct of those magicians of the past who stumbled upon primitive means of producing the effect that you have refined so spectacularly. We have no way of knowing how many there were, but we can be sure that those who attempted to traffic their secret to the temporarily powerful, as you have, did not enhance the likelihood of its preservation, let alone its publication. The same is probably true of other desirable discoveries that the ancient alchemists might have made.

"What I do know, however—and this is perhaps where you might cease to trust me, and raise the common psychological barrier of incredulity—is that the cult to which I and my ancestors have belonged for centuries has contrived to preserve one such secret, and to employ it, precisely by refusing to traffic it to the rich and powerful, sometimes in spite of extreme pressure to do so on the part of those who suspected that they had it.

"I believe that the reason for that successful preservation has been that very refusal to divulge the secret to those intent on making egotistical use of it, or likely to treat it as an object of commerce. I believe that the tradition has survived for longer than history is capable of remembering because of the investment of its objective with a sacred character, its insistence on regarding the quest for transfiguration and the enhancement of beauty as a quest undertaken for its own sake, a Grail whose achievement is esthetic and moral rather than something to be employed in the service of vanity and lust. I will not try to persuade you here and now that that attitude is morally correct, but I do ask you to think about the matter carefully. If you do, I believe that you will come to appreciate the logic of its survival in a hostile and avid world, which could so easily have destroyed it by attempting to monopolize it.

"The truth is that a means of transferring beauty analogous to yours has existed for thousands of years—unsurprisingly, given the avidity with which such means have been sought, often in blood, which, as you have proved, really was the appropriate source. We have recently modified our traditional methods of donation by substituting Pravaz syringes for lancets and other successive replacements for the original thorns, but much of the ritual remains the same. We shall not celebrate it while Sir Julian Templeforth is here, but that will not prevent my daughter gathering donors for a special donation—as many as you will need to collect sufficient serum for Sir Julian's initial treatment, without taking sufficient from any one of them to cause deleterious after-effects. That has always been our policy, and we have not seen the kind of drastic effects that some of your London volunteers, including Caroline, seem to have suffered.

"We do not know who made the initial discovery that we are carrying forward, nor the names of those who might have modified the formula of the compound potion thereafter. My son has analyzed the one we currently use as best he can, and he will show you his findings in due course. We suspect, but do not know for certain, that similar discoveries have been made at other times, in other places, and it is not impossible that some of those have been preserved in a similar way. But we suspect that those discoveries have never been devoid of costs of various kinds, and the possibility of their preservation has always been cursed with severe difficulties.

"I asked my children to find you and bring you here, Dr. Galmier, because I want you to join us. I want you to work with my son, externally to our cult—at least to begin with—but I understand that you will have to think long and hard about the implications and consequences of the decision even to work with us on that basis. What I have said to you this evening is merely an attempt to lay the intellectual foundations for your decision, and subsequent decisions that you will inevitably be called upon to make. My son and my daughter have ideas of their own, which they will doubtless communicate to you over time, which will probably complicate the decision-making process, but we believe it to be necessary that your decision is a matter of free choice, and we shall not attempt any coercion."

The Marquise paused, and looked at Caroline. "Do you understand what I have said to the doctor, my dear?"

"I think so," said Caroline. "May I ask you a question, milady?"

"Of course."

Caroline touched her face, lightly. "This will fade, will it not? Not just with age, but soon?"

"I fear so," said the Marquise, touching her own face. "It can be renewed, but each renewal is more difficult than the last. The beauty that we transfer has always been essentially ephemeral, just as the beauty produced by nature is ephemeral—even more so than that of life itself. I cannot say for sure that it will always be so, but I fear that it might. Dr. Galmier might be able to develop a means of slowing down its decay, as he hopes to do, but his dreams of reproducing an active agent outside a living human body might well be disappointed."

Caroline nodded. "I thought so," she said, and added, almost absent-mindedly: "Love is *essentially ephemeral* too, is it not?"

If the Marquise was surprised by what question, she did not show it. "Passion is certainly liable to fade, as it is blunted by familiarity, but love is a different matter. It is capable of lasting much longer, perhaps forever. I wish I could say that my own personal experience has confirmed that assertion, but I have not been so fortunate. I am, however, aware of sufficient examples to be certain of the contention. Are you asking me about love because you believe that your own recovered beauty is as much a product of your feelings for Dr. Galmier as for his serum?"

"Yes," said Caroline simply.

"You might be right. I have long thought something similar." She turned to Mathieu. "Do you have any questions, Doctor?"

"A great many," said Mathieu. "Some more indelicate than others."

"Of course. I can anticipate some of them. No, I do not renew my looks by drinking blood, and have only recently had recourse to injections administered by my son. Initially, before and after my accident, I used a method of external application employed by my community for centuries. The switch to injections seems to have inhibited the degenerative trend, but I might not have made it had I been aware of the risk that I might suffer a sudden catastrophe akin to Sir Julian's. I have read old accounts of similar metamorphoses, and other unfortunate side-effects, but all were construed by their observers in magical terms, as curses, deserved or undeserved. None of the donors who have offered their blood to me or my peers have ever suffered any such drastic reaction, but I believe that Sir Julian's situation was…unusual."

"And why, exactly, do your donors make their donations?"

"Because they are members of the cult, disinterestedly committed to the cause of the perfection of beauty, as we understand it. My own active role has been reduced somewhat by my injury, and will inevitably come to an end at some indeterminate point in the future, when my position will be taken by my daughter."

"As a matter of aristocratic right."

The Marquise smiled. "You might see it in those terms," she said. "Perhaps you would be correct, and our beliefs are merely a hypocritical disguise for predation in that particular instance—but I am not the only regular recipient of the gift, by any means, and we would like to think that our criteria of selection are not merely reflective of social status or wealth."

"Do you use your methods for the purpose of reparation—to compensate for ugliness, natural or induced, rather than for the maintenance or enhancement of existing beauty?"

"Yes, on occasion—but we have never, so far as I know, attempted to address a situation like Sir Julian's. We shall be very interested, I assure you, to see how successful you are in his treatment…and to see how enduring any success you achieve will be."

"Because, if it is successful, and if I can contrive to find a means of stabilizing the effect, it will change your entire world-view, and the logic of your determined esotericism?"

"Do you think so?" the Marquise countered. "You might be right, I suppose—but that is something about which I shall have to think long and hard. So will Sir Julian, I dare say. What will his reaction be to your success, do you think, if you are, in fact, successful? Personal satisfaction, obviously, but beyond that…do you think he will want to broadcast your success to the world, apply for a patent on it, or strive to keep it secret? I shall be interested to find out, if that situation does come about."

"But you don't think it will?"

"How can I tell? You have already worked one miracle; I have no way of knowing whether you are capable of others. But I do think you ought to ask yourself how you might want to proceed in the event that your success remains partial—if beauty like Caroline's or mine, or the attractions that you were initially able to transfer to Sir Julian, can only be maintained by renewal, with its inevitable costs and inevitable gradual decline. We have adapted to that situation as best we can, but you might be able to envisage better ways."

Mathieu, having reached a break in the series of his question, fell silent momentarily.

Again, the Marquise turned to Caroline. "I hope that you can be happy here, my dear," she said. "It's a very different world from the one to which you are accustomed, but it is a far better one. If happiness only depended on that…but things are never so simple. Whatever I can do, you may rely on me to do it. You are a miracle worth preservation, perhaps the finest exemplar of our quest presently alive. This is where you belong."

Caroline blushed, and looked away, but raised no objection, even though Mathieu had no difficulty in imagining the objections that had sprung to her mind.

"Thank you, Madame," he said to the chatelaine, on Caroline's behalf. He knew that the Marquise had no need to make a similar formal statement to him; it was blatantly obvious what she thought about the question of where he belonged, and her willingness to do whatever she could to persuade him to say. Alas, he reflected, just as she had, things were never so simple. And he had yet to discover what the ultimate outcome of his endeavors would be.

He shifted in his seat, ready to take his leave, but the Marquise made a slight gesture indicating that she had one more thing to say. "What I said to Sir Julian is true," she said. "I really do hope that you will be successful in your attempt to give him what he wants. But you have already discovered—have you not?—that these processes are more complicated than they might seem at first glance to the untutored eye. I cannot tell what the result of your experiment will be…but I hope you will not be too disappointed if it does not entirely live up to Sir Julian's hopes, or yours."

"That is a possibility for which I am trying to prepare myself," Mathieu said, dryly.

"Good," said the Marquise. She turned back to Caroline. "Please come back and see me in the morning, my dear, and every morning, so that I can contemplate your beauty in daylight."

Caroline attempted a kind of curtsey as they withdrew. Mathieu thought that only he could hear her mutter, as she turned away from her hostess: "For as long as it lasts."

XIV

The donation process seemed almost surreal. As soon as Mathieu had isolated and refined a sufficient quantity of the gel, which he contrived to do within the deadline he had set himself on the first evening, Myrtille de Valcoeur made haste to assemble a company of some twenty young women, all of whom she gathered in one of the château's reception rooms. One by one she brought them through to the laboratory, which they had evidently visited before, although Mathieu could not imagine that it was where the mysterious rituals of the Rosicrucian cult were held. All the young women knew Philippe, and they exchanged remarks with him in a familiar manner, verging on outrageous flirtation in some cases. None made any objection to Mathieu drawing blood from their arm or thigh. All of them looked at Caroline curiously, assessing her with their gaze, but none asked who she was or why she was present.

"Have you done this before?" Mathieu asked the first volunteer, a petite dark-haired girl who seemed to have put on her Sunday dress and bonnet in order to answer the summons to the château.

"Of course, Doctor," she said.

"Here? For Philippe's research?"

"Yes."

"And it doesn't trouble you?"

She laughed.

"It doesn't have any ill-effects?"

"None." Then, as an afterthought, she added: "I sometimes feel a little tired, but I'm not one of the silly ones who faint."

After removing a liter of blood from each donor, Mathieu ran it through the filter, gradually accumulating a supply of the golden fluid, and then handed the blood back to Philippe. Philippe made no attempt to restore it to the donor, but merely added an anti-clotting factor and then stored the blood, carefully labeled, in a huge refrigerator, for use in his own research.

Caroline watched with intense attention, sometimes getting up from the stool where she was sitting in order to take a closer look at the apparatus. At one point she said to Philippe, by way of explanation: "I need to study. I want to be useful. I want to be Mathieu's assistant as well as his secretary."

"Very commendable," was Philippe's only response.

It took some three hours to collect and process all the necessary donations, at the end of which Philippe separated out a small sample of the golden fluid on which to work subsequently *in vitro*, mixed the remainder with a liter of donor blood that he had checked for compatibility with Sir Julian's, and summoned the baronet.

Sir Julian came into the laboratory eagerly, alone, and immediately sat down in the chair beside which Mathieu had set up his delivery apparatus.

"I'm going to introduce the serum slowly, as usual," Mathieu told him. "Although the blood is from a single source the golden fluid is from a number of different donors, so there might be a possibility of some interaction that will reduce or obliterate its effect, but I hope not. With luck, that won't happen—as you've seen, the fact that some of the golden fluid extracted from your veins had originated from more than one source didn't cause any problems when it was reinjected into Caroline's veins.

"You've seen, too, that the effect of the injection on Caroline was far from immediate, so you know there'll almost certainly be a delay before you can hope to see any effect. In the meantime, I'll resume my attempts to find a means of cultivating the fluid, or at least stabilizing it so that its effect won't wane. Don't expect miracles immediately. We're in uncharted waters here."

"I know all that," Sir Julian growled. "But if I'm going to need repeated treatments, this is a hell of a long way to come to get them. If you're prepared to come to Ireland when I need you, I'm sure that I could gather enough farm-girls to play the part of milch-cows without suffering too much from the extraction, and hopefully without causing the peasants to riot, calling for me to be hanged as a vampire."

"I don't think that would be a good idea," said Mathieu, warily.

"That doesn't surprise me. And I suppose you wouldn't think that it was a good idea to give me detailed instructions as to how to manufacture your magic jelly?"

"It's a very delicate process," Mathieu told him. "I'm not sure that it would be wise to ask someone else to carry it out working from instructions on a piece of paper."

"You needn't bother with the fancy excuses—I understand no. And you can't just give me a supply, can you, because it doesn't keep, even when refrigerated?"

"Quite so."

"So, in effect, you and your friends have me over a barrel?"

"I have no intention of discontinuing your treatment, for as long as it might be necessary, Sir Julian," Mathieu told him, "nor of demanding money for its continuation. But it might be necessary for you to stay in the vicinity for a while, and perhaps for some time. Perhaps you could rent a property in the valley, or even in Bordeaux or Toulouse. There are surely some advantages for an absentee landlord in being absent, and pleasant as Holland Park or the west of Ireland might be, the south of France is surely even more so."

"That depends on your idea of enjoyment," said Templeforth. "If it were a matter of Paris...but it's no good building castles in the air. You need to fix me first. You'll understand me, I think, when I say that, at present, I wish I'd never made this diabolical bargain."

"Oh, I can understand that," said Mathieu, "although we might disagree as to which of us is playing the part of Mephistopheles."

"Well, at least we know who Helen of Troy is," retorted the baronet, glancing at Caroline. "I hope you remember, while you're fucking her, whose blood it is that's coursing though her veins."

"It's hers," said Mathieu, tersely, "and the golden fluid it contains probably contains measures from half a dozen innocent donors, although the bulk of it undoubtedly came from Judy Lee."

"Whores," said Sir Julian bluntly. "No wonder it feels more at home in her body that it ever did in mine."

"Perfectly understandable," Mathieu agreed. "Just as it's understandable that when a sufficient quantity of the innocent fluid was removed, the tainted remainder went sour. We'll just have to hope that Valcoeur innocence is made of stronger stuff. It might be advisable, though, to keep your bile under strict control, as that's rumored to be an interaction that can prove nasty. Think beautiful thoughts. Think of all the people you've ever loved."

Sir Julian probably scowled, although his inexpressively bestial face gave little evidence of it. "It'd be a longer list than yours, Doctor," he retorted. "And the list of people who've loved me would be longer by far."

"Good," said Mathieu. "Hold that thought. It might help."

"Get rid of her, then," said the baronet, looking at Caroline. "Having people who hate me stare at me doesn't help at all, however reassuring it is that her uncanny good looks haven't faded significantly as yet."

"She's training to be my assistant," Mathieu said.

Caroline, however, had got up from her stool and had come to stand within two feet of Sir Julian, looking him in the face. Had he been so minded, he could have reached out a hand and strangled her.

"I don't hate you any more," she said. "The Marquise is right. That only makes things worse. I forgive you for shooting Tom, and whatever

Mathieu says about the fluid he gave me, I think the fact that it had been in your body probably gave me strength that I needed, so I'm grateful to you for that. But I'll leave if you want me to. I'm not afraid of being on my own any more."

Sir Julian looked at her for a few moments, and then seemed to sketch an attempted smile. "Maybe there is a little of me in you after all," he said, "and not just the pretty face. You've acquired a certain dash. Stay—if you can stand to look at me, I can certainly stand to look at you."

Caroline sat down again, and resumed her attentive observation.

"There you are, Doctor," said the baronet to Mathieu. "There *is* a little bit of me in your image of perfection."

"Perhaps so," said Mathieu. "On the other hand, perhaps Tom Deangate had more common sense than he knew. Perhaps the golden fluid I took out of you was hers to start with, and had outlasted all the rest because of its own innate virtue. Perhaps it has only completed its educational tour.

The baronet had recovered from his fit of ill temper. "I doubt it," he said, "but it's a good story. Have *you* forgiven me for shooting her brother?"

"No," said Mathieu, "but then, I haven't forgiven myself, either. I'm not a very forgiving person. But I never hated you. I was scared of you, and still am, but I never hated you. You were there when I needed you, and not because you were a minion of the devil, sent to tempt me. I owe you a debt for that, and I'll do everything humanly possible to repay it. I'm sorry that I lapsed in that duty temporarily, by leaving you in the burning house and running away. That was cowardly of me."

The baronet tilted his ugly head to one side. "You were saving the girl," he said. "You can't do everything at once. It's always women and children first—that's the rule. I'd have done the same if the situation had been reversed. The only reason I don't forgive you is that there's nothing to forgive.... God, did I really just say that? Hand me a mirror, Doctor, I think all that virgin fluid you just pumped into me is already having an effect."

Mathieu remembered the flirtatious conduct of a few of the donors in regard to Philippe, and had doubts about the virginity of the blood, if not its innocence. He handed the baronet a small mirror.

"Well, obviously it takes time to work its way outwards," Sir Julian said. "But if it does, and you really do find that means of making it permanent you've been promising me for years, you and I could make a colossal fortune out of your gel...unless you have other partners in mind."

Mathieu shook his head. "No," he said. "I don't want to start a commerce in innocent blood. The world has troubles enough without that. You're the first and last of your kind, Sir Julian...and you ought to be capable of being exceedingly glad about that. If I marketed your treatment, with your help or that of any other partner, you'd soon be just one more dandy in a legion. This way, you'll be a phenomenon, even if the treatment fails to achieve the perfection for which we hope.

The baronet's gaze flicked to Caroline yet again. "And you get to keep Helen of Troy to yourself," he said, "at least until someone better looking runs off with her."

Caroline shook her head, but made no verbal protest.

"I think we can be happy here," Mathieu said, in a neutral tone.

Sir Julian pursed his thin lips. "I think you might," he said. "I couldn't, but you might. I might stay for a while though, if you can fix me up—long enough to have Myrtille, at least, and perhaps the old lady, if she still has some feeing below the waist. You seem skeptical—and your friend's trying to stop himself splitting his sides; but he's only seen me like this. Just give me my face back, Doctor, and leave the rest to me."

Mathieu looked at his patient quizzically, wondering whether the injected serum really might be having an effect—but he didn't know Sir Julian well enough to judge whether his mercurial character might extend this far.

The injection apparatus had now completed the introduction of the new fluid into the baron's veins. Mathieu detached it gently from his arm. "It might be as well if you were to go and lie down for a while," he said. "Try to relax—and I really did mean what I said about thinking positively, about the people you've loved as well as those you have still to love. I'll come to check on you before dinner."

"Not a difficult prescription to follow," Sir Julian assured him, and limped away.

"Have you seen a reaction like that before, Philippe?" asked Mathieu.

"No," said Philippe, "but I've never seen a case like his before...and blood is said to have an intoxicating effect, in many ancient accounts. It's probably more psychological than physiological, but even so... What you said to him, Mademoiselle Deangate, seemed to turn him around completely, but a beautiful woman can always do that to a man."

"Is that true?" Caroline asked Mathieu.

"How would I know? Not always, I suspect...but you're a phenomenon."

"Beauty is a phenomenon," said Philippe. "Mother's mysticism might be overdone, but of that, at least, there's no doubt. Beauty is a phenomenon, and the quest for its perfection is, or ought to be, essentially spiritual and sacred. Did you mean what you said to Sir Julian about being happy here."

"Of course. With what I have here, right now, there's only one thing I lack."

Caroline sat upright, in slight alarm, but left it to Philippe to ask: "What's that?"

"A chance to make amends to Judy Lee and the others, as I have to Caroline…at least to give them a chance to be themselves again, and not to be whores, if that's their desire."

"No one I ever knew desired otherwise," muttered Caroline.

"And what you said about not wanting to make a commerce out of innocent blood?" Philippe added.

"Very much so. How could I make amends to anyone, if I gave the world the means to repeat my crime endlessly? It will probably happen eventually, just as cruder technologies have probably been discovered repeatedly, as your mother says—but I see what she means about there being reasons why those other discoveries disappeared, or were maintained in the strictest secrecy. I don't think it's any kind of divine design, as your sister seems to think, but it does have a logic to it. There are some discoveries that could spoil the world even more irredeemably than gunpowder. As I said, I think I can be happy here. Far happier, probably, than I could have been in Paris or London, even if things hadn't gone awry. "

"Mother will be pleased. Myrtille too—although she always said you would come around to our way of thinking. I wasn't at all sure, but Myrtille says that she knew the first time she looked into your eyes, in the hotel in Rockley Road. She has these intuitions, sometimes. I don't believe in them, obviously, but I haven't yet found an opportunity to prove her wrong."

"She only had to look into my eyes to know everything about me," Caroline observed. "Even things that I didn't know yet—but they were true."

"If Myrtille is spectacular now," mused Mathieu, "imagine what she'll be like when we've helped her to become a perfect representation of ideal beauty."

A shadow passed over Caroline's face, but he knew that there was nothing that he could say to soothe her anxiety, so he said nothing. The trick, he knew, for himself as well as her, was not to focus one's mind on such anxieties, but to concentrate on the love.

He went back to work, patiently and methodically, while Caroline watched him carefully. He did not find her presence discomfiting. Indeed, eventually—some three hours after Sir Julian had left the laboratory—he reached out and took her hand.

"I have made amends, to you at least, haven't I?" he said.

She almost smiled, but suppressed the impulse. "Oh no," she said, "not yet. That might take a lifetime. Deep down, you see, I'm not a very forgiving person either. But we will be happy here, if you keep working on it."

Mathieu did smile—but before he could say anything further, the laboratory door was thrown open, and Michael MacBride ran in.

"Come quickly, Doctor," he said.

Mathieu felt all the color drain from is face. "Is it the Marquise?" he asked, already moving toward the door.

"Oh!" said MacBride. "No, sir—it's Sir Julian. Cormack grabbed and told me to fetch you. He's with him in his room. He thinks he's been poisoned."

"Poisoned!" Mathieu exchanged a rapid glance with Philippe, who was following him along the corridor.

"Yes sir," said MacBride. "He lay down in his bed, and everything seemed fine for a while, according to Cormack, but then he started having convulsions. Horrible convulsions, Cormack said—and he started changing. His face, that is."

"Already! My God, Philippe! Have we overdosed him?"

Philippe was biting his lip, and did not answer.

When they got to Sir Julian's room, Myrtille was already there, sitting beside the recumbent baronet. Cormack was standing up, in a state of high agitation. "You did this!" the butler cried, pointing an accusing finger at Mathieu, and moving to block his path. "You've killed him! I told him not to trust you! I told him you were a charlatan, and you'd do him harm! Murderer!"

Mathieu shoved him aside and bounded toward the bed.

Sir Julian Templeforth did, indeed, seem to be in the grip of a *grand mal* fit, shaking uncontrollably and foaming at the mouth. It seemed worse than the seizure he had had in London, but he had been standing up then, and exerting all his might to remain in control. This time, he was lying down, abandoning himself to the effect. Mathieu turned him on to his side and pulled the pillow under his head.

"It will pass," he said. "It won't last. It's just a seizure, a side-effect. He hasn't been poisoned."

But he knew, even as he spoke, that he could not be certain. He was in uncharted territory—and Sir Julian was, indeed, visibly changing, as abruptly as he had changed a few days before. His features were visibly altering, mainly, no doubt, because of alterations in the tension of the many facial muscles, but not entirely.

Mathieu had witnessed the stages of the baronet's first metamorphoses, as well as the accelerated process in his laboratory, so he knew that there was nothing impossible about what was happening, but even so, it seemed marvelous, and bizarre. He could hardly blame Cormack for having been frightened by it.

"It's all right!" he shouted, but immediately lowered his voice considerably to say: "He's getting better, don't you see? The metamorphosis is reversing. He's recovering his old self. Don't you see?"

He hoped that he was right. Internally, he was thinking, although he knew how irrational it was: *She forgave him. The curse is lifted.*

He knew that it wasn't really a curse, but he also knew that what was happening was nothing as simple as a mere reversal of a simple physiological change. The golden fluid still retained all its mystery, all its magic, and all its power.

The convulsions calmed down, exactly as they would have done in a conventional epileptic seizure, and the writhing features eventually calmed down too, seemingly stabilizing.

Sir Julian Templeforth was no longer the paragon of ugliness that he had been a few moments before, and although he was not quite the dashing romantic cavalier that he had been once he had absorbed Caroline Deangate's golden fluid the first time, he could have passed for a moderately handsome man even if he had been ten or fifteen years younger than his actual age. Mathieu was certain that he had not been as good looking as he was now becoming when the two of them had first crossed paths at the Institut.

The baronet looked around, his expression as unreadable now as it would have been an hour before, although Mathieu thought he could detect signs of both puzzlement and panic. He experienced a strange sinking sensation himself as he watched that gaze scan the people gathered around the bed, with not the slightest flicker of recognition.

Cormack, like the good servant he was—or pretended to be—stepped forward. "Thank God you're all right, sir," he said. "I was afraid..." He trailed off. Sir Julian's expression was no longer unreadable, and there was definitely puzzlement in it...as well as more than a hint of panic.

"Who are you?" he whispered.

"Cormack, milord," the butler replied. "I'm Cormack."

Sir Julian was no longer paying any heed to him. He put his hands up to his face and palpated his forehead, cheeks and chin. Then he scanned all the faces in the room again, with a long and deliberate circular glance. A host of questions seemed to be hovering on his lips, but the one he finally asked was: "Who am I?"

Cormack made no reply, but simply looked bewildered. Mathieu shoved him out of the way. "You're Sir Julian Templeforth," he said.

Again, there was no sign of recognition in the baronet's face when he heard the name.

"Do you know who I am, milord?" Mathieu asked. "Try hard to remember. You know me. Who am I?"

Templeforth stared at him. He seemed to be doing as he was bid, and trying with all his might to remember. Finally, he said: "A doctor?"

"That's right," said Mathieu. I'm a doctor—your doctor. Can you remember my name?"

That, apparently, was a step too far, at least for the moment.

Mathieu looked around, and the addressed Cormack. "I think it might be best if we cleared the room," he said. "Your master is suffering some after-effects of the seizure. It's probably temporary—but I need to examine him, to see how extensive the problem is. Caroline, would you go back down to the laboratory with Dr. de Valcoeur. Myrtille, would you please tell your mother what has happened, and ask her whether she knows of other effects similar to this one. Cormack, and you too, Mac-Bride, will you please wait nearby, so that you can come immediately if I call you.

Everyone seemed ready to obey his instruction except Myrtille de Valcoeur, who was still sitting on the bed. She took the baronet's hands in hers, and looked into his face.

"Let me see," she said.

For two full minutes, she peered into the baronet's eyes. He blinked several times, but did not look away. Then Myrtille looked up at Mathieu, and nodded. "You're right," she said. "I'll go consult Mother. Do what you can for him, Doctor, but…don't expect too much."

She stood up, then, and everyone else seemed to take that as a signal that Mathieu's plan had to be put into operation. There was a general movement toward the door. As she moved away, though, Myrtille de Valcoeur met Mathieu's gaze, and what her eyes said, silently, underlined what she had said aloud. Witch, mesmerist or whatever she might be, she had not been able to read anything behind Sir Julian Templeforth's eyes.

The treatment had worked, in returning his good looks, with a little interest. But at what cost?

XV

When they were alone, Sir Julian Templeforth looked Mathieu in the eye. "Doctor?" he said. His voice was uncertain—not exactly plaintive, but seeking help, in meek fashion that Mathieu had never seen before in any of the baronet's previous incarnations.

The physical examination that he carried out revealed only slight nervous and muscular aftereffects of the rapid metamorphosis. Sir Julian had lost a certain amount of weight—perhaps half a stone—with remarkable rapidity, and he was certainly weak, but his heartbeat was sound and his lungs were functioning well.

The examination of his state of mind showed much more considerable losses. The baronet was still able to speak English perfectly and French with as much competence as before. He had no difficulty solving elementary arithmetical problems, and his general knowledge of the geography and history of the world did not seem badly impaired, although his awareness of recent events was vague. He was aware of the political demands being made in the English parliament for Irish Home Rule, but he could not remember any political involvement of his own, or any personal interest in the matter. He knew that Holland Park was in London, but not that he owned a house overlooking it. He recognized the name of the Pasteur Institut, but had no memory of every having visited it— or, indeed, Paris. He recognized the name of Simon de Montfort as the leader of the Albigensian crusade, but did nor claim descent from him. Apart from a vague recollection that Mathieu was a doctor, he had no further memory of their relationship or of the particular treatment that he had received from him.

In the end, Mathieu had to yield to the interrogations addressed to him and repeat the baronet's name, adding his place of residence and his status as a significant landowner in the west of Ireland. He told him that he had just suffered a seizure, but did not tell him about the infusion of golden fluid he had received beforehand—or, indeed, anything at all about the golden fluid or the use he had made of it. He gave the baronet a mirror in order that he could examine his own features, but was not in the least surprised when Sir Julian declared that he did not recognize himself.

Mathieu told him that he was in a château in the south of France, but did not explain how he came to be there, except to say that he had come in search of medical treatment. He added that the baronet would now be able to go home, and that the return to surroundings that had previously been familiar might well provoke at least a partial return of his memory.

"You think that I'll recover, then?" Sir Julian asked, anxiously.

"I don't know," Mathieu admitted. "Numerous case studies of amnesia have been reported recently in Paris and London, but not sufficient to allow us much in the way of confident generalization. Some patients recover completely, others do not, and we have little or no idea of what determines the difference. I can't give you a confident prognosis. Physically, however, you're in good shape for a man of your age."

"Which is?"

"Fifty-nine."

The baronet was still holding the mirror. He gazed into it with slight surprise.

"I don't look like a man of fifty-nine," he said, frowning slightly, as if not entirely sure what a man of fifty-nine ought to look like."

"As I said," Mathieu replied, in a neutral tone, "you're in good condition for a man of that age."

"And I'm fit to return to my home—to London, you say?"

"Physically fit, yes, I think so. Perhaps I ought to warn you, though, that there might be a certain…inconvenience when you return. You recently shot and killed three men. The police seem satisfied that you did it in self-defense, but the investigation of their deaths is still ongoing and the officer in charge might be displeased that you left the country."

"I shot three men?" The baronet's tone was scrupulously even.

"Yes."

The baronet thought about that for a few moments, frowned again, and said: "Am I the kind of man who shoots people, then?"

It was Mathieu's turn to hesitate. "You've served in the army, in India. I don't know, but I think it likely that you had numerous occasions to shoot people there. Since then…again, I don't know, but your reputation suggests that you have killed more than one man in duels."

Sir Julian digested that information, seemingly with more curiosity than alarm, but finally asked: "Am I an evil man, Doctor?"

"That's not for me to judge, Sir Julian," Mathieu said, without any hint of irony. *Am I?* he wondered.

"You say that the man you called Cormack is my butler?"

"Yes, he is."

"Does he know me well?"

"He's known you for a long time," Mathieu replied, conscientiously making the slight adjustment. "I believe you first met him in India, some thirty years ago."

"But he's my butler—he knows all the details of my life?"

Mathueu could not help feeling a sinking feeling at the thought of what Cormack might tell Sir Julian about the details of his life, but he could hardly prevent the butler from telling him exactly what he wanted, for whatever reason seemed good to him."

"A good many, I dare say—but as your doctor, perhaps I ought to point out that amnesia, catastrophic as it might seem, is not necessarily a total disaster. We all have things that we might be glad to forget, and many of us would relish an opportunity to make a new beginning in life, with the slate of the past, if not wiped clean, at least less imperious in its demands."

The baronet looked hard at Mathieu then. Arithmetical calculations were not the only kind that he was still capable of making."

"Including you, Doctor?" he asked.

"Including me," Mathieu admitted. *And how*, he added, silently.

The baronet paused for another ten or twelve seconds, examining Mathieu curiously. "It's odd, don't you think," he said, "that I have no memory of any of the other people that were surrounding me when I woke up, or even of myself, but I did remember that you're a doctor?"

"Perhaps—but such idiosyncratic details are often reported in the case studies I've read. The workings of the human mind remain largely mysterious." *And how*, he refrained from adding, once again.

"But you are important to me? You've helped me?"

Mathieu had no idea what would qualify as an honest answer to those questions. "I've tried, Sir Julian," he said, feeling that it was, at least, true. "I haven't entirely succeeded…but medicine, at present, is a very imperfect science and art. Experimental medicine—and we are living in an era of such rapid discovery that almost all scientific medicine is experimental—inevitably carries risks."

"And the fit I suffered? The fit that wiped out my memory? That was…a risk?"

"Yes, sir, it was. It was an effect of the treatment that I was giving you—an unintended effect, but an effect nevertheless. My intentions have always been good, but when the final balance is added up, it might not be easy to tell whether I have done more good than harm, or even added anything very significant to the sum of human knowledge."

"But you intend to continue the treatment? You can help me recover my memory?"

Mathieu took a deep breath. "The first principle of medical ethics is: *if possible, do no harm*," he said. "The second is the principle of informed consent. The first is difficult enough in application, but the second, in your case…until two hours ago, I was always acting with your full consent, as fully informed as you could be. Now, the information has been lost, at least for a while, and your informed consent may be very difficult of achievement. I ought to warn you, however, that I can't go back to London with you. Although I haven't shot anyone, I might be in considerably more danger from the law than you are. The work in which we have been complicit…well, let us say that there are people who might judge both of us reckless, if not actually evil."

"But not that woman who looked into my eyes before she left? The one who seemed to be searching my soul…and did not seem to find it."

Mathieu contrived a slight smile. "No, not her," he agreed. "I have friends here, and colleagues. I will be able to continue my work here, more tentatively and less optimistically than in the past, but necessarily. I have to discover the truth…while doing no harm, if possible. If, when you are more fully informed, you wish to continue to consult me, you will know where to find me."

The baronet's mild expression changed slightly, and a little of his old self seemed to surge forth within him. "Stop playing games, man," he said. "From when I sit at present, the world is mysterious enough without you beating around the bush. If you're so keen on the principle of informed consent, the least you can do is inform me instead of teasing me. What have you been treating me *for*, damn it?"

"Ugliness," said Mathieu, flatly.

The flicker of Sir Julian's old self seems to be snuffed out by that word. "Ugliness isn't a disease," he said.

"No," Mathieu agreed, "but that doesn't prevent people seeking remedies for it. You discovered that I might be able to develop one, and were eager to try it. With no standard for comparison, the mirror won't allow you to judge the extent of my success, but Cormack is able to affirm that I'm no charlatan, and that my method worked…to a degree, Unfortunately, there have been side effects, Including, most recently, a quasi-epileptic seizure and amnesia."

The baronet looked in the mirror again, creasing his eyes slightly with attention and concentration. "The operation was a success," he muttered, "but the patient died."

Mathieu did not bother to point out to his patient that he was still alive; he knew what the baronet meant.

Sir Julian looked up at him again. "I'm not your only patient?" he queried.

"No," said Mathieu."

"And there have been…other side-effects?"

"Indeed. But the third principle of medical ethics is professional confidentiality. I can't discuss my other patients' cases with you."

The baronet nodded. "Of course," he agreed, complaisantly. His old self had definitely retired, for the moment. After a moment, he added; "I sought you out, then?"

"Yes, Sir Julian, you did."

"And I knew that you method was untried?"

"Yes."

"So, I accepted the risk…insisted on it, even?"

"Yes."

Again, there was evidence of an internal stir, or surge. "I'm a self-made man, then," he said, sarcastically. "Or a self-made un-man."

"In some measure, Sir Julian, that's true—but I can't deny my part of the responsibility. I was, at best, foolish in my optimism, and at worst, criminal in my carelessness. In trying to repair the harm that I did, albeit without meaning to, I compounded my culpability. And I don't know whether it will be possible for me to expiate my sins…or even whether I dare try, for fear of piling error upon error."

Sir Julian smiled, wryly. "I'm not in any position to judge you, at present," he said. "Or myself, either. But I do seem to be thinking more-or-less lucidly, and apart from a few aches and twinges, I feel reasonably well in my flesh. So I take back what I said about the patient having died. He's merely…left the room."

The baronet got to his feet, and stretched his limbs. "You mentioned a man named MacBride," he said. "You told him to wait outside with Cormack. He knows me too?"

"He's one of your tenants…or was. He's in service now with Ma-demoiselle de Valcoeur. But no, he doesn't really know you, except by reputation. He did see you shoot two of his friends, but he saved your life thereafter, so he, at least, is far more saint than sinner—far more than either of us, I believe."

"In that case," Sir Julian said, decisively, "I think I'd like to see Cormack now, if our consultation is concluded."

"I'll fetch him for you," Mathieu said, meekly, and went to the door to do as he said. Cormack was not waiting outside, however and nor was MacBride. The only people there were Caroline and Philippe de Valcoeur.

"Where's Cormack?" Mathieu asked.

"Myrtille took him with her to see Mother," Philippe replied. "Mac-Bride too. How complete is the amnesia?"

"In personal terms, almost complete. Apart from the matter of his identity, however, he doesn't seem to be at all disorientated."

"You think it's a temporary lapse, then? That it will all come back, in time?" Philippe sounded more anxious that Mathieu would have expected.

"I don't know. Myrtille thinks otherwise?"

"Myrtille thinks in non-scientific terms," was Philippe's only reply to that.

Mathieu nodded. "Perhaps you'd like to carry out your own examination," he suggested. "A second opinion wouldn't be unwelcome—or a third, if you're prepared to count Myrtille's. At any rate, someone needs to stay with Sir Julian until I can fetch Cormack. He's with your mother, you say?"

"Yes. I'll be happy to stay with Sir Julian—as you say, a second opinion can't do any harm."

Mathieu nodded, and set off along the corridor, after barely a glance at Caroline, He did not have to invite her to go with him. She did not ask him any questions, but her curiosity was almost palpable.

"Don't be afraid," he told her. "I don't believe that Sir Julian ever intended to harm you, but if he did, he's forgotten it now."

"I'm not afraid of *him*," she retorted, but there was a hint of anxiety in her voice. Presumably for the sake of honesty, she added: "Not any more."

Mathieu knocked on the door of the Marquise de Valcoeur's study-bedroom. Myrtille opened it.

"Come in, Dr. Galmier," she said. "We're trying to make arrangements for Sir Julian's safe return home."

The atmosphere in the study seemed more than a little tense, and Mathieu judged at a glance that the responsibility for that was entirely Cormack's. The butler's expression was thunderous, and more than a little fearful. The way in which he stared at Mathieu was clear evidence that in his eyes, the one and only guilty party in the entire affair was the doctor who had guided his master to this awkward impasse.

Having not the slightest desire to start an argument, Mathieu simply said, addressing the Marquise: "Sir Julian is asking for Cormack, if you've finished with him, Madame."

"Of course," said the Marquise. "I believe that we've agreed the necessary arrangements for Sir Julian's return to London—assuming that that is your recommendation, Doctor? Myrtille anticipated that it would be."

Mathieu glanced at Myrtille whose expression was deliberately bland.

"It is," he said. "Case studies of amnesia suggest that familiar surroundings can be invaluable in helping to repair memory loss, and Sir

Julian is perfectly fit to travel, physically and mentally, even though his sense of identity has been prejudiced. Doubtless Cormack will be an enormous help in helping him to rebuild his memories—probably the only person who can, in fact."

Cormack, as a conscious simulation of a polite butler, should have asked the Marquise for more formal permission before leaving, but in fact he barely sketched the most tokenistic of bows before hastening out of the room. Apparently, he disapproved of her and her daughter almost as much as he disapproved of Mathieu and MacBride. When the door closed behind him, it seemed that all four of them relaxed.

"I'm not wrong, Doctor Galmier, am I?" Myrtille said, in a soft voice. "I know that you don't believe that I can make judgments based on looking in someone's eyes, but his memories of himself have gone completely, have they not?"

"Almost," Mathieu conceded. "Philippe's making his own assessment, but I think it will conform mine...ours, that is." He made the concession to Myrtille with only the barest hesitation.

Myrtille nodded in acknowledgement, and said: "Mother and I were trying to impress upon Mr. MacBride the necessity of his accompanying Cormack in escorting Sir Julian back to London."

Mathieu was startled by that. "Necessity?" he queried, looking at MacBride, who sketched an imperceptible shrug of the shoulders suggestive of his own uncertainty.

"Necessity," said the Marquise, supportively. "We fear, you see, that if Sir Julian only has Cormack to guide him in...finding himself...he might lose a valuable opportunity for...shall we say self-repair? Whereas, if Mr. MacBride can help to educate him in the duties and responsibilities of a landowner toward his tenants, a certain amount of improvement might be possible. Don't you agree, Doctor?"

"Ah!" said Mathieu. "I see what you mean."

"It is, after all, in the hope of making personal progress that Sir Julian approached you in the first place, Dr. Galmier," said Myrille, with a characteristic inflection of irony. "We are obliged, are we not, to help him in that quest? Handsome is as handsome does, is that not the English saying, Mr. MacBride?"

"Not being English, Mam'zelle, I wouldn't know," said MacBride, "but I do take your point. Having caught a glimpse of paradise, I can't say I'm not reluctant to be turned back at the gates, but Ireland is home, after all, and I owe it to Sean's widow and boys to do what I can for them. I'm still a loyal member of the Association, after all. Whether Sir Julian will lend me an ear is a different matter, especially with Cormack whispering in the other."

"Don't underestimate yourself, Mr. MacBride," said Myrtille, in a voice redolent with coaxing flattery. "You've saved the man's life once; now you have an opportunity to save his soul. But I can't compel you to go."

It was, of course, blatantly obvious that she could. He was in her service, after all.

"I'll do it, obviously," MacBride said. "Can't leave the poor fellow at Cormack's mercy, can we? And Sean's ghost would haunt me till the day I die if I even thought about shirking the task."

"Good," said the Marquise. "Myrtille, would you please make the arrangements that we've just agreed, in collaboration with Mr. Mac-Bride. I'd like to talk to Dr. Galmier and Caroline."

"Yes, Mother," Myrtille replied, and accompanied MacBride out of the room. MacBride met Mathieu's eye as he left, and favored him with a wry smile, which Mathieu attempted to match.

"Sir down, please, Doctor," said the Marquise. "And you too, my dear. I'm getting a crick in my neck looking up."

When they had obeyed the injunction, Mathieu said: "You knew this was going to happen, didn't you, Madame?"

"Of course not," the Marquise replied. "How could I possibly know? The experiment had never been tried, and my ancestors' archives are certainly not replete with accounts of induced amnesia—but that isn't what you mean, is it? Yes, I did have reason to suspect that your trans-formative serum would not be restricted to purely physical effects. You surely knew that yourself. You had seen changes even in Sir Julian, let alone Caroline, and you are surely not so shallow as to think that beauty is only skin deep. Even in butterflies, birds and roses, the matter is more complicated than that."

"The previous metamorphosis was far more drastic," Mathieu point-ed out," but it hardly seemed to alter Sir Julian's personality at all." Even as he said it, though, he was not sure that it was true. Thinking back to the strange lamplit interview aboard the *Pendark*, he wondered whether he had not been simply interpreting the baronet's words in the context of his previous knowledge of the man's inclinations. But if the collapse of his good looks had been reflected in his soul, should it not have become even blacker than it had been before? Evidently, the matter was more complicated than that…which he should, by now, have learned to expect.

"Even if you think about it entirely in your own scientific terms," the Marquise said, quietly, "in terms of the logic of natural selection, and its effects on our microbial commensals, I think you will see that it is not merely effects on physical appearance that might be expected. And even if physical appearance is the principal guide of that evolution, the physical cannot be separated from the psychological in such matters. Even if beauty *were* merely skin deep, self-esteem, self-confidence, vanity, coquetry and a host of other associations are not. But we are not simply talking about the effects of natural section on benign parasites, are we?"

"Probably not," Mathieu agreed.

"Nor do we have to depart from a materialistic philosophy in order to begin considering the matter in a more enlightened way, although we do have to deal with phenomena that the vocabulary of spirit and magic is at least as well-equipped to describe. The fundamental point is that what we think of as ourselves, the constitution of our self-consciousness, is not simply a product of the neural connections in the brain and their chemical signaling. The fluid that you have contrived to extract, which Myrtille would like to identify with the alchemical azoth, actually makes a contribution to our mentality, our thought-processes; it is part of what makes us who we think we are. And by definition, who we think we are is who we really are. You cannot filter, remove and transfer that fluid without altering the minds as well as the bodies of those from whom it is removed, and of those to whom it is transferred, in ways that are difficult to specify, evaluate, or predict…but which can become catastrophic under stress."

"And because you knew that, you expected that an extreme case like Sir Julian's might have an extreme result, even though you couldn't predict exactly what it would be?"

"Indeed. I'm sorry that I didn't offer you a more elaborate warning when we discussed the matter in advance, but I am enough of a scientist myself to have been curious about what might happen."

Mathieu considered the situation for a few seconds, and then said: "He'll be back, though. His good looks will start to fade again, exactly as before."

"The change in his appearance is probably inevitable," the Marquise agreed. "That does necessarily not mean, however, that his reaction will be the same."

"You think he might be content to let it happen this time, to accept his fate?"

"Who can tell? We have no way of knowing the extent to which his memories will return, or whether, if they do, he will be able or enthusiastic to be the same person that he was before. Perhaps he will return, again and again—but we should not take anything for granted. In the meantime, there is still work to do, exploration to be conducted."

"You really want me to continue experimenting with the golden fluid, in spite of what you've just said about the complications and dangers?"

"Of course. I've inherited a tradition of three thousand years of groping in the dark toward our particular Holy Grail. Now that a chink of scientific enlightenment has finally penetrated the darkness, do you really think that I would not want to take the fullest possible advantage of it? I've had high hopes of Philippe for many years—now that you and he can work in collaboration, and Myrtille too, I have very high hopes indeed."

"In spite of the risks?"

"Absolutely. The rose has thorns—we have always known that. You belong here. Dr. Galmier. You know that as well as I do. You know, too, that in spite of the difficulties you have had, and doubtless will have, you have already made great progress. You only have to glance sideways to realize how much."

Mathieu glanced sideways with reflective obedience. Caroline put her hand up to her face, and said: "It's already beginning to fade."

"Not yet, my dear," said the Marquise. "That's anxiety speaking, But if and when it does, you know now that there are means…"

"No," said Caroline, flatly.

The Marquise did not seem offended by the rudeness of the reply, but did seem slightly surprised. All she said, however, was: "Why not?"

"Because I've been listening to what you said. I don't pretend to understand all the words, but I get the drift—and I saw what happened to Sir Julian."

"You won't…," Mathieu began.

"I'm not afraid of that," Caroline interrupted. "But I heard what Madame said: you can't just change appearance. I don't want any more injections. I don't want to lose who I am right now at this moment. The person I was before, certainly—she was only fit for the scrap heap, which is where she was. But not the person I am now. Now, I'm who I want to be, and I want to hold on to that. I won't say I don't care about the looks, because I do, but I care a lot more about the way I feel. I care a lot more about what I have inside, and what I have inside me now is too precious to risk. I'll look after it myself. Maybe I won't succeed in holding on to it, but I'll do my damnedest, and that's all I'll do, if I have any choice in the matter."

"Of course you have a choice," said the Marquise—but Caroline was looking at Mathieu, challenging him. She already knew that he would never dream of trying to deny her the choice, but that wasn't what the challenge was about.

"If effort were all that it took to hold on to who we are," he murmured, "or to become who we want to be, there wouldn't be a problem." But Caroline already knew that, and had said so in so many words. Maybe she wouldn't succeed, but she would do her damnedest. It was up to him to do the same.

The Marquise had caught up by now. "The magic does help," she said, softly. "Or the symbolism, if you'd rather put it that way. The commitment, the ritual…it all helps. There are no guarantees, but if you want to make the effort, there are other kinds of ways of helping it along, as well as the blood."

"I don't need that kind of help," said Caroline. "All my life, things have been done to me, and I've never seen any alternative but it let it happen. Not any more. I'm different now. Now, I can take responsibility, for my body, for my mind. And whatever happens, I will. Maybe Sir Julian was right, and that's a little bit of him that's now in me—well, if so, it's mine now. But I don't think it's anything of him at all. I think it's me. It's who I really am, and always would have been, if it hadn't been beaten out of me, and it always will be, if I can hold on to it. I know that neither of you is not going to throw me out, at least for a while, but even if you did, and even when you do, I won't let it be beaten out of me again. I'll die first. But no more injections. I'll do it on my own."

It seemed to Mathieu that there was nothing to say to that, so he said nothing, but secretly, he envied her. He wished that he had the same certainty about who he was, and who he wanted to be, and the same stubborn desire to hold on to it. *Perhaps*, he thought, *I ought to have. Perhaps I ought to know exactly who I am and what I want, and perhaps the fact that I don't reflects the fact that I'm simply too weak to be in love in the same way that she is—but I can work on that.*

At any rate, he decided, he envied her that certainty, that stubbornness.

Perhaps the Marquise herself was not entirely free of a hint of envy. Respect, though, she certainly had. "I wish you the best, of luck, child," she said, softly. Then she turned to Mathieu, and said: "Isn't that worth fighting for?"

Mathieu didn't have to say anything in reply; it was a rhetorical question. He understood, though, that it was the right rhetorical question. He was in no position to offer any guarantees, to the Marquise or to Caroline, as to the success of his scientific endeavors or the durance of his affection, but what he was doing, and what he already felt, was certainly worth fighting for.

Which was perhaps as well, given that he had no alternative.

"I think I can be happy here," he said, to both of them. "And if there's anywhere in the world that my work can bear fruit—the right fruit—it's here. Whatever can be done, I want to do it. Whatever it takes."

All the Marquise said to that was: "Myrtille was right."

"Of course she was," said Caroline, "She's a witch."

"No," said the Marquise, shaking her head. "She just has an inkling of what she calls the design—the way that things ought to be—and a naïve faith that because it's the way things ought to be, it's they way things will work out. But she seems to be able to tell whether things, and people, fit into the design or not. I never could, even before my accident. But I've had my compensations, and still have. Thank you, Dr. Galmier—and you, my dear."

"I haven't done anything," murmured Caroline.

"You have no idea, my darling," Mathieu, even more softly. "No idea." Then he stood up, and bowed to the chatelaine. "If you'll excuse me, Madame," he said, "I have work to do."

And he had. As Myrtille had said to him, and as he had said to Sir Julian, almost in as many words, the path of progress was a thornier than it seemed at the first naïve glance, in both general and personal terms, but once one had embarked upon it, the only possible way was forwards.

There was no turning back.

EPILOGUE

After the funeral, Mathieu went up to the top of the tower in order to think, intending to stay there and watch the sunset, hoping that he would not find it too symbolic. The valley was, as always, peaceful. He mapped the changes that had overtaken it during the twentieth century, as the farms had been modernized and the cottages in the hamlets renovated, but did not find them too drastic to have changed the essential identity of the domain.

His mind was dominated by a single, absurd question for which he knew that he could not possibly find a satisfactory answer.

Why had Caroline died?

The fact that she had been a hundred and forty eight years old made the question seem ridiculous. Why had she not died seventy or eighty years sooner? Obviously, that was because she had been one of the five original recipients of the longevity serum. But of the other four, all of whom had been older than her, two were still alive, at the age of a hundred and sixty. So the question might more reasonably be formulated as: Why were he and Myrtille still alive?

Myrtille, of course, had always been convinced that the serum could not take full effect in isolation, that its effect needed to be complemented by other factors. Her long-held belief that her eternal chastity was her shield against the advent of decrepitude that had eventually afflicted Caroline was plausible, if one considered that Philippe the libertine had died more than thirty years before, and if one assumed that Caroline's wretched childhood had left ineradicable scars on her body and soul alike. The Marquise, too, had been far from chaste in her youth, and had already been well over sixty years old, as well as paralyzed from the waist down, when she had taken the serum—it was hardly surprising that it had had far less effect on her than anyone else.

But in that case, why was he, Mathieu, still alive, giving that he had been living in intimacy—in sin the Catholic Church to which he still belonged in theory, would reckon, given that they had never undergone any kind of marriage ceremony—for a hundred and thirty years; in active sin, thanks to the effects of the serum, for all but the final months. Did monogamy count as chastity? And was the judgment of the Catholic

Church in regard to sin irrelevant in Valcoeur, where the institution had no purchase and a secret paganism still ruled all lives—even Mathieu's and Caroline's, in spite of the fact that neither of them had ever been initiated into the cult of the Rose Cross?

His own longevity, not Caroline's death, he thought, was the real enigma—but how long would that last now, now that he was alone? Would he deteriorate rapidly himself, under the affliction of loss and loneliness? If that turned out to be the case, should he really care? Had he not lived long enough? Did he still have sufficient reason to carry on living, isolated as he was by being an outsider, a man who did not truly belong to Valcoeur, and never had? He had his work, of course, but was he not continuing his research, in desultory fashion, by virtue of habit and inertia, having lost any authentic intellectual impetus many decades ago? What did he still to offer Valcoeur—and what did Valcoeur still have to offer him, now?

He reflected, with bitter irony, that for a full century, he had been secretly unsure in his own mind whether he actually loved Caroline, and whether it was not responsibility that maintained their relationship, the debt that he had contacted, and his sharp awareness of her dependency on his affection. That doubt had faded, slowly, but it was not until she had been on her death-bed that he had realized the full force of his love—and then he had immediately felt that he had failed her, and himself, because he had not fully appreciated it before. Did he deserve to live, while she had died? Her love for him, he felt sure, had never wavered in its force since it had first awakened, even before they had reached Valcoeur. If love were a fact in maintaining the vitality and force of the golden fluid, as Myrtille had always claimed, then surely Caroline should still be in the best of health, and he should the one whose mortal remains were dispersed in the air with the smoke of his pyre?

It's over, he thought. *Whether I'm dead or not, my story is over now. For decades, I thought that the perfection of the elixir was the adventure, extracting the full advantage from the golden fluid, in spite of the fact that it couldn't renew itself* in vitro, *and decayed even within a body to which it was not native—albeit far more slowly in some than others, with the right support. But even if that had been the adventure, it ended decades ago, and in truth, the real adventure, the real core of my personal progress, was Caroline. And now, Caroline's dead.*

Dusk had only just begun to fall when Myrtille came to find him. He would have known that it was her even if he had not recognized her footsteps on the stairway, so he did not turn round immediately when she reached the top. There was no point in trying to hide his emotion—when had it ever been possible to hide anything from Myrtille?—but even so, he did not want her to see his tears and measure his distress with her typical clinical accuracy, so he maintained his stance, staring out over the valley.

When she came to stand beside him, he still did not look at her, even when she placed a hand in his shoulder, a trifle awkwardly. She seemed to be respectful of his wish, deliberately standing slightly behind him as well as to his right, apparently gazing in the same vague direction.

"Well," he said, dully. "The experiment's over now. How did it work out, do you think?"

"What experiment?" she asked. She did not sound surprised by the slight tone of surly provocation in his voice, but her retort did not sound blatantly disingenuous.

"Your experiment—the one you planned and set in motion a hundred and thirty years ago, aboard the *Pendark*. I suppose, even though you couldn't have had the slightest inkling that it would run for so long, you must reckon it a tremendous success—or at least a triumph of scheming."

"I never thought of it as an experiment, Mathieu," she said, with a studied mildness that he found a trifle irritating. "I was just trying to do what I thought was best—and you mustn't give me too much credit for scheming. I thought of it as simply greasing the wheels of inevitability."

"But you did know what you were doing, didn't you. Even before you made us share a cabin on the ship, instead of putting Philippe and me together and taking Caroline in with you and Isabelle. You knew when you extracted the formal declaration from me that I would take responsibility for her at the hotel in Rockley road."

"But the design had already been put in place by then. My contribution was belated, and probably unnecessary. You had carried the poor child out of a burning building. Given her dire past and her fragility, how could she not cling to you thereafter, and fall in love with you? All I did was facilitate the process slightly."

"But you did manipulate me."

"Did I? You had incurred a debt that was already weighing too heavily on your conscience for you ever to think of abandoning her. Perhaps you weren't absolutely bound to fall in love with her, but whether you did or not—and I suspect that even after a hundred and thirty years, you've never quite admitted it to yourself that you did—you were never going to let her down. All I did was to make it easer for you not to do so. Do you really resent that?"

Mathieu shook his head, but refused to emphasize the weak negation with any verbal admission.

"She never really believed it," he said with a sigh. "No matter how many times I told her, and no matter how many times you told her, she never trusted either of us fully. Right to the end, to the day of her death, she still thought that I was just being kind. And she never believed in your chastity. Not only wouldn't she believe that I wasn't sexually attracted to you, she wouldn't believe that you weren't sexually attracted to me."

Myrtille shrugged. "She wasn't wrong, was she? The point is, that neither of us did anything about it."

Mathieu almost turned round at that, but suppressed the gesture by putting his hand up to his forehead.

"Oh, come on," she said. "I've always been able to read you like a book—you're not exactly difficult. As for me—well, chastity is a decision, not a natural inclination. I had urges, like everyone else—and still have, now and again, thanks to your magical elixir, in spite of my antiquity. Given the proximity in which we've been living these last hundred and thirty years, how could my temptation not settle on you as a potential target, at least occasionally. It was worse for Mother, of course, in the early years—her urges were always stronger than mine, and less afflicted by conscience."

"The Marquise?" Mathieu queried, not particularly surprised, except by the fact that Myrtille had never mentioned it before, in the eighty years that her mother had been dead. He had got to know the Marquise quite well, even if he had never been able to read her like a book.

"Of course. Don't be too flattered—proximity was a much more important factor for her, given that you and Philippe never did manage to find a cure for her paralysis. Wheelchair or no wheelchair, though, and the twenty-odd year age gap notwithstanding, she'd have had you fifty times over if I hadn't forbidden it, no matter how much she liked Caroline."

"You forbade it?"

"Of course. I had to. You're not laboring under the delusion that you'd have had enough moral fiber to turn her down, are you? Don't tell me that you resent that too?"

Mathieu shook his head again, this time with more bewilderment than negation in the gesture. "Didn't she resent it?" he asked.

"Of course she did—but she saw the logic of the argument. She knew that I was saving you and Caroline from a lot of heartache, and her from a burden of guilt. She just needed to be strictly forbidden, to save her from her own weakness."

"Is that what you've been doing with me all these years—saving me from my own weakness?"

"If you like. In saving you from Mother's seduction, certainly. As for anyone else's, I didn't think you were in much danger."

"Because you didn't think that any of the women in the valley would ever try to seduce me?"

"No, because I thought that if they did, you probably wouldn't even notice, and that if you did notice, your loyalty to Caroline would stop you. Mother was a special case—she had a power of command that no one else could match."

"Except you."

"Except me."

"But you never tried to exercise that power it over Philippe, while he was alive, before or after his marriage. Or did the fact that he was your brother give him a special immunity to you commanding authority?"

It was Myrtille's turn to shake her head, but because Mathieu was still refusing to look around, he was unable to see whether she exercised the option.

"Why would I have tried to forbid Philippe anything?" she queried. "I didn't stop Mother on moral grounds—I did it because it would only have done harm if she'd let herself surrender to temptation. Philippe needed his dalliances, before and after his marriage—his *droit de seigneur*, as he insisted on calling it. Trying to forbid it would have rendered him unhappy, and wouldn't have been of any real benefit to his... *willing donors* as Caroline used to put it. You and he were very different. He needed his distractions in order to stabilize him in his endeavors— including his marriage—whereas you needed exactly what you had: certainty and reliability: a secure anchorage. You were never made for philandering. Fortunately, you're a hundred and sixty years old now, so I'm hoping that you won't feel Caroline's loss too badly."

The extent to which he might feel bereft without the love of his life was not a topic that Mathieu wanted to discuss with Myrtille at the moment, or even to think about.

"Philippe's womanizing could have had long range repercussions in a community as closely knit as the estate," he said, "but all the DNA test results are in now, and he doesn't have quite as many descendants as one might have imagined. He seems to have been careful, at least after the marriage. It's way too late now, anyhow, to worry about any of his unacknowledged children getting together, but the situation still needs monitoring. Given that his sons seem to be taking after him in that regard, the possibility of unwitting sibling marriages won't disappear."

"Étienne and Raymond aren't short of common sense, mercifully," said Myrtille. "Even when I'm not here to guide them any more...well, I have high hopes of Esclarmonde, even though she isn't exactly a carbon copy of me."

"I thought you were convinced that the interaction of the serum with your chastity would ensure that you'd outlive all of us, including the boys?"

"Perhaps so," she retorted, seemingly more amused by the slight bitterness of the remark than annoyed by it, to judge by her tone. "But you've never believed in its relevance, have you? And I have to respect your expert opinion. I dare say that you'll make every effort to outlive me just to prove your point—and I won't hold that against you, even if you succeed."

Mathieu grimaced, not wanting to talk or think about that either, for the moment.

In order to change the subject, he said: "There is one slight oddity in the DNA analysis, concerning Isabelle's son—her firstborn, that is, the one conceived before her marriage."

"I'd always assumed that he was fathered by Michael MacBride before he returned to Ireland," said Myrtille, with a hint of puzzlement.

"So had I. The tests couldn't confirm that, of course, because we don't have a stored sample of MacBride's blood—but the son's DNA does make an interesting comparison with one of the samples we do have in store."

"Whose?"

"Sir Julian Templeforth's."

Myrtille must have let a little amazement show, because her left hand, which was still resting on Mathieu's shoulder, twitched slightly. "Are you saying that Templeforth fathered Isabelle's first child?"

"No, not that. Isabelle might have been a slut and a half, as Caroline used to put it, but she didn't lack taste. There's a margin of uncertainty, obviously, but what I'm saying is that there's reason to believe that Templeforth might have fathered the father of Isabelle's child. The *droit de seigneur* isn't just a French institution, after all."

"Sir Julian Templeforth was Michael MacBride's biological father? Perhaps it's as well that they're both long dead—I'm not sure that's news either one of them would have be glad to hear. So some of Sir Julian's genes were imported into the valley without our knowing it—and they're still around?"

"Much diluted, and harmless in context. There is a certain irony, though, isn't there, in Sir Julian Templeforth having fathered a hero of the Easter Rising and an eventual member of the parliament of the Irish Free State. He was from a military family, though, so Sir Julian might have been able to find a little consolation in the rank to which Michael rose in the IRA."

"He must have had a beautiful mother," Myrtille mused.

"Certainly—and beautiful without any artificial aids, unlike his father…or Isabelle, eventually. Not to mention…"

Mathieu knew perfectly well what Myrtille looked like: still beautiful, even at the age of a hundred and sixty, but with a kind of beauty never seen on earth before, superior to the one that her mother had briefly attained, and superior too, to the remnants of her former beauty that Caroline had been able to preserve once had had passed the age of eighty. Whether that beauty was associated with a special spiritual enlightenment, as Myrtille had always hoped and sometimes claimed, he did not feel that he was in any position to judge, even though he had made prolific and productive use of the serum himself. Myrtille had always claimed that his commitment to the rigidities of science would bar him from true enlightenment; given that her version of enlightenment seemed to be essentially mystical, she was probably right, although he still clung to the stubborn assertion that he was he enlightened one and she a mere dreamer. They had agreed to differ a century ago, and it was no longer a bone of active contention.

"So, even if Simon de Montfort's reputation for chastity was overstated," Mathieu observed, maliciously, when Myrtille did not respond to his latest provocation, "some of his genes might have made their way into your Rosicrucian utopia anyway, if Sir Julian was telling the truth about his ancestry. Not that it matters, now that you've got your revenge."

"Revenge?" Myrtille queried, her voice taking on a slight edge for once as he finally tempted her into a hint of reaction.

"Of course. By hoarding my elixir in the valley, you've lopped more years off the lives of far more northerners than the butcher of the Midi stole in the course of all his massacres."

"Let's not rake up all that again, Mathieu. It was settled long ago, with your consent." There was no anger in her tone, and even a slight hint of supplication. That, combined with the fact that Mathieu thought that his tears had now dried up, caused him to look over his shoulder, at last.

Myrtille's tears had not quite dried up—which amazed him, and made him feel slightly guilty about trying to needle her in order to release a little of his own ill-feeling. He had seen her in tears before, obviously, but it was more than thirty years since Philippe had died, and he had been her brother, whereas Caroline…

Obviously, Caroline had not been nothing to her, and certainly more than an experiment.

Mathieu made no comment, but she could read him like a book. "Don't be so surprised," she said. "I loved her too. Not in the same way as you, obviously, but she was every bit as close as a sister. And it wasn't just you that felt a sense of responsibility to her, even if my so called scheming did only amount to smoothing the path of inevitability."

Mathieu sighed, feeling that now that feelings were out in the open, there was no reason to put on a show of bottling them up. "It's going to be difficult," he admitted. "It's going to leave a hell of a gap...."

"I forbid you to die on me, Mathieu," Myrtille said, abruptly. "You hear me—*I forbid it*. There's just the two of us left now. I need you."

Mathieu raised an eyebrow, genuinely surprised by the outburst.

"There isn't just the two of us," he said, pedantically. "In spite of your strict rationing there are half a hundred people in the valley now who have had the full dose of the longevity serum."

"You know what I mean," she retorted, bluntly. "Of the original five, there are only two. Only a handful of the others are over a hundred, and you and I are more than thirty years ahead of the oldest. That's a generation—or used to be, before we started engineering the valley's demography. It still is in the deceptive statistics we continue to send to Toulouse and Paris, in which you and I are now on our fourth identities and still in our fifties."

"Before you started engineering the demography and falsifying the records of births and death," he corrected her. "As you never initiated me into the cult, in spite of the preparation you put in before we arrived here, I'm still an outsider. Not that I mind—but Caroline did, a little. She thought there was an element of insult involved."

"There wasn't, but I couldn't initiate her without you. And the tentative preparation that I put in was a way of testing the water. By the time we arrived here, I could see that you'd never be able to take it aboard. It's not your fault. You weren't born here; you hadn't grown up with the traditions. Other people who've married out have never gone very far from the valley, but you're a Breton by birth and a scientist by vocation. Philippe could look at the work from both sides, although Mother would have hesitated before initiating him if she hadn't need his active involvement so desperately. She always thought that you'd do better work outside, and I always agreed with her. But you're right—you have always been an outsider, in that sense. I still forbid you to leave me alone, though. I really do need you—not for the science, any more, but for the company. You're only other person on earth of my antiquity, and you're my doctor...and the only person still alive to whom I have a debt that I can never repay."

Mathieu stared at her for a moment, and then smiled wryly. "Likewise," he said. "With regard to the unrepayable debt, that is...and I still feel that I've short-changed you with the serum. We both know, now, what its limits are. I never did manage to make the effect of the golden fluid truly permanent. We're still vampires, you and I. As you say, three out of the five vampire elders are dead, and I…"

"Will go on until you I give you permission to stop, damn it." The edge in her voice almost became a snap, although he had given up trying deliberately to needle her, and his own tone had been wistful, without a hint of accusation.

Mathieu nodded, by way of weak assent, but then changed his mind, and shook his head. "Sometimes," he said, "even befor Caroline began to deteriorate, when I tried to weigh things up retrospectively, I wondered whether all I've achieved is to waste a long life on a futile quest."

"Don't be ridiculous," said Myrtille, sternly "I forbid you to wallow in self-pity, too. I'm trying to be sensitive to your loss, but you really aren't making it easy. We'll both be better off if we both make every effort to console one another and build up one another's morale, don't you think?"

Mathieu knew that she was right, as usual, but it really wasn't that simple. "In that case," he said, after a pause, "speaking as your doctor, may I give you a prescription?"

"Have you developed something new?" she asked, taken by surprise and suffering a slight lapse of foolishness. "Why haven't you mentioned it?"

Again, he smiled, wryly. "No," he said, "It's something very, very old, but it worked wonders once. Would you like me to hold you or a few minutes? Just to hold you, with no further agenda…to help you feel a little better."

She considered the offer for twenty seconds, and then said: "Yes, I think I'd like that.

So he held her, just for a few minutes. He knew that it was completely different in its implications from the time that he had held Caroline all those years ago, because there was no possibility at all that Myrtille was going to fall in love with him. In retrospect, as Myrtille said, it had been inevitable that Caroline would, because it was the first kindness she had ever known in a wretched life in which she received nothing but violence and violation even from the people she loved. It was equally inevitable that Myrtille would not.

He knew too, however, that the situation was not completely different, in that he was deriving just as much benefit from the gesture as she was, and was not at all sure that he had not issued the prescription entirely for his own benefit. No matter how much Myrtille might think that she needed him, he was very well aware that he needed her far more, if he really was going to go on living—and he did not have the authority to forbid her anything.

When he let her go, she immediately stared into his eyes, plumbing the depths of his soul. He made no attempt to hide anything, not because it would have been futile, but because he no longer had anything to hide, now.

"I'll try," he promised. "I won't say that it's going to be easy, because it won't, especially if your conviction that you're far better equipped for emortality than I am turns out to be true—but I'll do my best to make a new start, to find new goals, to manufacture a reason for going on. At the very least, I can set myself a target—two hundred's a round number. Assuming that the world at large lasts that long, of course—which, given the way things seem to be going, it might not."

"Things could be worse," she told him. "You could have published your results...and that really would have precipitated disaster...but as I say, let's not rake up old arguments. Let's concentrate on the future, and what there is for us still to do. Is there really no hope left of stabilizing the fluid?"

Mathieu shook his head. "We've tried everything," he said. "It can't be isolated from an organism, and even switching the organism accelerates its deceleration. You know how hard it was even to get the result we did. I need a new direction, a new preoccupation. And at my age..."

"Stop it," she said. "You just need time. Talk to the boys, and Esclarmonde...or even the grandchildren. They've all got work in progress. You'll find something. You have to."

"I'll try," was all the Mathieu would say, again. He did not feel confident. But even her insistence that she needed him was something, and the authority of her prohibition. Simply knowing that somebody cared was always a plus...as witness Caroline, who had seemed virtually finished at eighteen, and had almost managed a hundred and fifty, with various kinds of assistance.

"I'll do my best too," Myrtille told him, still looking at him, but no longer trying to plumb the deaths of his thoughts, merely holding his slightly distraught gaze. "I need a renewal of my motivation too, a reason to go on. And I will go on—not for the sake of vanity, or love, and perhaps not even for the quest for perfect beauty and spiritual perfection, or the search for the soul of blood and the authentic elixir of life, but I will go on. If all else fails, I'll do it for the sake of sheer stubbornness."

"And progress," Mathieu added.

"That's true," she replied as they clasped hands to seal the optimistic bargain. "There'll always be progress."

www.ingramcontent.com/pod-product-compliance
Lightning Source LLC
Chambersburg PA
CBHW020641180626
46816CB00003B/1078